Fiona Leitch is a writer  written for football and illegal raves and is a st commercial, even appear cleaning product called 'Soa Oii . and Cornwall, she's finally settled in sunny New Zealand, where she enjoys scaring her cats by trying out dialogue on them. She spends her days dreaming of retiring to a crumbling Venetian palazzo, walking on the windswept beaches of West Auckland, and writing funny, flawed but awesome female characters.

Her debut novel, *Dead in Venice*, was published by Audible in 2018 as one of their Crime Grant finalists. Fiona also writes screenplays and was a finalist in the Athena Film Festival Writers Lab, co-run by Meryl Streep's IRIS company.

twitter.com/fkleitch
facebook.com/fionakleitch

Also by Fiona Leitch

The Nosey Parker Cozy Mysteries

A Brush with Death

A Sprinkle of Sabotage

MURDER ON THE MENU

A Nosey Parker Cozy Mystery

FIONA LEITCH

One More Chapter
a division of HarperCollins*Publishers* Ltd
1 London Bridge Street
London SE1 9GF
www.harpercollins.co.uk

HarperCollins*Publishers*
1st Floor, Watemarque Building, Ringsend Road
Dublin 4, Ireland

This paperback edition 2021

1

First published in Great Britain in ebook format
by HarperCollins*Publishers* 2021

A catalogue record of this book is available from the British Library

ISBN: 978-0-00-843656-8

Printed and bound in Great Britain by
CPI Group (UK) Ltd, Croydon CR0 4YY

This book is dedicated to my parents,
and to
Jacinda, Ashley, and the #TeamOf5Million

Prologue

I'm not superstitious. I never have been. I make a point of walking under ladders and I positively encourage black cats to cross my path. My old partner on the beat, Helen, used to laugh and tell me that I was tempting fate, like I was standing there glaring at it, fists raised, going, *Come on then, is that all you've got?* But I wasn't, not really. I've never tempted fate; I just can't help poking at it. If I see something wrong, I can't resist getting involved.

I'm not superstitious, but I do have a few rituals, which is more to do with avoiding bad karma or Murphy's Law. Lots of coppers do. Stuff like, when you go out to a café or restaurant, always sit facing the door, so you can see everyone who's coming in and going out (which makes life difficult when you're out for a meal with another police officer, because if you can't get the right table and neither of you gives way, you end up sitting next to each other). Or not polishing your shoes before a Friday or Saturday night shift because if you do you're bound to run into a drunken hen party trying to stab each other with their stilettos outside a nightclub at 3am, one of whom will definitely unload seven Bacardi Breezers and one doner kebab all over your shiny black footwear as you get her in the van. That kind of thing.

The other ritual I have is always leaving a good-luck card for the new occupants whenever I move house. I've moved house *a lot*. There was the skanky bedsit I lived in when I first relocated to London. I loved it because it was the first place which was *mine* (even though it was rented) and I had become a grown-up and my life was just getting started and it was all so exciting. I was away from my parents and following in my dad's footsteps without being in his shadow for once. All this despite the bedsit having hot and cold running mould and a wicked draught from the one solitary window, and a landlord who refused to get anything repaired until I told him I was a copper. And then he *still* didn't repair anything; he just put the rent up by another hundred quid a week until I moved out. There were the shared houses – often with other police officers from the same nick – which kind of made sense until we all ended up doing different shifts, so it didn't matter what time of day it was, there was always someone trying to sleep and someone else waking them up as they came home and someone getting ready to go out. That had been particularly stressful. There was the nice flat I finally found myself in, just before I met Richard; it was small but perfectly formed, and quiet. I bought a cheap poster print of a famous painting of the coast near my home town in Cornwall and I would sit there, in the peace and quiet of my lovely flat, staring at the picture and thinking about the way the light reflected off the sea back home, and I would cry because I was so flipping lonely and homesick when I wasn't actually at work, but I wasn't about to give in and go back and admit I'd been wrong to leave.

And then there was this place. This was the first house I'd ever actually owned – *we'd* owned, me and Richard – and although it wasn't perfect, it was full of memories. Memories of Richard carrying me over the threshold after we got married, banging my head on the door frame as he did so. *That* was bad karma and should have made me wary of what was to follow. Of bringing our daughter Daisy back from the hospital after a long-drawn-out labour that put me off having any more children, at least for a year or so, and by then Richard had gone off the idea anyway. It was a few more years before I found out why.

The good-luck card lay on the kitchen counter, which had been cluttered with cookbooks and gadgets the day before but was now empty. They were inside a box, inside the removal van, which had already left. The picture on the front was of a lovely country cottage made of stone with climbing roses around the door. It was ironic because it looked nothing like this house but wasn't too dissimilar from where we were moving to. I picked up the pen and composed in my head what to write.

Good luck in your new home. I hope you are as happy here as I was.

…Or as happy as I was before I found out that my stupid useless can't-keep-it-in-his-pants husband was cheating on me.

I hope you are as happy here as I was once I got him out of this house and our lives, before he moved in with his new girlfriend ten minutes away, but STILL constantly let his daughter down by turning up late when he'd promised to take her out (if he turned up at all). If we're living miles away he can't let her down anymore, as she won't expect anything from him (she already knows better than to do that, but she's only twelve so she can't help hoping).

I hope you are as happy here as I was when I could still afford to pay the mortgage, before he started kicking up a fuss about paying child support and before I left the job that I absolutely loved but which (after a particularly nasty incident) my daughter didn't. I could see her point. If anything happened to me she'd have to go and live with her dad, who, as I think we've already established, is a total waste of space, oxygen, and the Earth's natural resources. So I left and retrained and now we're both ready to start again somewhere else.

I hope you are happy here spending an absolute fortune on this cramped house with its tiny garden, noisy neighbours, and busy road outside while I'll be paying considerably less for somewhere bigger with a lovely view of the sea and neighbours who are more likely to wake me up at 6am with their loud baaing than at 3am with their drunken return from a club.

Hmm. Maybe I was overthinking it. I opened the card and wrote inside it.

Good luck.

It was definitely time to go home.

Chapter One

Funny how things turn out. I only went in to buy a sofa.

Penhaligon's was one of those old-fashioned family-run department stores – the type that once upon a time every town had but which were now disappearing (and with good reason, to be honest; most of the stock looked like it had been procured in the 1950s and came at such an exorbitant price you were forced to step outside and double-check you hadn't inadvertently wandered into Harrods by mistake). But Penhaligon's had persisted, remaining open through world wars, recessions, and the rise of internet shopping. The zombie apocalypse could hit Cornwall (*I know, I know, would anyone even notice?*) and Penhaligon's would *still* be there, clinging stubbornly to its prime spot on Fore Street, serving the needs of both locals and the undead brain-hungry horde (or 'holidaymakers', as they were otherwise known).

I wouldn't normally have bothered with Penhaligon's, but we'd been at our new house for four days now and Daisy and I were sick of sitting on my mum's old garden chairs – they were literally a pain in the backside – so as I was passing I ventured inside.

It hadn't changed much since the last time I'd been there. It had barely changed since the *first* time I'd been there forty years ago. But I was pleasantly surprised to see that someone had given the furniture department a bit of a makeover and there were a few lounge suites that looked like they'd actually been designed sometime after the fall of the Berlin Wall (as opposed to before the building of it).

I sank gratefully into a big, squashy sofa, stroking the fabric appreciatively and reaching for the price tag. The figures made me suck in my breath in mild horror (along with an unfortunate fly who was just passing), but the words 'Next day delivery!' had an immediate soothing effect.

I stood up to get a better look at it and jumped as a voice boomed across the shop floor at me.

'Oh my God, Nosey Parker! Is that really you?'

I turned round, already knowing who it was. Tony Penhaligon, great-grandson of the original Mr

Penhaligon, old classmate and sometime boyfriend (we went out for two weeks in 1994, held hands a bit, kissed but didn't – *ewww* – use tongues), stood in front of me, a big smile on his face. Like his family's shop, he also hadn't changed all that much over the last forty years and every time I looked at him I could still see a hint of the annoying little boy with the runny nose who had sat next to me on my first day in Mrs Hobson's primary class. But he had a good heart and it was nice to see a friendly face.

I did a double-take as I took him in properly. Hang on a minute; he actually *had* changed. The last time I'd seen him, on one of my trips back to see my mum, he'd been sporting a dad bod, a paunch brought on by too many pasties and pints. But that was gone and he was looking rather trim. Also gone was the unflattering store uniform of white polo shirt and black chinos, replaced by a sharp, well-tailored, and expensive-looking suit. A little voice in the back of my mind went, *I'd blooming well let him use tongues now*, before I shut it up with a contemptuous internal glare.

'It's been a while, Tone. I haven't seen you since—'

'New Year's Eve, three years ago.'

I laughed. 'You've got a good memory.'

'Last time anything exciting happened here. Did you stick to your resolution?'

'That was the first Christmas after I broke up with

Richard,' I said. 'I think I probably made a lot of drunken resolutions that year.'

Tony grinned. 'Yeah, there were one or two. Tell me you've stuck to the main one though? "Avoid idiot men"?'

'Oh, *that* one I live my life by these days. What was yours?'

He shook his head. 'I never announce my resolutions. That way nobody knows whether I followed it up or not.'

'And did you?'

'Nope. But it doesn't matter now anyway. So what're you doing here? Visiting your mum? I heard she'd been ill.'

'Buying a sofa,' I said.

'You do know we don't deliver to London,' he said.

'That's just as well because I don't live there anymore.'

He looked surprised. 'Since when? Are you back, then?'

'Yeah.'

I could see that he was dying to ask me more but the thought of pushing it too far and losing out on his commission was too much for him. Plus, he knew that if I was sticking around he'd get it out of me eventually.

'So what do you think of the sofa?'

I sat back down. 'Honestly? It feels like my backside

has died and gone to heaven where it's being caressed by the wings of an angel.'

He laughed loudly. 'Do you want a job in our marketing department? I always said you should be a poet, not a copper.'

'I'm not either anymore,' I said, fishing in my bag and handing him one of my new business cards.

'"Banquets and Bakes",' he read. 'What's this?'

'My new business,' I said. 'I've just started up—'

'Wait, are you a chef now? Do you do weddings?' Tony looked at me hopefully.

'Weddings, christenings, bar mitzvahs, you name it. If people want to eat there, I can cater for it.' I *hoped* I could anyway; I hadn't actually had any clients yet, but in theory…

'This is brilliant!' cried Tony. 'It's … what's that word? Serentipidy?' I thought about correcting his pronunciation but decided against it; it would only make both of us feel bad. And anyway, he was waving across the shop floor to a woman who was stalking proprietorially around a display of crystal glass vases. 'Cheryl! Come over here! I've found a caterer!'

He held out my business card as Cheryl approached. She read it, then looked me up and down, clearly not overly impressed with what she saw. Which was fair enough as I had really only popped out to get some teabags in between coats of paint and was looking more like the Michelin Man than a Michelin chef.

'We're getting married,' said Tony proudly, and I could understand why. Although the expression currently occupying Cheryl's face was reminiscent of a bulldog sucking a lemon, she was (probably, in the right light) quite attractive, and she had to be ten years younger than him, even if she did dress a bit like Dynasty-era Joan Collins. I couldn't remember the last time I'd seen shoulder pads that size outside of the Super Bowl. It also explained the dapper suit that Tony was currently sporting, as well as his newly svelte figure.

'Congratulations,' I said. He deserved happiness. Tony's first wife had left him for her driving instructor, the betrayal made all the worse by the fact that Tony had paid for the lessons and she hadn't had the decency to leave him until she'd passed her test (after three attempts), done a motorway safety course and a defensive driving course, and was halfway through getting her HGV licence. The driving instructor hadn't lasted long and, according to my mum, who knew her mum, she now drove tankers up and down the country with just her dog – a Pomeranian called Germaine – for company.

I hoped he was going to ask me to do their catering – I needed the money – but at the same time I wasn't sure I wanted to risk cocking up his nuptials. Oh, well, I would just plan everything really, really carefully.

'Our caterer let us down and the wedding's next weekend,' he said.

Next weekend? Holy—

'I was just saying to Jodie' – he turned to his fiancée, indicating me with a wave of his hand –'I was just saying, it's serentipidy—'

'Serendipity,' she corrected, smiling at him condescendingly. *Hmm.* 'So – Jodie, was it? – what are your credentials? How many weddings have you done? We've got a very upmarket venue – Parkview Manor Hotel, do you know it? – and lots of guests coming from all over the country.'

I opened my mouth to confess that I hadn't actually done any weddings but if they were this close to their wedding day, good luck finding someone else as willing (or as desperate for the money) as me. But Tony beat me to it.

'Her credentials are, she's an old friend and ex-copper, and you don't get better references than that,' he said. Cheryl pursed her lips but didn't argue, aware that if she didn't want to end up feeding her upmarket guests pasty and chips in the very downmarket Kings Arms in Market Square, she didn't have much choice. I smiled.

'I'll do it for whatever the last caterer was going to do it for, if you throw in the sofa.'

So that was how I found myself, six days later, standing outside the imposing entrance to Parkview Manor Hotel. It was early evening, the day before The Wedding of the Century™; many of the guests were staying overnight and Tony had (against Cheryl's wishes, I thought) invited me to join their welcome drinks. I tugged down my dress; I'd put weight on since leaving the force, and even more since doing my catering course, and my going-out clothes, which I didn't get the chance to wear much, were all starting to get a little snug. My shoes were already pinching my toes. They were hardly Jimmy Choos but they were the only ones in my wardrobe that weren't made by Nike or Dr Martens. I comforted myself with the thought that I'd be in the kitchen tomorrow and back in my eminently more sensible jeans and trainers, took a deep breath, and entered.

The hotel foyer was very plush and wouldn't have looked out of place in London, rather than in the Cornish countryside. Marble covered every conceivable surface and I got the feeling that if I stood there gawping for too long I'd get marble-ised as well. There were lush, exotic ferns and birds-of-paradise dotted all over the place, and the plant-killer in me (I have brown thumbs) immediately suspected they were plastic. I surreptitiously stroked a leaf as I passed (thereby condemning the poor unsuspecting fern to an early grave); they were real and all very well cared for.

I vaguely recognised the woman behind the reception desk. Although I hadn't lived in Penstowan for almost twenty years, I'd grown up and gone to school here, and seventy-five per cent of the inhabitants were either old classmates, siblings of classmates, or parents of them. She smiled and inclined her head slightly towards the sign that said, 'Penhaligon and Laity Wedding Party', with a photo of the happy couple and an arrow pointing towards a function room. It was forebodingly quiet, with very little in the way of music or chatter floating into the foyer.

Inside the function room, there were a few guests standing at the bar chatting, with Tony holding court. He was clearly very excited about his upcoming big day, chattering away with a boyish enthusiasm that was quite endearing. It was still fairly early so presumably this wasn't it; Cheryl had said they had guests coming from all over the country so maybe they just hadn't arrived yet.

'Nosey!' called Tony. Now *that* was less endearing. I really needed to have a word with him about using my childhood nickname. I plastered on a smile and tottered over, grimacing at the blister that was already threatening a little toe.

But I never reached Tony and his chums because

everyone's attention was suddenly drawn to the doorway of the function room. The double doors had been thrown open and Cheryl stood there, smiling beatifically at the assembled guests. She was dressed to the nines in a fitted cocktail dress of deep scarlet silk, while her hair had been seriously coiffured and hairsprayed to within an inch of its life. She was still rocking that 80s kind of vibe, but there was no denying that she did it well. My cheap chain-store dress and ugly shoes felt even more uncomfortable under her gaze and I could not wait to go home and put my pyjamas on.

She paused for a moment longer, milking her dramatic entrance, then opened her mouth to speak.

Her words were lost as she suddenly disappeared from view, bulldozed and tossed to one side by a screeching harpy in a khaki boiler suit.

Chapter Two

For a split second nobody moved; we were all wondering what the hell had just happened. And then came the sound of bitch-slapping from the foyer.

I yanked off my stupid uncomfortable shoes and ran outside to see Cheryl lying on the ground, her hands thrust upwards and attempting to choke the madwoman sitting astride her – a madwoman who was still managing to wheeze threats at her.

'Mel?' Tony arrived seconds after me, and stood staring in astonishment.

'Is that really Mel?' I said, amazed. I hadn't seen Tony's ex-wife for years, and the last time I had she'd possessed a head of wonderful red curly hair. The harpy's hair was bleached blonde and cut very short and spiky.

'You can't marry him!' the harpy screeched. 'You don't love him! I won't let you ruin his life!'

'*You* already did that, you cow!' snarled Cheryl, who was having trouble breathing under Mel's not inconsiderable frame. I had to admit she had a point.

This was entertaining but getting out of hand. No one else was going to stop it – they were all still too gobsmacked – so I waded in. I've had the training, after all.

'All right, ladies, that's enough,' I said, as I tried to prise Cheryl's fingers away from Mel's throat. When that didn't work – she had a strong grip for someone with such well-manicured hands – I chopped her hard on the inside of the elbow with the side of my hand, making her yelp and let go. Then I dragged Mel to her feet and positioned myself between the two women.

I glared at Tony and the crowd (who were mostly male) gawping at us.

'It's all right, lads, don't bloody help or anything, will you,' I said, rolling my eyes. Tony shook himself and helped Cheryl to her feet.

'She can't marry him!' cried Mel, straining to get to the furious and not-so-blushing bride-to-be again. I shook her and made her look at me.

'Mel,' I said. 'Mel! Calm down. Do you remember me? Jodie?'

She looked at me and slowly recognition dawned.

'Aren't you the one who went off and joined the police? What are you doing here?' A look of relief washed over her. 'Are you investigating them? Are you—'

'Just calm down,' I said. 'I'm going to let go of you so we can talk properly, okay? I don't want a repeat of whatever that was.'

'I want the police here RIGHT NOW!' shouted Cheryl. She was understandably shaken, but I couldn't help feeling she was almost enjoying being the centre of attention, or help noticing that her lacquered hair had barely moved under the onslaught. She must've sprayed it with liquid Kevlar.

Tony looked at me helplessly. I seem to have that effect on men; at some point in our relationship they always look at me helplessly. I sighed.

'Let's not be hasty, Cheryl,' I said. She glared at me but I carried on before she could start shouting at me. I don't normally take an instant dislike to people but I really could not warm to her. 'It's the night before your wedding, all your guests will be arriving tonight, and you're meant to be having a party. Do you really want to spend the evening at the police station? It'll take hours for them to take statements. Your whole night will be ruined.'

Tony looked at me gratefully and I forgave him for being a helpless wuss. My kind heart will be the end of me one day.

'Jodie's right,' he said. 'Let's just go and have a drink and forget about it, yeah? No harm done.'

Cheryl looked for a moment like she was going to open her mouth and unleash such a stream of verbal abuse that it would make a navvy blush.

"Ello, 'ello, 'ello, what's going on here then?' The man's voice stopped Cheryl in her tracks. We all turned to stare at the small group of guests who had just arrived in the foyer and were looking on, bemused, obviously wondering if they'd missed the evening's entertainment.

I took in the appearance of the man who had stolen what was, by rights for an ex-copper, my line. He was in his early sixties, dapper and well dressed in casual but expensive-looking clothes. A Ralph Lauren polo player gambolled discreetly on the breast pocket of his shirt and the chunky diver's watch on his wrist did not look like a cheap knock-off from the local market. He radiated self-assurance and good humour, particularly if it was at someone else's expense. Behind him stood another, younger man, good-looking in a cocky kind of way – the sort of bloke you knew deep down you couldn't trust, but who could probably persuade you otherwise just long enough to get into your knickers. A sardonic smile, almost a sneer, crossed his face as he looked at Cheryl, who had gone uncharacteristically silent.

'All right, Chel?' His voice had a mocking, slightly

belligerent tone to it. 'My name weren't on the invite but I'm sure you didn't mean nothing by it.'

'We did send you one,' said Tony awkwardly. 'The post round here...'

The older man smiled – he was clearly very amused both by Tony's obvious discomfort and by the tableau in front of him – and inclined his head towards Mel.

'Is this the floorshow? I don't think much of your strippergram.'

Oh, so he was a dick. Good to know up front.

'That's really not helping, Mr...?' I said, in my best police officer's voice. These things never leave you.

'Laity. Roger Laity.' He held out his hand to shake, but my hands were still occupied with holding onto Mel. 'Uncle of the blushing bride.'

'Well, Mr Laity, if you and the rest of the group could make your way into the function room, rather than stand there making funny comments, that would go some way towards salvaging your niece's party, don't you think?'

He looked at me appraisingly. I got the impression that he expected me to blush or falter under his gaze but then, he really didn't know me. He turned away and patted Tony on the back condescendingly: *you can stand down now, son, the real man of the family has arrived.* Tony looked like he wanted to wash and possibly disinfect the spot his uncle-in-law-to-be had touched, and I felt a rush of sympathy for him. All he'd wanted was a nice wedding.

'Come on, babe,' said Tony, tugging at Cheryl.

The bride-to-be bestowed a murderous glance on Mel, who deserved it, to be fair, and on me, who didn't, and then allowed Tony to take her hand and lead her away. But she stopped and turned to me, hissing, 'Get that … that *thing* out of my sight or I really will call the police!'

We waited while Tony, Cheryl, and their guests left the foyer and then I led a now docile Mel out of the hotel and into the grounds. We found a bench in a secluded spot near a pond full of koi carp, and sat down.

'So what was all that about?' I asked. Mel looked remorseful.

'I'm so sorry,' she said, miserably. 'I tried to talk to her but she brushed me off and I just got this rush of blood to the head.'

'That was quite a rugby tackle,' I said. We looked at each other, the image of Cheryl and her hair flying into the air running through our minds, and both stifled giggles.

'You don't like her either, do you?' asked Mel.

'I hardly know her,' I said, and she laughed gently.

'That's not a no, then,' she said, and I laughed too.

'No, it's not.'

We sat quietly for a moment, letting her calm down and marshal her thoughts.

'I don't think she loves him,' Mel said finally. 'She's going to ruin his life.'

'At the risk of sounding judgemental...' I started.

'I know, I know, I already ruined it.' She sighed. 'I didn't do it lightly. And I did love him. I just fell in love with someone else as well.'

'Your driving instructor.'

She looked at me, surprised. 'I keep forgetting that everyone knows everyone's business in this town. Your mum and my mum—'

'They both go to the OAPs' coffee club at the church hall on Wednesdays,' I said. She nodded.

'Of course. Anyway, I fell for my instructor but I still loved Tony. I wasn't stringing them both along, I just didn't know who I wanted to be with.' She sighed again. 'If it's any consolation, I chose the wrong one. She did to me what I did to Tony.'

I looked at her miserable face. I remembered how I'd almost instantly fallen for Daisy's dad – PC Richard Doyle, to give him his official title, or 'that cheating swine' to give him the unofficial one my mum always used – spotting him across the room at a team briefing. He'd just transferred to the station and I had to show him around. I ended up showing him a lot more than that after a few drinks in the pub after work. I hadn't known he was married at first, and I didn't care about his wife when he left her because it meant he'd chosen me. I'd been a lonely workaholic and I wasn't letting him go. Doubtless the woman he left me for – who I was sure was just one of many sad extra-marital conquests – twelve years later didn't care how I felt, either. It had felt like he'd ripped my heart out and stamped on it. And stamped on Daisy's, too, because when he left me he left her as well.

There wasn't a finite amount of heartbreak in the world. It didn't make any difference how many people suffered from it, it didn't lessen the sting. I sighed.

'Of course it's not a consolation, not to anyone. Not even to Tony, because he's not like that.' I picked up a piece of gravel and tossed it into the pond, watching the ripples spread out. I turned back to Mel. 'But what makes you think she's going to ruin his life?'

'She's not marrying him for love,' she said firmly.

'What makes you say that? What's she marrying him for?'

'Money.'

I laughed. 'He hasn't got any, has he? I mean, I know the shop's still going after all these years…'

She looked at me steadily.

'The shop?' I said. 'You think she wants the shop?'

Mel shrugged but didn't say anything. Why would

Cheryl want the shop? It can't have been that profitable; I was amazed it was still going. Smaller shops were closing all the time in seaside towns like Penstowan.

I looked at her thoughtfully. 'You said to me earlier, was I here investigating them. Investigating who?'

'The Laity family,' said Mel without any hesitation. 'Are you?'

'I'm not a police officer anymore,' I said. 'I'm just doing the catering.'

'Oh.' She looked disappointed.

'I'm still nosey, though,' I said. I had to admit that my childhood nickname had become quite apt during my years on the force. 'Why should the Laity family be investigated?'

She looked around nervously. 'My cousin works for the council. Let's just say, that family have got plans for Penstowan that not everyone will agree with.'

'What sort of plans?' I asked.

'Everything okay?'

I looked up into Tony's concerned face. He looked anxiously from me to Mel, a worried smile on his face.

'Tony! I'm so sorry…' started Mel, looking like she might cry.

'Do you want me to leave you to talk?' I said, standing up. Emotional scenes are not my thing. But they both looked horrified at the idea. Mel grabbed my hand.

'I just wanted to make sure you were okay,' said Tony.

'I know it must be hard for you, seeing me move on and be happy—'

'Oh, for Christ's sake, Tony, this is not a bloody love triangle with you in the middle!' she snapped. He looked affronted, then annoyed.

'Oh, so you just decided to rock up and ruin my wedding for a laugh?'

Mel got to her feet and it was in danger of all going off again. I jumped up and stood between them.

'Tony, thank you for checking on us; everything is fine. Mel is going to go home now so you get back to your party and I'll be in for a drink in a bit.' I really needed a drink after all this. To think I'd been expecting to be bored. I gave him a little shove towards the hotel and took Mel's arm.

We left him standing there with his mouth open, catching flies.

'So what were you going to say?' I asked Mel, when we were out of earshot. But she shook her head.

'No. Balls to him. If he wants to marry her, let him get on with it.'

We were almost in the car park by now. She disentangled her arm from mine and stopped.

'Thank you for stopping me make an even bigger idiot of myself,' she said. 'I appreciate it, honestly.' She looked over at an old and slightly battered Vauxhall that was parked on the other side of the gravelled drive. A small, furry, and undeniably cute face peered out of it, nose sniffling at the window. 'I left my dog in the car. She must be hot.' Mel must have seen my disapproving expression; the window was open a tiny crack, barely enough to let any air in, and it had been a hot day. 'I can't leave the window down any further than that or she gets out,' she explained, and chuckled. 'She's so clever, she throws all her weight at the top of the window until she forces it down, and then wriggles out. I should have called her Houdini. I'll just let her out for a pee and then I'll be off.'

She went to leave but I grabbed her arm to stop her.

'If you ever want to talk...' I said. 'I'd give you my business card but I left my bag in the bar.'

She smiled softly. 'Thank you. If you've moved back to Penstowan I'm sure we'll run into each other.'

I watched as she opened the car door and made a fuss of Germaine, faithful companion and would-be canine escape artist. Then I went back to the bar.

I thought I should probably stick around long enough to have a glass of wine, and then I would make my excuses and leave. It really wasn't my kind of party. But there was someone else missing from the bar too: Cheryl.

Tony saw me enter, brought me a glass of champagne, and steered me over to the window.

'So, do you think she'll come back?' he asked.

I gulped at my champagne. 'Who, Cheryl?'

'No, you muppet. Cheryl's having an early night. Mel. Will Mel cause any trouble tomorrow?'

'Oh, right. No, I don't think so.' I shook my head. 'And anyway, if she does turn up, I'll be right over there in the kitchen, preparing vol-au-vents and making dinner for a hundred people. I will have access to a lot of sharp pointy things.'

'You could do your awesome ex-policewoman ninja stuff again.' Tony laughed. 'That was so hot…'

I gasped in mock horror and slapped him. 'Anthony Penhaligon! You're practically a married man!'

He smiled. 'I know,' he said. 'I'm very lucky.'

'Hmm,' I said non-committally, sipping at my drink.

'You don't like my wife-to-be much, do you?' he said.

'I hardly know her.' I was painfully aware that was the exact thing I'd said to Mel. He laughed.

'That's not a no, is it?' He stared out of the window for a moment then turned back to me. 'I know Cheryl can be a bit…' *What? A bit of a fricking nightmare?* 'A bit high maintenance. But she's not had an easy life.'

I thought about the things I'd gone through over the last few years.

'Lots of us have had a hard life—' I started.

'She lost her parents when she was fifteen.' *Oh crap.* 'That's how she ended up with her uncle. I don't know what her parents were like – they didn't live round here – but her uncle and his lot...' Tony shook his head and lowered his voice. 'They're not very nice people. So cut her some slack, yeah?' He touched me gently on the arm. 'I'm glad you're back, Jodie. I'd really like you and Cheryl to be friends. Will you try?'

'Of course,' I said. And I meant it, for him.

I finished my drink and left the bar. Should I go up and talk to Cheryl? Part of me wanted nothing more than to just go home and relieve my mum of her babysitting duties – Daisy liked to think she was a grown-up, but she was still only twelve – but the concerned (or nosey) part of me thought that maybe I should pop up and check on her.

I stood outside her room, hesitating. Maybe I shouldn't disturb her if she wanted an early night. But I could hear movement – a lot of movement – from the other side of the door. So I knocked.

There was silence. To my mind it was a guilty silence – like someone had been caught doing something they shouldn't. Don't ask me how a silence can be guilty, but it can. I just have this instinct...

Just as I was becoming convinced she wouldn't answer the door, she did, opening it a crack. She had a smile on her face which dropped as soon as she saw me.

'Oh, it's you,' she said.

'Just checking that you're all right after that little incident earlier,' I said sweetly. I can do sweet.

'I'm fine,' she said. Through the crack in the door I could see a suitcase on the bed with a mess of clothes half in and half out.

'Getting everything ready for your big day?' I said. 'Packing for the honeymoon?'

'Yes,' she said, attempting to close the door a little tighter. I had a horrible feeling that packing wasn't what she was doing.

'Look, we may have got off on the wrong foot,' I said. 'If you want to talk—'

'Not really.'

'Okay.' I was relieved. 'Tony's a really good guy, you know. He deserves to be happy.'

Her face dropped. *Uh oh.*

'I know he does.'

'So if you've got any doubts…'

She looked at me for a few seconds, then plastered on a fake smile.

'No doubts at all,' she said. 'Thank you for your concern.' And with that she shut the door in my face.

I went home and went to bed, first looking in on Daisy, who had given up waiting up for me and gone to bed, and on my mum, who was staying in the spare room. I'd mentioned her moving in with us permanently as she was getting on a bit and I worried about her being on her own (especially since she'd been diagnosed with angina a few months ago, which had helped persuade me now was a good time to move back), but she'd been almost indecently hasty to reject that idea, saying that she valued her privacy and she could hardly bring a man home if her daughter and granddaughter were there.

I turned the light off and stared at the ceiling before finally falling into a restless sleep. My dreams were filled with 80s hairstyles, rugby tackles, and dickheads in Ralph Lauren, and somewhere in the middle of it Tony saying he'd deliver the sofa tomorrow. Except of course he wouldn't because it already had pride of place in my living room and tomorrow was his wedding day.

I woke the next morning and saw the text from the groom, and in my sleep-fuddled state I thought, *He's arranging a time to deliver the sofa.*

When I opened it, I was unsurprised to read that the bride had disappeared.

Chapter Three

Tony was waiting outside the hotel, hopping about impatiently from foot to foot as I drew up in the van. He looked up and his mouth dropped open as I jumped out.

'What the—? What are you driving?' he asked, aghast, staring at the picture on the side of the van. 'Tell me it ain't yours.'

'My new company vehicle,' I said airily. 'I got it a couple of days ago off a bloke in Tavistock. He's closing down his fetish shop. Apparently Tavistock isn't the hotbed of perversion and kinkiness he thought it was. Who knew?'

Tony walked alongside the van, looking closely at the image while also quite clearly not wanting to look *that* closely.

'Oh my God…'

'Do you like our Gimpmobile?' Daisy smiled brightly at him, having clambered out of the passenger side followed by my mum.

'Don't call it that!' I said quickly, stifling a giggle, although I had to admit that description fitted it perfectly. I turned to Tony. 'You didn't give me much time to get prepared. I'll get it resprayed next week.'

'You could have peeled the decals off…' Tony looked at the picture of a cartoon figure holding a whip and shuddered.

'Yeah, I tried that and it was worse.'

'How could it be worse?'

'The outline was left behind, and it didn't look like it was a whip he was holding.'

Tony gulped.

'Oh, pull yourself together!' My mum shook her head. 'You young people are too easily offended…'

I indicated my fellow caterers. 'You know my mum, of course.'

'Yes, of course, nice to see you, Shirley…'

'And you remember Daisy? She must have been about nine the last time you saw her.'

'Yes, wow, haven't you grown…' Tony looked at me helplessly. It was starting to become a habit. 'Why—'

'My sous chefs,' I said. 'Like I said, you didn't give me much time to prepare.' In truth, Daisy had been getting bored – it was the summer holidays and she hadn't started her new school yet – and I didn't entirely trust her and my mother to keep each other out of trouble if I was out all day. 'They'll start unloading the van while we have a little chat.' I threw Daisy the keys and grabbed Tony's arm, marching him off before she could complain about being treated like a slave (even though I'd already said I'd pay her).

We walked through reception and started up the grand staircase that swept up to the first floor. We headed towards Cheryl's room, where Tony stopped to take a key from his pocket.

'We were doing the old-fashioned not-seeing-each-other-the-night-before thing,' he said. 'She sent me a text about half nine, quarter to ten, saying she wanted to talk to me after the party, but I didn't see it until later so I didn't reply straight away, and then she sent me another one telling me not to worry about it because she was going to bed. I sent her a goodnight text but she didn't send me one back, so I thought she was probably just asleep. Then this morning when her friend turned up to do her hair and make-up there was no sign of her.'

He opened the door and we went inside. The mess of clothes on the bed that I'd seen last night was gone, the suitcase was absent, and either the bed had not been slept in or Cheryl had been a hotel chambermaid in a previous life. Maybe she had, or maybe she was just tidy and into soft furnishings. My bedding never looks like that. Tony sat down heavily on it.

'I tried ringing her, but there was no answer. No one could get hold of her so I got the key from the manager and let myself in, and I found this.'

He held out a sheet of paper. *Oh no,* I thought. My instincts last night had been right. I took the sheet of paper.

'Dear Tony,' I read, and then stopped. There was nothing else on it.

'I didn't know who else to call,' he said. 'I didn't want to tell my mum because she'd have got into a right tizzy about it and the less I speak to Cheryl's family the better as far as I'm concerned.'

'I can't blame you,' I said. From what I'd seen of them the night before, Tony was marrying into a right bunch.

'I can't call the police; they'll just say she's left me. But she never finished the letter, did she? She could've been about to write anything.'

'She could…' I didn't want to tell him about the bad feeling I'd had after my brief conversation with her the night before. But I didn't need to.

'Who am I kidding?' he said, his face dropping. 'She's left me, hasn't she? That's why she wanted to talk to me. I should have known it would happen, especially after Mel turned up and had a go at her. She's so far out of my league, why would she want someone like me? I'm such an idiot.'

'Stop that right now!' I said, sitting down next to him. 'I'm only going to say this once because you know I'm not given to big displays of emotion, so you'd better listen carefully. You are a good man, Tony Penhaligon. Now you've grown out of that habit of wiping your nose on your sleeve—'

'I still do it occasionally,' he confessed in a low voice. I ignored it.

'You're a good man,' I repeated. 'You're as daft as a brush but you've got a kind heart and you deserve to be happy. Cheryl was a lucky woman and if she was too stupid to see it then you're better off without her.'

'I don't *feel* better off without her,' he said, mournfully. I sighed and leant my head against his shoulder.

'No, I know you don't.'

We sat in silence for a moment.

'What do I do? Do I cancel the wedding?' he said.

'Well, I ain't marrying you.'

'We've got a hundred people coming. I can't ring them all up and tell them not to come!'

'Then let them come,' I said. 'You've done nothing to be ashamed of. And you've already paid for everything. I've got 300 vol-au-vent cases downstairs, waiting to be filled. Let them come and all find out at the same time.

They can have a drink and some food, and a good old gossip. Let them pat you on the back and tell you how sorry they are—' He let out a low moan. I patted him on the back myself. He was going to have to get used to it. 'I know, I know, but at least you'll get it all over with on the same day. No point dragging it out.'

'This is a nightmare,' he said. I nodded. Then sat bolt upright as I spotted something on the dressing table: a bunch of keys, almost hidden by a crumpled hand towel.

'Are those your keys?' I asked.

Tony looked surprised, then shook his head. 'No, they're Cheryl's.'

Then she hasn't gone home if she's left her door key, has she? And her car keys. She must still be here somewhere.'

'She could've got a taxi.'

'Why would she do that? If I was doing a runner I wouldn't want to wait around for a cab.' I stood up and tugged Tony to his feet. 'Come on! She's probably just had some last-minute nerves and she's gone for a walk to clear her head. She might even be in the hotel grounds as we speak.'

We walked back down to the foyer and stopped in the doorway of the hotel, looking out into the grounds. Tony pointed to the other side of the car park where a very new, sporty-looking bright red Mazda was parked.

'There's her car,' he said. 'I didn't even think to look; I

just assumed she'd gone, what with the letter and her suitcase missing.'

I wandered over and peered in. Cheryl's suitcase was on the back seat.

'You're leaving for your honeymoon straight after the reception, aren't you? What car were you planning to go in? Yours or hers?'

'Hers. She wanted to have this big send-off after the reception – us driving away with the top down, and confetti and balloons and everyone waving us off – and she said my old car didn't really fit the bill.'

'There you go, then. She was just getting prepared.' Although it was a slightly odd thing for a bride to be doing on the morning of her big day when she should have been busy getting her hair done. And it didn't explain why she wasn't answering her phone.

The sun was shining. The gardens, where the ceremony was going to be held, were beautiful and it was already warm; it was gearing up to be a lovely day. The only blip was the barking of a dog somewhere nearby, but you couldn't have everything; the hotel was well known for being dog-friendly, and it was probably the pampered poodle or blinged-up bichon frise of a fellow guest.

'Go and have a walk around and see if you can find her,' I said. 'You've still got hours 'til the ceremony. Honestly, you're just as on edge as she is, jumping to conclusions like that. Now, I need to get into the kitchen.' I clapped him on the arm. 'We've got a wedding banquet to prepare!'

I left him standing on the steps leading up to the hotel, looking slightly less worried than when I'd found him, and headed for the hotel kitchens. The manager had been happy for us to use their waiting staff but I got the impression they were a bit miffed that Tony and Cheryl hadn't hired their catering services, so I really had needed to supply my own kitchen helpers. I just hoped they wouldn't be hinderers. And I really hoped we would still have a wedding to cater for...

Mum and Daisy were hard at work, if you could call drinking tea and looking mutinous 'work'. Daisy looked up from behind a huge pile of potatoes.

'Nice of you to join us,' she said. Sarky little madam.

'Hey, young lady, I'm not just your mum today, I'm your boss,' I pointed out. 'Don't be cheeky and make me fire you.'

'I really wouldn't mind,' she said. I pulled her into a hug, making her squirm.

'Thank you so much for coming to help Mummy, my little sugar plum,' I said, in a condescending baby voice.

She hated that voice and that pet name. 'Mummy can't do this on her own.'

'You'd better still be paying me,' she growled, her voice muffled against me. I laughed and released her.

'I'll take you to get your ears pierced on Monday,' I said. She tried not to look thrilled but I could see she was. She should have been; she'd been nagging me about it since she was seven.

'Two holes in each ear?' she asked. I hesitated, then nodded. Why not? It was probably against her new school's regulations, but she could always take one lot out and for once it wouldn't be me being the bad guy. 'Can I have one in my nose too?'

'Of course! And one in your belly button. And a tattoo. And Nana'll get a nipple ring while we're there.'

'Ooh,' said Mum. 'Just imagine getting *that* caught on your cardie.'

Daisy rolled her eyes. 'You only had to say no.'

'All right. No.'

My mum finished her mug of tea and began to whisk the bowl of Marie Rose sauce in front of her.

'How's Tony? What do you think, has she done a runner?' She dipped her finger in the sauce, licked it, then added a squeeze of lemon juice. 'I can't say I've really spoken much to her but I didn't warm to that woman.'

I gently grabbed her hand as she went to stick her

finger back in the bowl. 'Mum! Hygiene, please! Use a spoon and then if you want to taste it again, use another spoon. A clean one!' She harrumphed like I was making a fuss. 'You know I'm right. It's one thing to be a bit slack when it's just you eating it but I don't want my first foray into professional catering ending with us poisoning half the town with your geriatric cooties.'

'Bloomin' cheek!' she said, snapping a tea towel at the back of my legs in mock indignation. I dodged out of her way easily. 'No respect for your elders.'

'I think Cheryl just had an attack of nerves,' I said, changing the subject and deftly catching a freshly peeled potato as it rolled off Daisy's chopping board. 'I'm sure it will all go ahead without a hitch.'

Mum cackled. 'It's a wedding; *someone's* got to get hitched.' She grinned at me. 'That could have been you, you know.'

I rolled my eyes. 'Two weeks, Mum. Two weeks in 1994.'

'Oh no, you didn't go out with *Tony*, did you?' Daisy thought it was hilarious. God knows why; he'd probably have turned out to be a better choice than her useless father.

'No, I went out with Cheryl. She would've been about five at the time. Can we just get on with it, please? There's so much to do.'

I helped Daisy with the potatoes. It made my heart

swell to look at her standing in front of the chopping board in her pinny because it reminded me of my own childhood. Mum had never worked as a chef but she'd always loved to cook and I remembered the big dinner parties my parents had held when I was little. I would help her in the kitchen – I preferred assisting with dessert as there were more spoon-licking opportunities, but I could turn my hand to most things under Mum's supervision – and then, after an early dinner (usually fish fingers and chips) for one, I'd go up to my room so the grown-ups could eat all that lovely food and talk. I didn't really mind missing out on the posh food because for me the best bit was helping my mum. Quite often the Penhaligons would be among the guests, and me and Tony would sit on the stairs and listen to them all talking, giggling as we heard our parents getting tipsy and their conversations start to get more and more risqué as they forgot we were there. Then we'd sneak down and steal whatever pudding was left.

Those early days had really made me love food and I soon realised that if you loved food, you needed either to earn enough money to eat out regularly or to learn how to cook. On my police salary I'd had to go with the latter and when a late career change had been forced upon me it was the only thing I could think of doing that I actually enjoyed. And after a year at catering college, it had really become a passion.

We were serving a creamy truffle-infused mash, to go with some lovely free-range organic pork and fennel sausages (made by a local supplier), roasted apple purée and a cider jus. Mum got on with filling a hundred vol-au-vent cases with prawn cocktail; the rest were being stuffed with Mediterranean roasted vegetables or a West Country camembert and redcurrant jelly. Most of the guests would be having the sausages but there were also ten portions of parmesan-crusted aubergine and Israeli couscous for the vegetarian guests ready to go in the oven closer to the time. For dessert the diners could choose between rich chocolate tart with raspberries and clotted-cream ice-cream, or vanilla panna cotta with strawberries and more clotted cream. Cheryl had wanted to go full-on posh while Tony had been keen to stick with local suppliers and traditional West Country ingredients where possible, and I thought I had come up with a menu that combined the best of both worlds.

I checked the clock; we were bang on schedule, despite me being waylaid earlier by the worried bridegroom. I hoped he was just panicking and that everything was back on track. Surely nothing could stop this wedding now? And surely that blasted dog, which was still barking somewhere out in the hotel gardens, would shut up soon?

Both my questions were answered by a high-pitched, hysterical scream from just the other side of the window.

Chapter Four

All three of us flew out of the kitchen and into the service yard which backed onto the business end of the hotel. We followed the screams, which had subsided into panicky cries for help, around the corner of the building and out into the grounds. Over towards the fishpond, where only last night I had sat talking to Mel, a small crowd of hotel staff and guests was beginning to gather.

Tony, half-dressed in his morning suit, arrived at the same time as us.

'What the bloody hell's going on?' he said.

'I don't know,' I said, a horrible feeling starting to form in the pit of my stomach. Whatever was happening, it obviously wasn't good. 'Have you heard from Cheryl?'

He looked at me, his mouth open in shock. 'No. You don't think…?' We turned to the crowd.

'Let me through!' I said, with enough authority that the crowd had already parted before they realised I was just the caterer.

The dog had finally stopped barking but was still there, whining softly as a shocked early wedding guest – Tony's mum, Brenda – patted its head absentmindedly.

'Who is it?' Tony roughly pushed a woman in a big, stupid hat out of the way. 'Is it … is it Cheryl?'

'No,' I said. Even if I hadn't recognised the dog, the bleached-blonde crop was a dead giveaway.

Mel – ex-Mrs Penhaligon, tanker driver, and erstwhile wedding-crasher – lay on the ground, the peroxide hair matted with blood, her skin cold and pale, and her eyes lifeless. I thought at first that she'd hit her head on the bench we'd sat on the night before – much of the blood seemed to come from a wound at the back of her head, and it was pooled on the ground beneath – but there was another wound, caked with dark-red blood, on her forehead. Falling over and hitting your head twice, once on the back and then at the front, seemed pretty unlikely and would've taken some doing, meaning someone had done this to her. Germaine, faithful to the last, must've stood guard over her mistress's body for hours, barking in the vain hope that someone would come. But they'd come too late.

'Thank God,' Tony burst out, then realised what he'd said. 'Not that Mel's dead, that Cheryl—' He stopped, overcome with emotion, and sank to the ground next to his ex-wife's body.

The next hour was a blur. The hotel manager, Mr Bloom, was called into the grounds. He was a well-groomed, fastidious little man; he reminded me of Hercule Poirot, if the Belgian detective had neglected the little grey cells and gone into the hospitality business instead. Bloom took one look at the corpse and swayed violently, and for a moment I thought we'd have another body laid out next to poor Mel, but he rallied magnificently, if somewhat effeminately, and organised his staff with the efficiency of a general going into battle.

The hotel and wedding guests were herded into a function room – not the one we'd used last night, which overlooked the gardens, but one on the other side of the building which was rarely used as it afforded a not-so-lovely view of the car park and long driveway. Tea, coffee, and the odd nip of something stronger were offered around to calm nerves as the police were called, and velvet ropes, which were normally used to cordon off wedding ceremonies in the garden, were press-ganged into use in place of police incident tape.

I corralled Daisy and Mum back into the kitchen before either of them could get a look at Mel's body. I could see that Daisy was a bit peeved at missing out on the spectacle, but there is such a thing as being too young to see such an upsetting, grisly sight. Poor Mel.

I set my sous chefs back to work preparing the vol-au-vents and throwing together some canapés. I didn't imagine that the wedding would still go ahead, even if Cheryl showed up, but there was a room full of guests next door, all of whom were in varying degrees of shock, excitement, or titillation. Nibbles are always good for calming people down and it's hard to gossip or speculate when your mouth is full of prawn cocktail.

I found Tony sitting alone in the hotel dining room, which had been beautifully laid out by the hotel staff for the wedding banquet. The wedding cake, a magnificent five-tiered creation decorated in crisp white icing and purple sugar-paste flowers, had pride of place on a table at the back of the room, next to the head table. Tony hastily dried his eyes as I approached and sat down next to him.

'Mum's having a lie down,' he said. 'Dad's keeping an eye on her. It's given them both a bit of a turn. I forget sometimes that they're getting on.'

'Are you okay?' I asked, although I could see he wasn't. 'Have you got hold of Cheryl yet?'

'No.' He stood up and strode to the window, looking

out into the garden as if searching for his erstwhile fiancée. 'Where the hell is she? I'm going out of my mind. What if—' He stopped, not wanting to say it, so I said it for him.

'What if Mel isn't the only victim?'

He whirled round to look at me. 'You don't think something's happened to her, do you? You said she was just suffering from last-minute nerves.'

'I don't know,' I said simply. Another alternative had occurred to me, but I wasn't sure how he'd take it. 'There are three possible scenarios, as far as I can see. One, she's done a runner.' I held my hand up to stop him talking. 'Whether that's because she's changed her mind and she's not coming back, or she's just gone to clear her head, I don't know. Two, whoever killed Mel didn't stop at just one victim.' Tony shuddered, turning away from me to look out of the window again. 'And three…'

'Three?'

'She killed Mel. And that's why she left.'

My words hung in the air between us. Tony didn't turn round but I could see the set of his shoulders had changed.

'Tony.' Through the window I saw two police cars arrive, lights flashing but no siren. They were followed closely by a van – the scene of crime guys, I guessed. Or the funeral home.

'Tony, the police will ask you—' I reached out and put

my hand on his arm. He spun round to look at me and I was taken aback by the anger in his eyes. In all the years I'd known him, I'd never seen him look so furious; but then, how well did I know him these days? We'd been friends for a very long time and I'd always made sure to look him up when I came to visit my parents, but I hadn't lived here for nearly twenty years and in that time the longest I'd spent in his company was the odd evening in the pub with a big group of old school chums.

I automatically took a step back. He stepped forward, closing the gap again.

'How dare you say that!' he hissed. 'Cheryl would never do anything like that. You didn't know her; you didn't even like her—'

'Didn't? Or don't?' I didn't like the way he was talking about her in the past tense. He looked confused for a moment, then shook his head.

'Don't twist my words! Bloody typical. Once a copper, always a copper.'

I stared at him, holding his furious gaze steadily, until his shoulders sagged and he dropped his eyes. He pulled out a dining chair and sat down heavily, knocking over an empty wine glass that had been set out on the table. He reached out to set the glass upright again, his hand shaking.

'I just meant, she's gone, hasn't she? She's not d— She can't be. She's left me. I hope.' He laughed humourlessly. 'It's supposed to be my wedding day and I'm hoping my bride-to-be has jilted me at the altar.'

I pulled out the chair next to him and turned it around, sitting astride it to face him.

'The police are here and they'll want to talk to you,' I said softly. 'They'll ask you about the argument between Cheryl and Mel last night.'

'I know.' He reached out to fiddle with the dessert spoon on the table in front of him, twisting and tapping it on a side plate seemingly without realising what he was doing. *Tap, tap, tap.*

I took a deep breath. He might not like what I was going to say, but it was preferable for him to get angry with me rather than the police.

'Mel made some … accusations against Cheryl,' I said.

Tony looked at me anxiously. 'What kind of accusations?' he asked. *Tap, tap, tap.*

'She said the Laity family were after your shop and that's why she was marrying you.'

Tony dropped the spoon and looked at me for a second, then gave a short laugh.

'Is that what she thought? Trust Mel to bark up the wrong tree.'

'So there's a right tree to bark up, is there?'

He picked up the spoon again but didn't speak. I

reached out and grabbed his hand before he started with the irritating tapping again.

'You were expecting me to say something else then, weren't you?' I had this ... this *feeling* that there was something Tony wasn't telling me. 'Is there something else? Something you've found out or thought of since this morning?'

He looked at me as if trying to decide whether or not to speak. He'd just opened his mouth when—

'Mr Penhaligon?'

We turned to see a tall, fair-haired, and (it has to be said) absolutely gorgeous guy of about thirty-five standing in the doorway. He was square-jawed, oozed testosterone, and looked like he should be in a Hallmark movie wearing a lumberjack shirt and running a pumpkin farm somewhere in the Midwest. The mid-west of America, obviously. The mid-west of England would be Birmingham, which wasn't known for either its romantic heroes or its cucurbit agriculture. Behind him I could see a couple of uniformed police officers talking to some guests who were loitering in the hotel foyer, along with what I assumed were more plain-clothed coppers.

Tony stood up. 'Yes.'

'I'm DCI Withers' – Withers was not a good name for a Hallmark romantic hero, but you couldn't have everything, I supposed – 'and I'm leading the investigation into Mrs Penhaligon's death.'

'The ex-Mrs Penhaligon,' said Tony sharply. I put my hand on his arm warningly.

'I was under the impression she still went under that name?' said Withers. Tony shrugged. I wanted to slap him; he was making himself look guilty – if not of murder, at the very least of being an unsympathetic, stroppy bugger.

'She did. Poor Mel. Tony's just upset,' I said. 'Understandably.'

Withers gave me an appropriately withering look up and down. 'Who are you? The chef?'

'Jodie Parker, ex-Metropolitan Police officer. I was based at Kennington.'

'And now you're a chef. Based in the kitchen.'

Arrogant git. 'Yeah.'

He dismissed me. 'Okay, someone will possibly want to talk to you at some point, so don't leave. Mr Penhaligon, let's you and me have a little chat about what happened last night...'

Chapter Five

I had no idea what else to do so I went back to the kitchen and started chopping apples with the biggest, sharpest knife I could find. *And now you're a chef.* The implication being that I couldn't hack it – I brought the knife down hard on an innocent Granny Smith – in the police force. Git. He had no idea why I'd left the force and no idea how much I missed it, despite loving spending more time with Daisy and being able to do something I enjoyed almost as much: cooking, or, at the moment, pulverising fruit into tiny pieces.

'Everything okay, is it?' Mum said carefully, exchanging wary looks with Daisy as I executed another apple and tossed the core aside. 'Didn't we need to peel them first?'

Ah crap. I stuck my knife in the wooden chopping

board, ramming the pointy end into it and leaving the handle sticking up – the blade vibrating with a small but satisfying *boing* – and swept the apple pieces into a bowl.

'Here.' Daisy took the bowl from my hand and replaced it with a mug of tea, immediately making me smile and reflect on the fact that I really was lucky to have such a great life, regardless of what DCI Withers, with his clean-shaven but rugged jawline and his chiselled abs (which obviously I hadn't seen but could imagine only too well), thought.

'I brung you up proper, din't I?' I said, in my worst Cockney accent. She shrugged.

'Put the kettle on, Daisy, and don't ask questions,' she said, and Mum and I laughed.

'That's my girl. Thank you.'

We stood around drinking tea for a while, not sure what to do. Was there any point in preparing the rest of the food? The wedding was due to take place in an hour and, as far as I was aware, there was still no sign of the bride. Plus, the ceremony was meant to be happening right next to a crime scene, which was not terribly conducive to romance and didn't bode well for a happy marriage. *If there is such a thing as a happy marriage*, I thought cynically, but then I was off men – even (especially) good-looking detectives – so who was I to judge? And Cheryl must have heard about Mel by now; surely if she'd just changed her mind and bailed out of marrying Tony, she would at least have texted him to let him know she was okay? To my mind that left just two of those possible scenarios: she was dead too, or she was the murderer…

But why would she have murdered Mel? Mel's accusation – vague and enigmatic as it was – was hardly earth-shattering, and by the sounds of it Tony wouldn't have taken it seriously enough to call off the wedding. Or had she uncovered more about the Laity family than she'd let on to me? We'd kind of been friends through Tony, but we'd never been really close and there was no reason for her to trust me. Then again, I was beginning to suspect that Tony himself knew something; he'd definitely looked shifty when I told him what Mel had accused Cheryl of. And I'd left him to walk around the grounds that morning, to see if the runaway bride was just outside getting some air. How could he have missed Mel's body? The dog had been barking when I left him and if it had been me, I probably would have headed that way to see what all the noise was about or at least ask the owner to shut the mutt up.

Another unwelcome thought rose into my mind. If Tony had suspected that Mel knew something bad about his wife-to-be, could *he* have decided to shut her up? Or had he discovered Cheryl packing her suitcase and, realising she was leaving him, lost his temper and killed her to stop her going, then Mel because it was her fault?

Or had I just lost my entire mind? Tony wasn't a killer, my treacherous thoughts whispered to me again, *but how well do you even know Tony these days?*

'Penny for your thoughts,' said Mum. I shook myself; I wasn't going to share what were probably – hopefully – completely unfounded suspicions with anyone, particularly not my mum, who, bless her, had no real filter when it came to gossip and would more than likely share everything I said at the next village coffee morning, even if she didn't intend to.

'They're not worth as much as that,' I said, smiling at her and Daisy. 'Come on, let's pack up everything and just stick it in the fridge for the moment. I can't see this wedding taking place now, can you?'

So we clingfilmed everything and put what we could in the hotel fridge; there was more room for it here than at my house, and I wasn't sure what Tony would want me to do with all the uneaten food anyway. I was just about to go and find Mr Bloom, the manager, to tell him what I'd done and that I'd be back to move everything when I knew what was happening, when DCI Withers came into the kitchen.

'Mrs Parker?'

'Yes?' My mum looked up and smiled at him; he looked at her, then at me, confused.

'No, I meant—'

'I'm *Ms*, not Mrs. Mrs Parker is my mum,' I said.

58

'Shirley,' said Mum, ingratiatingly. She had an eye for a good-looking young man, which was sometimes rather embarrassing.

He nodded impatiently. 'Okay, *Ms* Parker. Can I ask you some questions about last night?' He stood back slightly, as if indicating for me to follow him.

'Of course,' I said, not moving. Petty, I know, but I wasn't going to make it easy for him. I'd noticed the slight, mocking emphasis on the *Ms* too. Mum held up a mug.

'Do you want a cup of tea? Kettle's not long boiled.'

'No, thank you. Can—?'

'You sure? I can always boil it again; won't take me a minute.'

'No, thank you, I'm fine.' DCI Withers was indeed starting to wither under my mother's charm offensive. 'If we could go somewhere a little quieter?'

'We'll be quiet,' said Daisy innocently. She was almost as nosey as me. It's a family trait. Withers was not going to be beaten by a twelve-year-old, though.

'Thank you, but no. Ms Parker? Shall we?' He stood back and firmly indicated the doorway. It would have been churlish (although entertaining) to mess him around any more.

He followed me out of the kitchen. I stopped and turned to him and he pointed towards the function room we'd used last night.

I went in and sat down at a table, waiting for him to join me. He took out his notebook and pen and sat opposite me.

'So, Mr Penhaligon tells me you're an old friend,' he said conversationally. He was well spoken in a BBC newsreader kind of way with the lingering hint of a regional accent, which I couldn't quite place. Maybe he was from a pumpkin farm in Birmingham, after all...

I nodded. 'Yes. We were at school together.'

'A *very* old friend, then,' he said. *The cheek!* He must have seen my face tighten because he said quickly, 'I just meant you've known him about as long as anyone else in town. What about Mrs Penhaligon – Melissa Penhaligon?'

'She moved here when we were in high school, so yeah, I've known her a while as well, but only really through Tony.' I stopped as it hit me again that poor Mel was dead. 'That is, I knew her...'

'You saw the altercation last night between her and Miss Laity, didn't you?' Withers looked down at his notebook, a lock of floppy fringe falling across his face. I wanted to reach out and tuck it behind his ear in a way that was half-maternal, half-frustrated divorcée. What was happening to me? I shook myself.

'I stopped it getting out of hand. Everyone else was too gobsmacked to move.'

'And then you took her outside to calm down?' I nodded. 'Did she tell you why she attacked Miss Laity?'

I hesitated, but only for a moment. Mel's accusations might now seem trivial but they'd been important enough in her mind to justify her approaching Cheryl.

'She thought Cheryl – Miss Laity – was only marrying Tony to get her hands on his shop.' Saying it out loud made it sound ridiculous. It was a small department store in a seaside town, for goodness' sake, not an oil empire or something. This was Penstowan, not Dallas. Withers obviously agreed, as he couldn't stop his eyebrows raising. 'I know, I know, it sounds daft. I suppose she just meant she was marrying him for his money or something.'

'Do you think she was? Do you think that's why she's disappeared?' So the police were taking Cheryl's no-show seriously. Good.

'I honestly couldn't say. I only met her for the first time a week ago. I didn't— I *don't* know her very well at all.'

Withers studied my face closely, in a way that made me feel a little uncomfortable; I wasn't sure if it was because he was making me feel like I was hiding something (like my stupid, momentary suspicions about Tony) or because he was super hot and it was a long time since anyone – let alone someone that good-looking – had actually looked at me with such deep interest. Except of course he wasn't interested in me; he was interested in what I was saying. Or rather, what I wasn't saying.

'Guv?' A uniformed officer stood in the doorway. Withers looked at him and nodded then turned back to me, snapping his notebook shut and getting to his feet.

'Thank you, Mrs … *Ms* Parker. We may need to speak to you again, so please give your details to one of the uniformed officers before you leave.'

———————

I thoughtfully made my way back to the kitchen. Mum looked up as I entered, a twinkle in her eyes that I knew only too well.

'Well, he was a nice young—'

'No, he wasn't. Let's grab what we can and get out of here.'

We made our way through the hotel lobby, where I stopped to give my contact details to a young copper near the door. As I turned to leave I spotted Tony through the open door into the dining room where I'd left him. He looked shattered. He was being fussed over by his elderly parents, Brenda and Malcolm.

'Tony!' I said. He looked up and smiled wanly at me as Mum hurried over to the Penhaligons. She embraced Brenda and reached out to pat Malcolm on the arm.

'How you all holding up?' she asked. Brenda smiled

bravely while Malcolm shook his head.

'Terrible business this, innit, Shirl,' he said. He looked like he couldn't believe it. 'Terrible business.'

'We're making a move,' I said to Tony. 'There's nothing more we can do here. I know food is the last thing you're thinking about, but if you let me know what you want me to do with it all, I'll pop back later and sort it out.'

'Okay,' said Tony. He seemed completely bewildered. 'I don't really know...'

'Don't worry about it now,' I said. 'It's fine where it is. What about you? Have the police said you can go? They seem pretty keen to get everyone out of the way.'

'They said we could leave but I want to stay in case Cheryl comes back...' Out of the corner of my eye I could see the Penhaligons and my mum exchange concerned looks.

'I dunno,' I said. 'What if she goes home? She might not want to come back to the hotel if she thinks all the wedding guests are still here. The police will contact you if she turns up.'

'*When* she turns up,' said Tony.

'When, yes, that's what I meant.' I couldn't meet his eye. I leaned in closer. 'Between you and me, I think Brenda needs to go home and she won't if you stay here. She won't want to leave you on your own, and your dad won't want to leave *her* on her own, so ...

maybe you should go back to theirs and keep an eye on them.'

'A nice cup of tea and put your feet up for a bit,' said Mum, and Brenda nodded.

'That sounds like a good plan,' she said. 'What do you reckon, love? Come back to ours for a bit. You can always come back and sort things out here later, when you feel up to it.'

'I suppose so...' He didn't sound very keen but with a bit of gentle cajoling, Malcolm got him to his feet.

'I should probably drop in and see Mel's mum on the way,' he said. 'She's going to be devastated.'

'You don't need to do that,' I said quickly. 'Mel had other family, didn't she? Cousins and an aunty and that. The police will have called them so her mum won't be on her own. She won't want a house full of people at a time like this, even if they do all mean well. Go home, Tony.'

He looked at me uncertainly for a moment, then nodded. Together we headed for the door to the car park.

The sight of the van, windows blacked out and the words 'Private Ambulance' in discreet lettering on the back, stopped us in our tracks. Two sober-looking men in black shirts and trousers gently unloaded the stretcher between them, the black-bagged occupant literally a dead weight. It was done without fuss or ceremony but it still felt somehow respectful; they were taking as much care of Mel as they would have done with a sick or injured patient.

We watched as the doors were firmly closed, then both men got into the van and quietly drove the body of Melissa Penhaligon away.

Chapter Six

W e drove home in silence, or in as much silence as the Gimpmobile allowed, anyway; it was making a nasty grinding noise every time I changed gear.

I offered to drop Mum off at her house but the events of the day had obviously shaken her more than she was willing to admit.

'I think I should come back to yours,' she said, leaning in to whisper conspiratorially to me. 'I think Daisy's upset and I can help you take her mind off it.'

I glanced over at Daisy, who had definitely heard but diplomatically (I don't know where she got *that* from) didn't say anything. She certainly didn't seem upset, humming to herself and texting one of her old London friends, no doubt telling them about all the excitement.

'Yeah, you're right,' I said with a wry grin. 'You'd better come back with us.'

I unloaded the bits and pieces we'd brought back with us (I'd made sure to bring the leftover canapés with some crisp lettuce and a nice potato salad; they'd make an easy dinner) and then flopped on the sofa, suddenly exhausted. What a day. And it was still only 3.30pm.

We spent the next couple of hours nibbling the leftovers (there went dinner), drinking tea, and gossiping.

'I didn't like that Cheryl,' said Mum, firmly. I had to agree; she had been a bit of a Bridezilla over the last week, picking holes in my menu suggestions until Tony had gently but firmly put his foot down and pointed out that if she didn't leave me to get on with it, there'd be no food at all. All the same, it felt wrong to come out and say it, now that she was missing-presumed-dead. I couldn't believe she would leave Tony in the dark if she was still alive; she owed him that much.

'She wasn't a warm person,' Mum continued. 'Not like her mother.'

I hastily swallowed a mouthful of flaky pastry. 'You knew her mum?'

'Of course I did.'

'Nana knows everyone,' said Daisy, and apparently she was right.

'You remember when I worked in the Co-op?' I

nodded. I didn't actually remember, but I knew Mum had worked in most of the shops in Penstowan at one time or another when I was a child. 'I worked with her mum then. She was younger than me, of course, only about eighteen or nineteen. What was her name?' Mum racked her brains; there was practically smoke coming out of her ears. 'Clare, that was it. She was— Oh no, not Clare. Eileen. I always get those two mixed up.'

Daisy looked at me and I could see the unspoken question: *how can you get Clare and Eileen mixed up?* I shook my head gently.

'Or *was* it Clare?' Mum looked thoughtful. I wanted to scream.

'Anyway…' I said, hinting.

'Anyway, yes, this Clare, she was a lovely girl, very pretty.' Mum stopped with a satisfied smile. I wanted to scream again. Was that it?

'Tony said Cheryl's family didn't live around here,' I prodded. Mum nodded.

'That's right. Clare – no, it *was* Eileen' – I didn't dare look at Daisy – 'she was a lovely girl, full of life. She grew up here in Penstowan but the Laity family didn't; they had a campsite down Boscastle way. They got a string of them now, of course.' Mum shook her head but I got the feeling it was more in admiration than disapproval. 'She was a one! Both the Laity brothers had their sights on her and she didn't exactly discourage them. Had them both eating out of the palm of her hand at the beginning! I don't know how she met them, but they used to come up here and wait for her to finish her shift. The older one was a right smoothie, but the young one, he was a nice lad. Very good-looking. I think there was a bit of bad feeling there, when she chose him over the other one.'

I tried to keep up with the gossip. 'So the older one, that would be Cheryl's uncle? Roger Laity?'

'That's right. He always dressed so nicely…' Mum smiled, misty-eyed. 'I said to your dad, why can't you dress like that Laity lad?'

'What did he say?'

'"Because I'm not a ponce, that's why."'

Daisy burst out laughing and I smiled. 'Yep, that sounds like Dad. So what makes you think there was bad feeling?'

'Am I under caution?' Mum raised her eyebrows.

'I'm just interested,' I protested.

'Smooth as he was, he was very keen,' said Mum. 'I can't imagine he was very happy when his little brother swept Clare—'

'Eileen,' Daisy mumbled.

'… off her feet like that. I think that's why they moved away.' Mum reached out to take another vol-au-vent. 'It caused a bit of a rift, I reckon. They went upcountry somewhere – Bristol, if I remember right. That

Roger was heartbroken; took him years to get over it, I heard.'

I remembered the sneering young man who had turned up with Roger Laity the night before, the one who had made Tony so uncomfortable.

'He's got a son, hasn't he? He was at the party last night, a right cocky little bugger.'

Mum nodded. 'Stepson. Craig. He's a bit of a bad boy, that one, always getting into some kind of trouble. His mum was married to one of Roger's business partners, and when he had a heart attack—'

'How do you know all this?' I asked, incredulous. She shrugged.

'Old girls' network,' she said. 'We like a bit of a gossip.'

Daisy guffawed. 'And the award for Understatement of the Year goes to…'

'We have to make our own entertainment,' said Mum defensively. 'Nothing ever happens here.'

We all looked at each other then and got into a fit of hysterics. Because nothing exciting at all had happened that day.

'So what about that nice young detective?' said Mum, when we'd all calmed down.

I groaned. 'Don't.' Mum tried to look innocent, but it wasn't working. 'I mean it, don't. You know I'm off men. You and Daisy are my priorities these days.'

'You can't tell me he's not a looker.'

'I can,' I said. But not very convincingly. 'Oh all right, yes, he's bloody gorgeous. But he's arrogant with it.'

'I thought he'd be the type you'd go for.'

'La, la, la!' sang Daisy, putting her fingers in her ears. 'Can we not talk about Mum having a type? That's dangerously close to saying she has a sex life.'

I laughed. 'I wish…'

'LA, LA, LA, LA, LA, LA!'

'Your mother's still young…' said Mum.

'Thank you,' I said.

'… and relatively attractive,' she continued.

'Relatively?'

'There's this game I heard some young girls on the bus playing,' said Mum. 'They'd name three boys and say which one they'd marry, which one they'd—'

'Oh, I know that game!' said Daisy. 'It's called Fu— Snog, Marry, Avoid.'

I looked at her warningly. 'Yeah, I know what it's called.'

'Okay then,' said Mum. 'That nice policeman—'

'DCI Withers,' I said.

'Withers? That's a terrible name. *Jodie Withers.*'

'Does she?' said Daisy.

I laughed. 'Exactly!'

'Okay, DCI Withers, Craig Laity and Tony.' Mum

folded her arms and looked at me. 'Which one would you fu— snog?'

'It's got to be the copper,' said Daisy knowingly.

'I thought you didn't want to think about my love life?'

'It is, though, isn't it? Who else are you going to snog, Tony?'

I gave a big mock shudder, although to be fair the thought of it wasn't actually bad, just a bit weird. 'God, no, it'd be like snogging a … a cousin or something.'

'Although technically kissing your cousin isn't classed as incest or anything,' pointed out Daisy thoughtfully.

'That's easy for you to say; you haven't got any. And you probably don't remember my cousin Kev. The one who moved to Hastings.' I shuddered, for real this time. 'Breath that could strip the paint off a barn door at twenty feet.'

'What about Craig Laity? He's pretty hot,' said Mum.

'Nana!'

'He is! He's a real bad boy. If I was twenty years younger … all right, thirty—'

'You'd still be too old for him. No, I wouldn't trust him as far as I could throw him,' I said. 'Avoid. Like the plague.'

'So you're going to avoid Craig, and you don't want to kiss Tony, so that means snog DCI Withers, and *that* means you become the next Mrs Tony Penhaligon!' Daisy and Mum laughed.

'I don't think so. Neither the ex nor the intended Mrs Penhaligon have fared very well, have they?' I said, and they both stopped laughing.

'No,' said Mum. 'Poor Mel.'

We all sat quietly for a moment, thinking of poor Mel. And poor Tony. I wondered how he was doing and hoped that he was still being fussed over by his parents.

'I might give Dorothy a ring, see how she is,' said Mum. 'I can't imagine how it feels, losing your daughter like that.'

We sat in sober silence again until my phone rang, making us all jump.

Chapter Seven

'And this is my responsibility why?' I asked.

'This' sat back on her fluffy white haunches and gazed up at me with her head to one side, her eyes full of the kind of expression that makes grown men descend into baby talk and melts the hardest of hearts. But I was (I told myself) made of sterner stuff. Besides which, I'd only just moved into my house and I was still in the middle of decorating. Plus, although I had savings I didn't have a regular source of income yet. Another mouth to feed and another body to get under my feet was the last thing I needed, even if it was cute and so soft and … and *floofsome* (totally a word) that you just wanted to grab it and hug it and bury your face in it…

I shook myself and looked into the pleading face of the hotel receptionist.

'I'm sorry, but I didn't know what else to do,' she said. 'I took her in when the police got here, to keep her out of the way, but Mr Bloom says we need to find her owner…'

'Her owner's dead,' I pointed out, not unkindly. She nodded.

'I know,' she said. 'I didn't know who to call so I rang Mr Penhaligon and he suggested I contact you because, and I quote, "Jodie always knows what to do."' I sighed. Sometimes being calm and unflappable in a crisis is a right pain in the backside. 'He also said he thought your little girl might like to look after the dog until you found a home for her.'

Until we found a home for her? *Yeah, right.* The minute that dog put one paw over the threshold I knew there'd be no way I'd ever be able to get rid of her. Daisy would never forgive me.

I squatted down so I was eye to eye (almost) with the dog. She immediately stood up and came over to snuffle at my hand, and I knew deep down that I was done for.

'I don't know if I should take her. Legally, she must belong to Mel's mum…' I said desperately. The receptionist smiled – she knew I was floundering now – and shook her head.

'Mr Penhaligon said that she lives in a retirement complex where they don't allow pets,' she said, 'so it's you or the RSPCA. And the poor thing's just lost her mum; she needs a family to make a fuss of her and give her cuddles…'

Oh, I could give her cuddles all right. No! I told myself. *Stop it!* Germaine gave a little whine and licked my hand. Were these things bred to play on your emotions or what?

'I haven't got a lead…' I said weakly. The receptionist smiled triumphantly and produced one.

'We have a dog walking service for our guests,' she said, handing it to me. 'It's a spare; you can have it. And these.' And she gave me a bundle of poop bags, all emblazoned with the hotel crest. 'She's just been fed as well, so you don't have to worry about getting food for her straightaway, she won't need any more until the morning.'

'Thanks…'

I stood in the doorway of the hotel, fumbling with the lead. It was one of those retractable ones, with a long lead curled up inside a plastic case and a button to lock it in place, or to let it spool out as the dog ran. Germaine was a very good girl and sat patiently while I clipped it to her collar and stuffed the poop bags into my pocket.

Should I take her for a walk so she could do her business? I rolled my eyes. *Do her business.* I was already talking like a true dog owner. I didn't know how long she'd been cooped up for and as much as the Gimpmobile – in which I'd driven over against my better judgement, as I hadn't known what the hotel had wanted me to collect – as much as it already smelt a bit funny (I did not want to know why, bearing in mind what sort of business the previous owner had run), I didn't want to risk the newest member of the family having a dump in it. And it was early evening, the weather was good, and it was still light. A brief walk around the grounds it was, then.

Germaine led me down the stairs and out into the car park. She turned straight towards the battered old Vauxhall, which hadn't moved from the night before and which had police tape all round it; I supposed it was evidence. The only thing I could see was different was that the window in the back – which I'd previously seen Germaine's snout sniffing at – was now open much wider. I looked down at her.

'Did you do that, Houdini?' I asked, remembering what Mel had said about her escaping from cars. The dog just wagged her tail and waited to be let into the car. I sighed and bent down to stroke her. 'I'm sorry, sweetheart, you'll have to come for a ride in my stinky old van.'

The phone in my back pocket vibrated. I took it out and looked at it. A text from Tony:

Everything okay with you?

Cheeky sod. He knew that right about now I'd be knee-deep in Pomeranian.

I'd just started to type out a slightly snarky (but not too snarky, as he was bound to be feeling emotional) reply, when Germaine picked up a scent.

I obviously hadn't clicked the button on the plastic housing properly because she was off and across the other side of the car park before I recovered my senses. I tried to reel the lead back but her momentum was too great and there was too much dog leash, well, unleashed. I hauled on the nylon lead; she was heavier than she looked. I felt like a fisherman on one of those extreme fishing shows they have on TV, you know the sort, where they're fishing off the Bahamas for barracudas or something and they have to strap themselves in so the massive beast on the end of the line doesn't pull them overboard. It was just like that, only with a small dog instead of a shark. I had no choice but to set off in pursuit.

It soon became apparent where she was heading. It was obvious, really. I ran towards the ornamental fishpond and got there just as Germaine reached the spot where she'd left her late mistress. She plopped herself down and start to howl, a tiny, high-pitched howl which broke your heart.

The crime scene itself was covered by a tent, erected by the forensic team to keep the prying eyes of the guests away from the victim's body and to protect any evidence. Police tape criss-crossed in front of it and I was mildly surprised that there was no officer on duty outside it; but then, maybe the scene of crime guys had finished, and we were, after all, in Penstowan, which at the best (or should that be worst?) of times was probably quite short-staffed. It had been in my dad's day anyway.

I squatted down in front of Germaine; if nothing else, my calf muscles would be getting well toned with a dog of this size. I reached out and stroked her soothingly.

'I'm sorry, fluffball, but your mum's not in there anymore,' I said, feeling a lump form in my throat. Poor Mel. Poor Germaine. The dog looked at me and I had to blink back tears. Ridiculous. Years in the force had made me, not hardened but able to control my emotions in the face of bereaved or angry relatives, but put a dog in front of me and I turned to mush.

Germaine licked my knee, which was comforting in a bizarre way, then she put her head down and began to snuffle around in the grass. I watched her for a moment. It was well trampled here, both where Mel and I, and then Tony, had strayed off the path to sit on the bench, and where later on the small crowd had gathered to gawp at her body. Later still, the heavily shod feet of the police had crushed it even further.

Germaine turned away from the tent and sniffed; she'd picked up a scent. I should really reel her in and get her away from there. I stood up, but halfway up I stopped, then hunkered down again. It wasn't really noticeable when you were standing, but from down here there was a faint but definite path in the undergrowth, leading away from the bench. Germaine started up that path, tail wagging, obviously following some kind of scent trail.

I stood up again and looked around. There was no one about. I felt pretty sure the police wouldn't really want anyone fumbling around so close to the crime scene but there was no one on duty and I could hardly help it if my dog managed to slip her lead…

I followed the ridiculously fluffy, waggy tail in front of me. The path was quite faint but it was also wide, stalks of grass flattened and bent, forming a track almost a metre across. *It could be nothing*, I told myself, but my copper's intuition was nagging at me.

Germaine ran on ahead, all thoughts of her mistress left behind with the tent. The trail wound through the grass for a good five hundred metres, and I was just starting to think that it was nothing more than an animal track or something when we reached a rather rickety wooden picket fence. On the other side of the fence was a lay-by, with the main road between Penstowan and Launceston next to it.

Germaine stopped and sat down, looking pleased with herself, and began to wash her unmentionables. I sighed and turned back to look towards the hotel, which was pretty well hidden behind the bushes. I must've driven past this spot thousands of times and never realised it was here.

I looked down at Germaine and reeled in the lead, then stared in astonishment. Caught on a bush next to her was an earring, a big gold flashy thing. A small yelp told me I'd reeled in the leash as far as it would go, so I loosened it and bent down to study the discarded jewellery.

I recognised it, I was sure. It was a large, hammered gold disc, about 5cm in diameter, with a red jewel set in the centre. I was ninety-nine per cent certain it was Cheryl's. She'd been wearing it the night before with her swanky red cocktail dress and I'd noted it at the time as I remembered my mum having some similar earrings when I was little. I'd coveted those earrings, but I'd been too young to have my ears pierced and by the time I could have them done, fashions had changed and so had my taste in jewellery.

I reached out to pick it up but stopped myself just in time. How had it ended up here? I stood and stared at the trail leading back towards the hotel; how had it been made? It was too wide to have been made by a runaway bride, even if it did lead to the freedom of the open road… I thought for a moment then, watched by a bemused Germaine, lay down.

The trail was the width of my body with my arms draped casually by my side. So the trail could have been made not by feet, but by a body. A body being dragged, all the way to the road.

I got up and inspected the fence. It was just about low enough to climb over, especially if you put a foot on one of the cross beams. The wood was old and rough under my skin and I yanked my hand away as a splinter found its way into a finger. I tied Germaine's lead to the fence and climbed ungracefully over it, hoping no one would drive past and find me in such an undignified position.

There was a scrap of material caught on the fence this side. White cotton, with a thin blue thread running through it. Nothing particularly distinctive, nothing like the red silk Cheryl had been wearing the last time I'd seen her, although of course she probably would have changed into something a little less restrictive if she'd been fleeing from her nuptials. But then, why come this way when she had a car in the car park? And why leave her suitcase?

I looked around the lay-by. There was nothing there except for the ubiquitous litter and suspiciously smelling damp patch you seem to find in all lay-bys where there're no toilet facilities. On the tarmac, where a car using the lay-by would have sat, was a dark stain, probably from engine oil or something. And that was it.

I climbed back over the fence. I momentarily

considered bagging up the earring as evidence, but then I remembered that 1) all I had in my pocket was a bundle of hotel doggy-poop bags, and 2) it wasn't my job anymore. Instead, I took out my phone and called the police station.

Chapter Eight

DCI Withers gave a big exaggerated sigh, which I thought was probably meant to make him look like a world-weary cop but just made me despise him all the more.

'And do you want to tell me exactly why you were poking around in the undergrowth near my crime scene?' he asked. *No*, I thought, but I didn't say it.

'I wasn't poking around. The dog slipped her lead and ran off.' It was more or less true.

'Hmm.' Withers did not look convinced. 'If you weren't sneaking around, how did you manage to get past the officer who was guarding the crime scene?' He indicated a young uniformed officer who was standing behind him nervously. The young man immediately looked terrified and shot me a pleading glance.

'I didn't sneak past him,' I said. 'I explained the situation and the officer used extremely good judgement and let me pass. We obviously couldn't leave the dog roaming around and I didn't want to make him desert his post and get into trouble.' The young officer sagged in relief and gave me a look of deep gratitude. So it clearly wasn't just me who thought Withers was an annoying git.

'Hmm.' Withers examined the trampled grass carefully, ignoring me. I let him look for a few seconds, but couldn't keep quiet any longer.

'If you look at the grass, it's not completely flattened, not like where the body was found, so I reckon there was only one, maybe two people walking along here.'

'Before you, you mean,' said Withers, pointedly. I ignored the veiled criticism.

'And the width of the path is about the same as a body with the arms laid out by its side.'

'What makes you say that?'

'I lay down and tried it out,' I said. Withers looked surprised, and for a moment it looked like he'd almost forgotten himself and was going to laugh – but it was only for a moment.

'You lay down, contaminating the scene?'

Oh for God's sake! I rolled my eyes. 'I lay down in one spot, yes, but you'll be taking my DNA for elimination purposes anyway, won't you?' He looked surprised again, but this time not in a good way. 'You know, because I manhandled the victim when she had her fight with Cheryl? Or had that not occurred to you?'

'Of course it had,' he said, but I got the feeling he'd dismissed me so easily earlier that day that he'd not really considered that my DNA would be all over Mel.

'You'll need Cheryl's as well,' I said, 'but as she's disappeared you'll have to get a sample off one of her belongings, a hairbrush or—'

'Yes, *thank you*!' said Withers. 'It's all in hand. One of my officers will take a swab from you now.'

'Er, the forensic blokes have gone home, guv,' said the nervous uniformed officer. Withers sighed again.

'In the morning, then. Pop along to the station and— STOP THAT DOG URINATING ON THE EVIDENCE!'

Germaine and I finally escaped. I took her back to the Gimpmobile and settled her on the passenger seat – which didn't feel terribly safe, but I didn't know what else to do – then I patted her on the head.

'Good girl, Germaine!' I said. 'Someone deserves some doggy treats for annoying old Mr DCI Grumpy Pants, doesn't she? Oh, yes, she does, oh, yes, she does.' I stopped in disgust. Less than two hours had passed since I'd returned to the hotel and I'd already turned into a doggy person. By morning there was every chance I'd be unironically wearing jumpers with pugs on them.

Daisy, of course, was over the moon when Germaine bounded in through the front door. She momentarily forgot that she was a streetwise South London twelve-year-old who was too cool for school, and actually *squealed* with delight at the sight of the fluffy white ball of cuteness who was to be our new family member. I think she was about to clap her hands in her excitement but she remembered just in time that she had a reputation to uphold and stopped herself. She still dropped to her knees and hugged Germaine tightly, burying her face in her fur in exactly the way I'd envisioned myself doing.

By now it was starting to get late. I offered to take Mum home, but she looked so tired that I suggested she stay overnight with us again. I didn't have to insist too hard and I was beginning to suspect she didn't enjoy her freedom and independence quite as much as she had said she did.

Daisy reluctantly went to bed – reluctantly, because she didn't want to leave Germaine and she begged me to let her sleep in her room. But I wasn't sure how well she would settle (the dog, not my daughter), so with one last cuddle (for the dog, not for me) she trooped off upstairs.

I made Mum a cup of cocoa and we sat up, talking over the day's events, until she too took herself off to the spare room.

I was tired but my mind was buzzing and I didn't think I'd be able to sleep. Germaine had flopped down on the sofa; I wasn't sure how I felt about getting dog hair on my lovely new furniture but she looked so comfy that I didn't have the heart to move her... I was just wondering if I should take her out for one last walk around the block to relieve herself before going to bed, when my phone buzzed. Another message from Tony.

You still up? Can't sleep.

―――――――――

'I feel like a teenager, sneaking out to meet a boy at midnight.'

Tony was leaning against a railing, looking out to sea. He jumped as I spoke and turned around to greet me with a grin. He looked at his watch.

'It's only half ten,' he said. 'I felt knackered and thought I'd have an early night, but then I couldn't get to sleep, and I had to get up again.'

'Same here,' I said. Germaine wagged her tail and sniffed around his shoes.

'You didn't mind me lumbering you with the dog?' he

said. 'I'm sorry, I should've checked with you first but I wasn't really thinking straight.'

'It's fine. You are officially one of Daisy's favourite people for suggesting it.'

'I would've taken her, but Cheryl's allergic to dogs and I thought, when she comes back…' His voice trailed off.

The town was pretty quiet for a Saturday night. There were a couple of pubs open near the sea front and a few drinkers spilled out into the street, talking loudly and laughing, but the police had cracked down on people drinking on the beach in recent years (too many people getting drunk and deciding to go for a moonlit swim), so apart from a group of moody-looking teenagers skateboarding and smoking spliffs in the car park and a drunken couple snogging furiously in a shop doorway, we had the beach to ourselves.

We walked down stone steps onto the sand and sat on a nearby cluster of boulders. The rock felt cold through the thin yoga pants I'd changed into earlier and I could hear my mum's voice in my head warning me about getting piles, but I ignored it.

'How're your mum and dad?' I asked.

'They're fine,' said Tony. 'I'm staying with them tonight. I'd rather be at home but Mum worries, you know?' I nodded. 'I think that's why I can't sleep. Their house always makes me feel claustrophobic. Like the walls are closing in.'

'Old people like a lot of stuff,' I said, and he laughed softly.

'Yeah, Mum's collected a lot of knick-knacks over the years...'

We sat in silence, listening to the waves. The tide was a long way out and the wet sand reflected the moonlight above, shining like a mirror in the darkness. I couldn't quite decide if it was eerie or romantic – probably a bit of both.

Germaine was having a grand old time digging in the sand and I could see clumps of it sticking to her lovely white fur; I'd have to give her a good brush before I let her in the house again.

'How are *you* holding up? Have you heard anything?' I asked. I wondered whether I should mention finding Cheryl's earring. It was on the tip of my tongue but I stopped myself; it looked like something bad had to have happened to her and there was no point upsetting him. Let him at least have a few more hours of blissful ignorance. I wasn't sure if that made me a good friend or a bad one.

'No, nothing,' he said. 'Did you talk to anyone when you went back to get the dog? Did they let slip anything about the investigation? You being Eddie Parker's daughter and everything...'

I laughed. 'I don't think DCI Withers has heard of my dad,' I said. 'Before his time. Most of the officers who served under him must be getting close to retirement age now.'

'Yeah, I suppose.'

'I'm assuming there's no word from Cheryl? What about her uncle and aunty? Or her cousin?'

Tony shook his head. 'You met her uncle. He despises me, which is fair enough because I don't like him. Her aunty is nice enough but she just does as he tells her all the time. She wasn't there last night but she was at the hotel earlier today; she had a stupid hat on—'

'Half the guests had stupid hats on,' I pointed out, and he smiled.

'What is it with weddings and stupid hats?' he asked. 'You should see the one my mum wanted to get.' He shifted on his boulder. 'I don't know what's going on. That Withers asked me a lot of questions about my relationship with Mel, then he started going on about Cheryl and did I have any reason to believe she was going to leave me...'

'Did you?'

He sighed. 'I don't know.'

'You know something?' I said. 'When I told you what Mel had accused Cheryl of, you looked surprised. And a bit relieved.'

He shook his head. 'Not really...'

'Tony, tell me.'

'Nothing much to tell.' He stretched out his legs. 'What you said, about Cheryl being after the shop? Well, I know that's nonsense, because the shop doesn't belong to me.'

'It's still your dad's?'

'It's not even his, really. He used to go on about giving me the shop when he retired, so I suppose that's where Mel got the idea from that it's mine, but he just meant handing over the reins so I can run it. The actual physical store – the building – is owned by a family trust. If I ever wanted to sell it I'd have to run it past everyone named in the trust: my mum and dad, my uncle and aunty in Newquay, my sister, even though she's in New Zealand and shows no sign of coming back or having any interest in it; I've got some cousins somewhere as well who I barely know. The building is probably worth quite a bit of money but by the time I'd paid everyone their share... Anyway, Cheryl knows that, so she wasn't after the shop or my money or whatever Mel thought, because I don't have enough to make it worth her while.'

'There is something though, isn't there?' I wasn't going to let this go.

'You're like a dog with a bone, aren't you? You haven't changed.'

'No point changing if you're already perfect,' I said, and he laughed.

'If you say so, love...' He looked up at the full moon, and for a moment I thought he was going to throw back his head and howl. But he just turned back to me. 'It's a bit ... vague. It's probably nothing. I'd forgotten about it, really, until this morning.'

I smiled encouragingly at him but didn't speak. I'd found over the years that people quite often *want* to tell you things, but if you push it they clam up. Best to just sit quietly and wait.

'About two months ago, things started disappearing,' said Tony.

'Disappearing? What, from the shop?'

'No, no, from home. Nothing of mine; I'm not talking about stealing. I'm not sure what I'm talking about. The first thing I noticed was this figurine of Cheryl's. Hideous china thing. Her uncle gave her it for her twenty-first and it was worth quite a lot of money.'

'How much?'

'I dunno, £500? £600? Anyway, I hated it but she was very fond of it and insisted on keeping it on the mantelpiece, and then I came home one day and it wasn't there.'

'Did you ask her about it?'

'Yeah, she just said she'd knocked it off while she was dusting and it had got broken. I did think it was a bit weird, because she was so fond of it that I would've expected her to try and stick it back together, but she said she'd chucked it in the dustbin.'

'Okay… And then other things went missing?'

'Yeah, but stupid things like kitchen stuff. The blender and the food mixer went, and the juicer, but we never used that. She said she'd taken them to the charity shop because we'd probably be getting newer ones as wedding presents, but they were all top of the range and fairly new. And I didn't want people buying us presents anyway because I'm forty years old – I've got everything already – but I thought maybe she'd made a gift list or something.'

'Anything else?'

'Yeah. This was the weirdest one. She asked to borrow my laptop because she said hers was broken and she'd taken it to be repaired. Of course there's only one place in town to take stuff like that—'

'Wonnacotts,' I said, and he nodded.

'Yeah. I was going past it a few days later, so I thought I'd go in and ask when it would be ready, and they said they didn't have it. She'd never taken it in there.'

'You think she sold it?'

'I think she sold all of those things. I didn't mention it – I didn't want her to think I'd been checking up on her – but why would she be selling stuff like that? If she needed money, she knew she only had to ask me and I'd have given her what I could. I wondered if she was trying to raise money to buy … this'll sound stupid, but you hear about people selling everything they can get their hands on to buy drugs…'

'Cheryl was on drugs?' I knew you couldn't always tell; there were plenty of people out there with hidden addictions who managed to function quite normally (as long as they got their fix), but I could not imagine Cheryl being a junkie.

'Sounds stupid, doesn't it?' Tony said. 'I don't seriously think she was on anything. I thought maybe she was trying to do something nice for me, maybe buy me something without me noticing the money leaving our bank account. But after I found the note this morning, I thought maybe she was getting an escape fund together?'

'Escape fund? Escape from what?'

Tony turned away from me. He had kept himself together so far, but as I looked at him it was just like someone – okay, me – finally unzipping a pair of very tight jeans: everything that had been held back by that thin strip of material suddenly came bursting out and it wasn't a pretty sight. He put his head in his hands and sobbed and I only just heard his voice, muffled as it was by tears.

'Me.'

Chapter Nine

I left Tony on the doorstep of his parents' house. He'd had a good cry, which had left him exhausted but calm. As I walked up the road I looked back and saw the front door open, and Brenda pull her troubled son into her arms for a hug. I was glad I'd insisted on him going back to the family home and not to his own empty house, because you're never too old to occasionally need a hug from your mum.

All that emotion from my old friend had worn me out too and I could barely keep my eyes open as I brushed the sand from Germaine's coat with a soft hairbrush. I made a mental note to add a proper dog brush to the long list of things I needed to get from the pet shop the next day. I turned off the light, intending to shut her in the kitchen-diner overnight (I'd purloined the beanbag from Daisy's room for her), but she looked up at me so beseechingly that I couldn't close the door.

I sighed. 'Come on, then.' I climbed the stairs to my room and flopped onto the bed, and fell asleep with Germaine snuggled onto the duvet by my feet.

I slept much better than I'd expected and woke at 8am (which is late for me; I've always been an early riser). I looked down at the end of the bed but Germaine wasn't there and for a moment I thought I'd dreamt the whole thing. But a woof from downstairs and a high-pitched giggle soon told me otherwise.

Mum and Daisy were in the kitchen. The back door was open so Germaine could trot in and out as she pleased, but as the human occupants were currently cooking bacon for breakfast, the canine one was definitely more interested in what was happening indoors.

'I'm not sure we should be giving her bacon,' I said.

Daisy shrugged. 'It's just meat, innit? Dogs can eat meat.'

'I know, I just meant there'd better be enough left for me to have a butty!' I flicked the kettle on to make tea and smiled as Daisy hunkered down and taught Germaine to shake hands. The dog quickly responded to

Daisy's outstretched hand and lifted her own paw for a handshake. I got the feeling my daughter wasn't teaching this dog any new tricks but she looked so happy that I wasn't about to burst her bubble.

'You went out late last night,' said Mum, flipping bacon over in the frying pan. I normally grill it because it gets rid of more fat, but you can only get it really crispy in a pan.

'Yeah, I just took Germaine for a walk round the block before bed,' I said. I don't know why but my meeting with Tony felt a bit clandestine for some reason and I decided to keep it to myself for the moment. 'You having a butty? Sauce? Brown or red?'

'Brown, of course,' said Mum.

I shuddered in mock disgust. 'Heathen.'

I buttered some bread (for a proper, authentic bacon butty you really need floury white bread but I only had wholemeal, which makes better toast) and sent Daisy off to wash her hands, then we sat down and ate our breakfast. That luscious, fatty bacony goodness, dripping with melted butter and ketchup and combined with a good night's sleep, made me feel marvellous (if slightly greasy), until I remembered that I had to go down the police station at some point to give them a DNA sample, and I really needed to sort out all the food that was left at the hotel.

My phone rang. I expected it to be Tony but it wasn't a number I recognised.

'Hello?' I answered with a mouthful of bacon.

'Is that Jodie?' A man's voice with a thick Cornish accent spoke on the other end. I didn't have a clue who it was.

'Yeah, who's that?'

'It's Cal.' The caller obviously recognised the puzzled silence that followed, as he clarified it for me. 'Callum Roberts, from school?'

Oh my God. Callum Roberts might not have been my first boyfriend (that had been Tony, for those short-lived two weeks) but he'd been the first boy I had been absolutely madly and unrequitedly in love with. He was gorgeous. Thick, dark hair that had a tendency to curl when it got a bit long, which he hated but which all the girls had thought was lovely, and the brightest bluest eyes you've ever seen. They'd had a real cheeky twinkle in them.

Lots of boys tend to go through a geeky phase where they're a bit skinny and gangly, a bit pimply and hopeless, before getting past puberty and into manhood. Callum had skipped all of that and almost overnight had turned into a fully-fledged actual man with muscles, hair in unexpected places, and, I dunno, *sex appeal*. Which seems yucky, me saying it as a forty-year-old, but as a sixteen-year-old it had been enough to set the hormones of every girl in the Fifth Year aflame. It was like going to school one day and amidst a sea of Adrian Moles finding George Clooney. *Where's Wally*, the X-rated version.

I combed my hair with my fingers before remembering that I was talking to him on the phone and he couldn't see me, and found my voice.

'Callum! What a lovely surprise! How are you?'

He sounded a little bit taken aback by my enthusiasm and I made a note to dial it back a bit.

'Yeah, I'm good, thanks, Jodie. I thought I should give you a call so we can sort out the stuff at the hotel for Tony.'

'Oh, right, that's nice of you.'

'Well, I'm meant to be the best man…' *Oh, you ARE the best man, Callum – or you always used to be, anyway.* I had to remind myself that I hadn't seen him for twenty years; he'd completely dropped off my radar after I'd moved to London. 'So what you up to today? Can you meet me at the hotel?'

I closed my eyes. After the upset and aggravation of the previous day, a rendezvous at a hotel with Callum Roberts sounded good to me. The police station could wait.

'Of course. What time?'

'I dunno, an hour?'

I smiled. 'It's a date.'

Now, I don't want you to think that I was desperate for a man.

I mean, yeah, I *occasionally* noticed hunky men when I came across them in my day-to-day life (DCI Withers was a case in point; nice to look at, nice to imagine what was under that shirt, which was a little too tight-fitting, but far too smug to actually want a relationship with), but I was actually very happy with the way my life had turned out – current murder situation notwithstanding. However, I was intrigued to see what had become of Callum, because I'd spent several of my teenage years daydreaming about him and imagining myself as Mrs Jodie Roberts, and sometimes – normally when things are turning to custard all around you and you're berating yourself for the dodgy life choices you've made – sometimes you can't help wondering what your life would have been like if those early daydreams had come true, or those stupid mistakes hadn't been made. I'd often wondered what I would have done if I hadn't had a policeman father. If he'd been a bricklayer, or a barber, or a fisherman, would I have wanted to follow in his footsteps then? And if I hadn't, would I still have moved to London?

So I turned up at the hotel, having made *possibly* a little more effort than usual (though not much) in honour of those teenage daydreams, burning with curiosity about how my teenage crush had turned out, and about how my life might have been different had he just bloody well noticed me at the school leavers' disco in 1996.

I parked the Gimpmobile and went into the foyer. There was a family waiting by the reception desk, the wife chatting loudly to the receptionist in a Northern accent – Manchester, I thought, although I'd been brought up in a part of the country that thought of anything past Dorset as 'the North'. The children – a boy and a girl of about seven and ten – were laughing and whirling each other around, quite violently, and I knew at some point one of them would let go of the other and it would all end in tears. The dad, who was what you might diplomatically call *well-built* and whose bald head was shiny with sweat, stood looking at his phone.

No sign of my childhood stud muffin there. I walked through to the dining room, which was still half-set for the wedding; the hotel had cleared away all the cutlery, plates, and glasses, but the floral table decorations and cake (both of which belonged to Tony and Cheryl) were still on display.

I turned as I heard someone enter behind me. The fat, sweaty bald guy (oops, there went my diplomacy) was in the doorway.

'Jodie?' he said, in that strong Cornish accent.

'Callum?' I tried to keep the amazement out of my voice. I'm not sure I succeeded.

'Well, I'll be jiggered, Nosey Parker, you ain't changed a bit!' he said, striding over to shake my hand heartily.

'No,' I said, 'nor have you...' I was still trying to get over the fact that not only had Callum become at least twice the man he used to be, apparently he was also now the type of person who said 'jiggered'.

''Ere, Debs, this un's Jodie! Come and say hello!' he called over his shoulder. The Northern woman from the foyer, who was blonde and had more make-up on than the cosmetics counter at Boots, came over and looked me up and down, then gave me a big smile and shook my hand. She might be a bit brash but she was open and friendly, and I immediately liked her.

'Hiya, I'm Debbie,' she said. 'Married to this one, for my sins.' She gave Callum a warm smile.

'It's lovely to meet you,' I said. Just then, Callum's phone rang and he wandered off a little way to answer it. Debbie looked at me again and grinned.

'So, don't tell me, you're another one of his schoolgirl groupies,' she said, amused.

'No, not really,' I protested, but she could see I was lying so I gave in and laughed. 'Yes, I have to admit I did have a massive crush on your husband twenty-odd years ago, along with most of our year.'

'And he hasn't changed a bit,' she said, still smiling.

'No, he hasn't changed a bit; he's changed *a lot*,' I said before I could stop myself, and she laughed.

'Oh, I know he has.' She watched him affectionately. 'We met years ago when he came up to Manchester to work on the children's hospital; he's in medical gases, engineering, that sort of thing. I don't understand any of it... Anyway, I was a nurse and he turns up with this gorgeous head of dark, curly hair, those beautiful blue eyes, and that lovely accent. Swept me right off my feet.' She sighed melodramatically. 'The only thing he sweeps off these days are quarter-pounders.' She noticed my look of discomfort. 'Oh, don't worry, I still love him. He's still got the beautiful blue eyes and the accent.'

'He's definitely got the accent,' I said, and we both laughed. 'I'm glad Tony chose him to be his best man. He needs some good friends around him at the moment.'

'Yeah, he does.' Debbie looked serious. 'What do you think's happened to her? Do you think the same person that killed Mel—' She broke off as Callum approached.

'Tony'll be here in about twenty minutes,' he said. 'He just wants to swing by his house first. He says we need to get rid of all the flowers and the cake.'

'We could drop them off at the one of the local nursing homes,' suggested Debbie.

I nodded. 'Yes, that's a lovely idea. Or the hospice. They'd really appreciate the flowers. And there's tons of food in the kitchen, too. Is there a food bank round here? Anything that'll keep for a while could go to them.'

We talked for a while longer and Callum proudly introduced me to their two children, Matilda and George, then I left them in the dining room and headed for the kitchen.

Chapter Ten

I started off by getting everything out of the fridge and making a list of what was there. Luckily, the guests had eaten most of the canapés and starters, as we'd ended up giving them out while the police were questioning everyone. But I'd ordered 200 sausages for the main course and, although they could be frozen, there wasn't room for that many in my freezer. Maybe we could give them to the Salvation Army for their food bank? They must still have a few days before they had to be used or frozen. Or maybe we could sell them on to one of the pubs; they all did food, and tourists to Cornwall always loved local, organic produce (as did the landlords, because it meant they could charge two quid extra per sausage). I also had ten parmesan-crusted aubergines, which had to be eaten today, and apart from the vegetarian wedding guests, who had now all gone home, there wasn't much call for aubergines in Penstowan – certainly not ten of them in one go. I hadn't made up the couscous to go with them, so that was easily dealt with, but Daisy and I had peeled most of the potatoes (which had been destined to be turned into truffle mash to go with the bangers). They were now chopped up and waiting in the fridge in some big empty ice-cream tubs I'd found in the back of a cupboard and filled with water. I hate throwing food away, but what else was I going to do with them?

I wondered if the hotel chef would take them off my hands but when I'd briefly met him the day before, he had been surly and unhelpful. It seemed that he had taken the decision to hire me as a personal slight and a slur on his cooking abilities, which, to be fair, it might have been; I'd not had a chance to sample his work. He was conspicuous by his absence from the kitchen, and I suspected he was keeping out of my way. All in all I doubted he would do anything to help with my predicament. First of all, though, I really needed to talk to Tony...

Debbie entered the kitchen in a rush.

'Jodie, come quick!' she said, already turning round again to leave.

'What's the matter?' I said, shutting the fridge.

'It's Tony, he's going mad...'

We ran out of the kitchen, along the corridor, and out into the foyer, but long before we got there I could hear crashing and shouting, and Callum's voice pleading for him to calm down. The receptionist was on the phone and she looked up at me as I skidded on the marble floor.

'Don't call the police!' I said. 'I'll sort this out.' I hoped I would. But she didn't need to call the police because through the big glass doors into the car park I could see two police cars already parked outside. Of course, they obviously weren't finished with the crime scene yet.

'He's in the dining room,' said Debbie, completely unnecessarily, because it was quite clear where all the noise was coming from.

Tony stood by the top table where yesterday he should have been toasting his new wife and being embarrassed by his best man's speech. Instead, he was holding the middle tier of the beautifully iced wedding cake. I didn't need to ask where the top tiers were; they were on the floor, dropped and then trampled on, absolutely destroyed. His face was flushed with anger as he raised the cake above his head.

'Tony!' I cried. He stopped for a moment and looked

at me, but it was as if he didn't recognise me. 'Tony, calm down. Don't take it out on the cake! Or the hotel carpet.' It was a right bugger getting fondant icing and marzipan out of a deep-pile carpet; I'd learnt that the hard way after one of Daisy's early birthday parties. Half a mermaid had ended up ground into the Axminster when a game of Pass the Parcel had turned bad.

'What's the point?' he said. He shifted the cake – which was a big, hefty fruitcake, going by what was on the carpet – and looked at the delicate purple sugar-paste flowers that decorated it. 'Do you know how much this cake cost? Two grand. Two grand on a bloody cake.' He lifted it over his head and threw it as hard as he could across the room, where it hit a sideboard covered in glasses. I heard something smash.

'Tony, mate…' Callum held his hands out in a placatory gesture, but Tony just glared at him.

'Callum, *mate*, did you know? I bet everybody knew.' He reached out and pulled a chunk of cake off the next layer and I couldn't help but look at it, rich with mixed fruit, and think, *Damn, that looks like a good cake.*

'Know what?' Callum genuinely didn't seem to know what Tony was talking about.

'I bet everyone knew but me,' said Tony, smearing the cake between his fingers and then studying them. He was losing the plot. 'I bet even Nosey knew about it.'

'Tony—' I started, watching as he began to pick up

lumps of cake and throw them at the glasses stacked up on the sideboard, like a petulant child at a coconut shy.

'You knew she was a wrong un, didn't you?' He threw a lump, but his aim was off. 'You didn't like her. No one liked her except me.' He threw another, hard. It hit a glass, knocking it on the floor where it shattered into tiny pieces. He did a mini fist pump and picked up another piece of cake.

Bloom trotted into the room and stopped, aghast at the devastation before him.

'Mr Penhaligon!' he spluttered, as Tony turned to him holding the baked projectile. I stood in front of him, my arms spread out wide to protect the hotel manager.

'Tony, stop it now!' I said.

'Or what? You'll arrest me?' he said sarcastically.

'She won't, but I will,' said a voice behind me. DCI Withers. *Damn.*

Tony shrugged and lobbed the fruitcake in his direction but I darted forward and caught it, staggering slightly under the force behind it. Two uniformed officers appeared from behind Withers and ran at Tony before he had a chance to reload with cake so he just picked up what remained of the tier and smashed it onto the carpet before they grabbed his arms and pinned him down on the table. I ran over to them, closely followed by Withers, who reached out to pull me out of the way.

'Oh, come on, there's no need for that,' I said, as one

of them began to cuff him. Tony struggled and swore and somehow managed to wriggle one hand free before the cuff went on, flinging his arm out and accidentally smacking Withers in his perfectly formed nose. Despite the fact that the situation was rapidly going pear-shaped, I felt dangerous laughter rising. The whole scene must look so ludicrous, and Withers getting slapped was the icing – I nearly choked – on the cake.

'Anthony Penhaligon, I'm arresting you for breach of the peace, resisting arrest, and assaulting a police officer,' began Withers, although what with him holding onto his wounded nose it sounded more like 'Andony Pendalion'. If the situation hadn't been so serious, I really would have laughed.

'Come on. It was an accident!' I said, getting in Withers's face, 'caused by you sending the boys in when we could've talked him down.'

'Get out of my way, *Ms Parker*, before I arrest you as well for obstruction.' Withers did not look like a happy bunny; I think he felt a bit daft clutching his nose, which had just started bleeding.

Tony had finally calmed down, only now of course it was too late.

'I'm sorry,' he said, looking like he was going to cry again, 'I didn't mean to. I just don't know what's going on…' He looked lost and I felt my heart break for him. 'Jodie, I'm sorry, don't let them—'

But I couldn't stop them. With one last glare at me, Withers and his two officers marched Tony out of the room, out of the hotel, and into a waiting police car.

Chapter Eleven

My first instinct – and Callum's – was to jump in the Gimpmobile and hotfoot it to the police station in pursuit. But I knew that it would take some time for them to process Tony, and that they would probably leave him to stew in the holding cells for a while until he properly calmed down. I also had the sneaking suspicion that the breach of the peace charge had been a bit of a pretext. Withers had been very quick to arrest him, when in normal circumstances most of the coppers I'd worked with would have tried much harder to smooth things over and get a mate to take him home. It made for less paperwork. I thought maybe Withers wanted him at the station so he could ask him a few more questions about Mel's murder.

So instead of flying into the car park, Callum, Debbie,

and I got some cleaning things from the kitchen and began to clear up the mess Tony had made in the dining room. Even the two children, Matilda and George, who had been quickly sent to play outside in the grounds when Uncle Tony began to have a meltdown, came in and helped. George picked up a big lump of cake from the floor and put it in his mouth when he thought no one was looking, and once or twice I caught Callum looking like he wanted to do the same. I will neither confirm nor deny that the thought crossed my mind once or twice too. It was a damn good cake. I was just glad I hadn't been the one who'd made it. All that work wasted…

I was hoping to get Bloom to drop any potential charges and I thought if we showed willing, scrubbed the carpet, and offered to pay for the damages, he might come around. Debbie had been threatening to wade in and 'persuade' the hotel manager to cut Tony some slack, but Callum – who I was beginning to see was something of a gentle giant – got there first and he proved successful. I could imagine only too well how 'persuasive' his wife would have been, as, much as I liked her, there was definitely a touch of the Ena Sharples about her.

We got as much sugary icing out of the carpet as we could and, after offering to pay for a carpet cleaner, headed into the kitchen with the last tier of the cake, which had managed to avoid contact with the floor. I made some tea and looked longingly at it; it had been a stressful morning and stress makes me eat more. As does contentment. And depression. And joy. I just like cake, all right? Don't judge me.

'Shame to waste it,' I said, and Callum laughed.

'I was hoping someone would say that,' he said.

So we all had a slice of wedding cake – we didn't think Tony would mind at this point – and discussed our plan of action.

'If we go down there, will the police let us talk to him?' asked Callum. I shook my head.

'I wouldn't have thought so. Although...' I thought for a moment. 'I wonder if anyone from my dad's time still works there?'

'Your dad was a copper?' asked Debbie.

'Chief Inspector Eddie Parker,' I said.

'Bit of a legend round these parts,' said Callum. 'But it's been a while since he...' His voice trailed off. *Died*, I thought. *It's okay, you can say it.* 'Anyway, I wouldn't know. Debs and me live in Manchester these days; we only came back for the wedding.'

I absentmindedly reached out for another chunk of wedding cake and chewed it, looking for inspiration in its rich fruitiness (any excuse). And then it hit me. I smiled.

'I just remembered that I have an appointment at the

police station today anyway,' I said. 'Let's see if I can get anything out of them while I'm there.'

It felt weird pulling up outside Penstowan Police station. I'd been there so many times when I was little, meeting my dad from work. And then when he'd become Chief Inspector, he'd divided his time between here and the smaller stations at Wadebridge and Launceston.

Like the rest of the town, it hadn't changed much. It was an ugly 1960s pebbledashed monstrosity which stuck out like a sore thumb amongst the quaint stone cottages and the old church that surrounded it. The blue 'Police' sign over the door was the only thing that had been updated over the years.

It felt even weirder going inside. There was a row of plastic seats against one wall, empty save for a miserable-looking woman who kept glancing at her watch and letting out her breath in a big huffing sigh of impatience. I walked up to the enquiry desk, which was now hidden behind a Perspex screen; when I was a child it had been open, and it had loomed above me when I'd gone in to ask for my dad. There was no one there so I rang the buzzer.

'I hope you ain't in a hurry,' said the miserable woman. 'They like to keep us bleedin' waiting.'

'Now you stop your mithering, June,' said the desk sergeant, entering the room behind me. 'I always tells you, it ain't worth you waiting for him. He'll be out soon enough.' He looked over at me and winked. 'Husband can't take his ale and we end up giving him a bed for the night. What can I do for you?'

'DCI Withers asked me to come along and give a DNA sample for the Penhaligon case,' I said. 'I'm Jodie Parker.'

The sergeant had turned away and was swiping a pass card to let himself behind the desk but he stopped and turned back.

'Jodie Parker? Not Eddie Parker's daughter?' He looked delighted to see me.

'That's me,' I said. He rushed over and took my hand, shook it eagerly, then kept hold of it, peering into my face.

'Little Jodie! Well I never! How long's it been?'

'Twenty years,' I said, a little overwhelmed by his keen scrutiny. 'Obviously I've been back to visit, but it must be twenty years since I've been in here.' I wrinkled my nose. 'It smells the same.'

The miserable woman snorted derisively and mumbled something but we ignored her.

'You won't remember me; I was PC Adams last time I saw you—'

A flash of memory came back. 'No, I remember you! You always had jelly babies.'

He laughed. 'That's me. I'll let you into a secret; I still do.' He swiped his card again and went round behind the desk, where he pulled out a drawer, took out a bag of jelly babies, and offered them up. 'That's why me teeth are so bad.'

'Well, it's good to see you,' I said, selecting a red one, 'but I'd better get this DNA swab thing done. That Withers strikes me as a bit of a stickler.'

Sergeant Adams rolled his eyes. 'Oh, yes, you could say that. He's a young gun, ain't he? Only been here five months and knows it all.' He tapped a number into the phone on the desk and spoke quietly into it. I heard the words 'Eddie Parker's daughter' and smiled; maybe there were a few people here I could mine for information after all, making use of the affection in which my dad had been held.

Adams put the phone down. 'Someone'll come and take you through in a minute, if you want to take a seat.' He smiled warmly. 'It's nice to see you again. I was proper fond of your dad. It's down to him that I joined the police.'

'Really?'

'Oh yeah. I was a right tinker when I were a lad, always getting into some kind of trouble. Nothing malicious, mind you, just bored. Your dad, he was a copper on the beat back then; he stopped me when I was throwing stones at the old bakery on Fore Street – it was empty at the time and I was trying to break a few windows. He gave me such a telling off, it scared the pants off me. Told me what would happen to me if I carried on down that path. Made me join the other side, as it were.'

'And years later, you're still here.'

'Yep, still here, in uniform.' He drew himself up proudly. 'There's a few of us still here, you know. Eddie Parker's Recruits.'

My eyes suddenly got a bit watery. Hay fever, obviously.

'How much longer are you lot going to keep him?' moaned the miserable woman.

'Oh, quit your bitching, June,' I muttered, and sat down at the other end of the row.

A young female officer came and took me into the station proper. She left me seated in a corridor while she went to get the DNA kit.

'Why is it that every time I turn around, you're there?'

I grinned to myself. I hadn't necessarily expected to see Withers while I was at the station – I didn't hold out much hope of getting any answers from him – but any opportunity to wind him up was too good to miss.

'Why, DCI Withers, fancy seeing you here!' I said brightly. He smiled thinly.

'I work here. What's your excuse? Come for a job in the canteen?'

'DNA, remember?' I said. 'I need to give you a sample.'

'And there's me thinking you'd come to berate me for arresting your friend.'

I smiled. 'I'm a woman. I can multi-task.'

The officer came back with the DNA sampling kit.

'Would you like to do this in an interview room?' she said. I smiled at her.

'It's fine; it'll only take a second, won't it? And then I can get back to my nice chat with DCI Withers.' She looked surprised but then took out the cotton bud and wiped it around the inside of my cheek. She placed it in a plastic sample tube, then repeated the process on the other cheek. Withers watched. I wasn't sure why, but he seemed reluctant to leave.

'Thank you,' I said to the officer, who smiled and left us.

'You really didn't need to stay on my behalf,' I said to him.

He gave me another one of his thin-lipped smiles. 'On the contrary, I thought I should wait and make sure you didn't *accidentally* go blundering into any crime scenes again.'

'I left my dog at home today. So that was Cheryl's earring, wasn't it? Did you have any luck with the scrap of material left on the fence?'

He shook his head. 'Ms Parker—'

'Jodie,' I said, and immediately wondered why I had.

'Jodie,' he said. He looked slightly uncomfortable using my first name. 'You know I can't give you any information about an ongoing investigation, especially when you're in a close relationship with the chief suspect.'

I felt my cheeks reddening. 'A close relationship? With who, Tony? We're just friends...' And then my brain caught up with what he'd just said. 'Chief suspect? You can't suspect Tony?'

'Ms Pa— Jodie, think about it; his ex-wife turned up and ruined his wedding.'

'She didn't turn up at the wedding; it was the night before.'

'You know what I mean. She turned up and caused trouble. The next thing we know, the bride's disappeared, her earring's found in a bush, and the ex-wife is dead. It doesn't look good, does it?'

'Yeah, but I know Tony. He wouldn't hurt a fly,' I said, but as I spoke I remembered the angry look on his face when I suggested that Cheryl could be the killer, and the rage he'd taken out on the poor defenceless wedding cake. The Tony I knew wouldn't hurt a fly, but did he still exist?

Withers looked at me. 'Come on. You're ex-force. You know how this works, and you know as well as I do that the most obvious explanation is usually the truth. You know that most murder victims are killed by someone they know. And most female victims are killed by their husbands or partners.'

'But not Tony...' But he was right. If I didn't know him, I would probably have pegged Tony as the murderer as well.

'You know how this works. We have to do things properly, for Melissa Penhaligon, and for Cheryl Laity.' I opened my mouth to ask him if she'd been found, but he anticipated my question because he quickly added, 'Wherever she is. Leave us alone to do our job. You're not a cop anymore. It's not your place to find the answers.'

Chapter Twelve

'Guv?' A plain-clothes officer, about fifty years old, arrived behind Withers. He saw me and stopped. 'Sorry, I didn't realise you were busy. Phone call.'

'Ms Parker and I have just finished,' said DCI Withers. 'Can you show her out?'

The newcomer looked surprised. 'Parker? Not Eddie Parker's daughter?' Withers turned to me sharply.

'Your dad was Chief Inspector Parker? I've heard a lot about him since I came to Penstowan. Big shoes to fill.' He looked at me, and it was probably just my imagination but I knew he was thinking, *Too big to fill; no wonder she quit.*

'Guv,' said the officer again, urgently. Withers nodded.

'All right, I'm coming. Ms Parker, remember what I

said. It's not your job anymore.'

I followed the plain-clothes officer back out to the enquiries office. He turned to me.

'Sergeant Adams said you were back,' he said, smiling. 'I remember your dad. When I was a rookie I went through a bit of a bad patch and he stopped me quitting. I'll always be grateful to him.'

'Thank you,' I said, but I was still thinking, *Big shoes to fill...* And that, in a nutshell, was why I'd joined the Met and not the Devon and Cornwall Constabulary. It's not easy, being the daughter of someone so highly respected.

'Hang on!'

I turned around. Withers stood in the doorway back into the station. 'Wait there, I've got something for you.'

A shamefaced Tony shuffled out. He looked thoroughly worn down. I glanced at Withers in surprise.

'Mr Bloom at the hotel dropped all charges. Apparently, Mr Penhaligon, your friends are very good at damage control.' He looked at me. 'I'm assuming that was you?'

I tried to look innocent but it probably just came off as smug. 'I couldn't possibly say...'

'Take him straight home,' he said. 'I'll be seeing you again soon, Tony.'

I tried to get some sense out of Tony on the drive back to his house, but he seemed exhausted and barely spoke. I pulled up outside the grey stone cottage and turned to him.

'Thanks, Jodie,' he said, fumbling with the seatbelt in his hurry to get out of the Gimpmobile. I put a restraining hand on his arm.

'Oh no you don't!' I said. 'I think you owe me an explanation, don't you? What the hell was all that about this morning?'

He sighed. 'Please, I just want to lie down.'

'Tough. Spill.'

He looked at me and his eyes filled with tears, but he swiped them away angrily.

'You'd better come inside.'

The house was a mess. It looked like it had been torn apart, a bit like the wedding cake. Tony saw my questioning face and looked away.

'I'll make some tea,' he muttered. I stopped him.

'No, *I'll* make some tea. You go and freshen yourself up, wash your face at least. And then you and I are going to have a chat.'

I put the kettle on and searched the kitchen for tea bags and mugs. I heard Tony banging around upstairs, and the water had just come to the boil when he came in, wearing a clean T-shirt and looking a bit more awake.

I fished the tea bags out of the hot water and dumped them in the sink. Tony passed me the milk and gave me a small smile.

'Sorry,' he said.

'What for? For only having full-fat milk or for all the nonsense you put us through this morning? Callum was proper worried about you. We all were.'

'I know,' he said, picking up a mug and walking through to the living room. I followed. 'I am sorry.'

'So what happened?' I sat down opposite him and watched him blow on the hot tea.

'I came back from my mum and dad's this morning. I wanted to get changed before I went to help you lot at the hotel.' He stared into the brew. 'There was a letter waiting by the front door, for Cheryl. It was a big envelope and it had "Do not bend" on it, so I wondered what it was.'

'Did you open it?'

'Of course I did. I thought it might have something to do with what we were talking about last night – about Cheryl's escape fund, or whatever it was. I thought it might help me work out where she is.' His hand shook as he leaned over to put the untouched drink on the coffee table.

'And did it? What was it?'

He stared at me and he looked sick to his stomach. 'Oh Jodie, I never knew her at all…'

'What do you mean? For God's sake, tell me what it was!'

A sharp rap on the door made us both jump. Tony got up and looked out the window then swore.

'Not them again! Why won't they just leave me alone?'

'Mr Penhaligon!' Withers was outside, with two police cars parked in front of the house. 'Can you open the door, please, sir?'

'What is he playing at?' I asked angrily. They'd only just let Tony go; this was looking like police harassment.

Tony looked around furtively and I could see what he was thinking. I stood in his way.

'No, you don't,' I said firmly. 'If you do a runner they'll just take it as a sign of guilt. And you're not guilty, are you, Tony?'

'Of course I'm not!' he cried, looking at me pleadingly. 'You know I'm not! I'd never hurt anyone!'

I looked into his eyes and nodded. I believed him. He was still the old Tony I'd always known. I trusted him like I would've trusted a brother.

'Sit down then and I'll let them in,' I said. He sat down and I knew he had complete faith in me to get him out of this. I just hoped it wasn't misplaced.

'Ms Parker,' said DCI Withers wearily. 'I knew you'd be here.'

I nodded towards the Gimpmobile, which was parked outside and was hardly inconspicuous. 'Great work, detective,' I said sarcastically. 'If you're expecting to come in I do hope you've got a warrant. Otherwise it's starting to look like you're harassing my client.'

He looked surprised. 'Client? I thought you were a cook. Don't tell me you offer legal advice now?'

'No,' I said. I wasn't entirely sure what I was going to say until the words were out of my mouth. 'I'm investigating the murder of Melissa Penhaligon and the disappearance of Cheryl Laity. I want to find the truth, even if you don't.'

Withers looked at me in amazement for a second, then burst out laughing. Honestly, you'd have thought it was the funniest thing he'd ever heard. I glared at him angrily, although I was really annoyed at myself for saying it. Because now I bloody well *had* to prove Tony's innocence, and while I didn't doubt him, I doubted myself.

I glared at him some more. 'All right, it's not that funny,' I muttered, and he shook his head weakly, still laughing.

'Come on, it is *quite* funny,' he said. 'Playing private detective. Who do you think you are? Miss Marple? No, no, wait … Magnum P.I.!' He laughed even harder. 'You just need the moustache.' He peered hard at my face. 'Hang on…'

I looked down – I'm at that age where any waxing going on is more likely to be on my upper lip than on my bikini line – and went to shut the door but Withers stopped laughing and stuck out his foot.

He held out a piece of paper. 'We have a search warrant, so unless you want to be charged with obstruction, you need to get out of the way.' He leaned closer. 'That's the second time today I've had to threaten you with that. Let's not make it three times, eh?'

I stood back and opened the door to let him in. He was followed by three other officers, including the one I'd spoken to at the station, who looked slightly embarrassed.

'Hello again,' he said, then shut up as Withers glared at him.

'What's going on?' said Tony, looking bewildered. I sat down next to him and held his hand.

'It's all right. They're just going to search the house,' I said. He looked alarmed.

'But … they're convinced I hurt Mel. They'll fit me up…'

'No, they won't,' I said. Whatever Withers was, he didn't strike me as a bent cop.

We watched as the police officers thoroughly searched the house. Tony was wound up so tightly he began to make me feel tense, too. One of the officers stood in the corner of the room while the others went through each room with a fine-tooth comb. I didn't know what they were hoping to find and I suspected they didn't know, either.

'What we were talking about earlier...' I spoke quietly to Tony, not wanting the officer in the room to overhear, but luckily they'd lost interest in us and were staring vacantly out of the window. 'What was in that envelope?'

Tony swallowed hard. 'Photos. Photos of Cheryl. She cheated on me, Jodie. She cheated on me and someone sent me the proof.'

'You mean these photographs, Tony?' Withers stood in the doorway of the kitchen, holding up a see-through evidence bag. Inside I could see an A4 size photograph. It had been ripped up, but Withers had put the pieces together and even from here it was easy to make out Cheryl's face. Her face wasn't the only part of her body in the picture, though.

'She was a good-looking woman, your Cheryl, wasn't she?' Withers said carelessly, turning the photo around and having a good look at it. 'Very nice. Very ... *photogenic*.' I could feel Tony tensing with anger next to me and I put my hand on his leg, giving it a warning squeeze: *keep calm, don't let him wind you up.* Withers took out another plastic bag from behind the first one. 'I particularly like this one. The lighting's quite artistic. You can see everything so clearly... Everything except who she's with.'

Tony leapt to his feet and was in front of Withers before I could stop him. I jumped up and grabbed his arms so he couldn't do anything stupid.

Withers didn't even flinch. 'This is what I think happened. I think Mel discovered that Cheryl was cheating on you and that's why she tried to stop the wedding.'

'I told you what Mel said,' I interrupted him. 'She thought she was after his money.'

Withers looked at me, waiting for me to stop talking, then carried on. 'I think Mel confronted Cheryl and told her she knew. What happened next? Maybe Cheryl decided to come clean, or maybe she thought it was best to just do a runner before you found out. Whatever, when you discovered that she was cheating on you, you saw red. You decided to teach her a lesson—'

'Woah, woah, woah!' I said, dropping Tony's arms and stepping forward. I was furious, and I was so close to Withers I could see the hairs growing out of his nose. 'Have you found Cheryl's body? No? Then you don't know what happened to her. At this point she's still a missing person. You cannot treat this like a double murder.'

Withers held his hands up in mock apology, forcing me to step back. 'Okay, okay, my mistake. I just got carried away. That's easy to do when your blood's up, isn't it, Tony? So let's say Mel scared Cheryl off and you blamed her for it. You went to have a go at her and she told you what she suspected, but that made you even more angry because, deep down, you knew a woman like Cheryl would never go for a man like you.'

I could see Tony's hands curling into fists. I put myself between him and the DCI, a gentle but restraining hand on his chest. 'Ignore him, he's trying to wind you up so you lose your temper.'

Withers raised his eyebrows as I turned to scowl at him. He continued, 'You were furious with Mel because you blamed her for Cheryl leaving you in the lurch, jilting you at the altar in front of all your friends and family, so you killed her. And then when you got home you found these photographs, and you realised you'd been a bloody idiot because Mel had been right. How am I doing? Am I right? Or did you already have these photos? Did you kill Cheryl when you found out and then you *had* to kill Mel because she knew about it, and if she'd told everybody it would have been obvious you killed Cheryl?'

Tony opened his mouth to speak but nothing

came out.

'What was that?' asked Withers, exaggeratedly turning his ear towards Tony.

'I didn't—' His voice was husky, his throat dry. He swallowed. 'I didn't kill Mel.'

'Then can you explain to me why your DNA was found on the victim's body? And we have witnesses who say you left the bar that night, who saw you going into the hotel gardens. We have witnesses who heard a man and a woman arguing loudly.'

'Did they identify the voices as Mel and Tony?' I said. Withers didn't answer, so I guessed it was a no. 'If not, that doesn't mean anything. And there must be a simple explanation for the DNA.' I turned to Tony. *Please have a simple explanation…*

'I did go out into the garden to see Mel,' he said. My stomach went cold. 'It was just after Jodie left…'

Withers looked at me, questioningly.

'I left the bar at about 9.30pm. I went upstairs to see if Cheryl was okay after the fight with Mel.'

'And was she?'

'Yes.' I didn't mention the fact it had looked like she was packing; I didn't know if it would help exonerate or convict Tony.

'I saw Mel out in the garden, walking her dog,' said Tony. 'I felt bad because I did have a bit of a go at her when Jodie took her outside, after the fight. Although we split up, I didn't bear her any ill will.' Withers looked sceptical. 'I didn't, I swear. I did at first, but after I met Cheryl I forgave her. I went outside because I just wanted us to be friends again. I was happy and I wanted Mel to be happy too.' Tony looked tearful again and I believed him. I knew Mel had broken his heart but Cheryl had apparently mended it.

'How long were you talking for?'

'I don't know, about half an hour?' Tony looked bewildered as one of the other officers made notes.

'And how did your DNA end up on her?' asked Withers.

'We talked for a bit, we made up, and then we had a hug,' said Tony. 'The only time I laid hands on her was to give her a cuddle.'

Withers stared at him. 'You *cuddled* the woman who had just tried to throttle your bride-to-be and ruin your wedding?' He shook his head in disbelief. 'Anthony Penhaligon…' he began.

'Oh, not again!' I said angrily.

'…I'm arresting you on suspicion of the murder of Melissa Penhaligon. You do not have to say anything, but anything you do say may be used in evidence against you. Do you understand?'

'Yes,' said Tony, in a small defeated voice. I watched as the police led him out of the house, then sat down and wondered what the hell was going on.

Chapter Thirteen

'So now he's back at the nick,' I said. I looked at the shocked faces in front of me.

I had returned home after checking over Tony's house to make sure the police had left everything as it should be, and had then called a council of war: Tony's mum and dad, Brenda and Malcolm, Callum and Debbie (the children were with Callum's parents), and, of course, my own mum, as she still hadn't gone back to her house and I had the feeling I wouldn't be getting rid of her any time soon. Not that I minded. Daisy had taken Germaine for a walk; they were already firm friends.

'I don't understand. They arrested him, and then they let him go, and then they arrested him again?' Brenda looked tearful, obviously out of her mind with worry over her son. I realised that it didn't matter how old your kids got, if they were in trouble, they were still your babies. 'That's just cruel, it's like they're playing cat and mouse with him.'

'I know it feels like that, but they're not,' I said. 'I reckon they took his DNA yesterday at the hotel, and when they got the result back today they applied for a search warrant. I think after the trouble this morning, Withers was probably hoping the warrant would come through while they still had him in custody. He was probably hoping to get the search done, and then if anything came up they could arrest him for Mel's murder while he was still at the station. But because Mr Bloom refused to press charges, they had to let him go and wait for the warrant to come through.'

'What were they looking for?' asked Callum. 'The murder weapon?'

'More than likely,' I said. 'I think a lot of the damage would have been done when Mel hit the floor, and the bench on the way down, but there was another wound on her forehead which looked like someone had bashed her with something. There was a lot of blood…' Brenda went white and I remembered that she'd been one of the first people on the scene. She'd always got on well with her ex-daughter-in-law, and to see her lifeless body up close must've been a terrible shock. 'Sorry, Brenda. So yeah, I think maybe the murderer used a heavy object to finish her off. But they didn't find it at Tony's house. Of course. Because he didn't do it.'

'Too right he didn't,' said Malcolm, and everyone murmured their agreement.

'I think they were looking for clues to Cheryl's disappearance as well,' I said. 'Although they haven't found a body, they seem pretty certain she's dead.'

There was another general murmur of agreement.

'But she might not be,' pointed out Debbie. 'She might have just left him. If she was having an affair, she might have decided to go off with the other man.'

I thought about it. 'Maybe. But why would she leave her car? And her suitcase? Tony said they were going on their honeymoon straight from the reception. I wonder…'

'Wonder what?' said Mum.

'I wonder what's in that suitcase.' The others looked puzzled. 'Think about it. Maybe she's trying to make it look like she disappeared, faked her own death or something—'

'What, *Cheryl*?' Mum looked sceptical. 'I don't know as she'd be clever enough to do that.'

'What if she had help from her lover?' I said. 'Or she might have just left her stuff there to throw Tony off the scent for a bit and give her time to get away. Which is why I wonder what's in the suitcase. Where were they going on honeymoon?' I asked Brenda.

'Corfu,' she said. 'Two weeks in Messonghi, half board. Lovely hotel.'

'So her passport, if she's been murdered, should be in the suitcase, or in her hotel room…' I mused. 'If it's not, then she must've taken it with her. Which would suggest she planned her disappearance.'

'Then I reckon we need to go and break into her car,' said Debbie, standing up and cracking her knuckles. Callum groaned. 'What? The kids are fine being spoilt by Nana and Grandad for a couple more hours. It'll be fun. I'm a mum; the most excitement I normally get is wondering which one of the kids will throw up first on a long journey.'

'George,' said Callum absentmindedly. 'It's always George. But you can't break into her car—'

'We don't need to,' I said. I remembered spotting Cheryl's keys on the dressing table when Tony had taken me to her room. 'But we might need to sneak past Mr Bloom…'

We parked outside the hotel. We were in Debbie and Callum's car; Debbie had taken one look at the Gimpmobile, shaken her head, and gone back to get the car keys from her unresisting husband. She had a point. We were trying to be inconspicuous and I could only imagine what DCI Withers would say if he went back to the crime scene and saw me there. Part of me relished the thought of crossing swords with him again – he really wound me up – but the bigger, more sensible part knew that it was unwise to antagonise him, at least while Tony was still in the frame for Mel's murder.

We strolled into the foyer. I did have a legitimate excuse to be there; I *still* hadn't got everything out of the hotel kitchen, having been so rudely interrupted by Tony's epic cake-throwing tizzy. But I really wanted us to get a look at Cheryl's room, to see if she'd left anything behind to suggest that her disappearance hadn't been planned after all and to get hold of her car keys, if they were still there.

Debbie strode confidently up to the receptionist and I remembered that they'd been having a natter when I'd arrived earlier that day. It seemed incredible that so much had happened so quickly, and I had to remind myself that Mel's body had only been discovered the day before.

'Hiya,' she said. 'Can we get the key to Cheryl's room? Tony said everyone was supposed to be checking out today, so we thought we'd come and get her stuff.' She leaned in towards the receptionist. 'Poor bloke, he's heartbroken. We thought, anything we could do to make it easier for him, you know.'

The receptionist lifted her phone. 'I'd better ask Mr Bloom if it's OK—'

'We don't want to disturb him,' I said quickly, 'and to be honest, we're a bit embarrassed after what happened earlier...'

The receptionist smiled but didn't put the phone down. 'I do understand, but Mr Bloom said I have to check with him if anyone connected with the ... the goings-on turned up. We've already had Mr Laity here wanting to get Miss Laity's things, but the policeman that was here earlier said no one was allowed in.'

Dammit. I had hoped that as she was still just a missing person, rather than a victim, the local police might have been concentrating more on Mel, but then Withers had seemed convinced that Cheryl was dead too and it was just a matter of time before they found her body. Why was I not so sure? Everything Withers had said earlier about Tony killing Cheryl after finding the photographs made sense. Tony had an obvious motive, and there was no denying that she had apparently disappeared off the face of the earth. And yet...

And yet *I knew Tony.* We'd been so close as teenagers, even after those ill-fated two weeks of being boyfriend and girlfriend. And, even though I had been away for such a long time, he'd always been among the small group of old friends I'd looked up whenever I visited. Most of the others had moved away or just fallen by the wayside, but we had the sort of friendship where it didn't matter how long it had been since we'd last seen each other, we'd just carry on from where we left off. And I knew he wouldn't – *couldn't* – kill anyone, least of all Mel or even Cheryl, however much I disliked her.

'The policeman—' I started, and the receptionist got a dreamy look in her eyes.

'The good-looking one,' she said. 'I can't remember his name.'

'DCI Withers,' I said immediately. I didn't know why Debbie looked at me with an amused grin on her face. 'He's not here now, is he?'

'I don't think so,' she said, with a hint of regret.

'That's a shame,' said Debbie, still grinning at me. 'Go on, let us just sneak in. We won't be any trouble.'

'You could always go up and ask the policeman outside her room,' she said, thoughtfully. She laughed. 'Old Davey's not quite as good to look at as the other one, mind you, but he's a nice bloke.'

I gave a start. 'Old Davey? You don't mean Davey Trelawney?' She nodded. *Bingo*, I thought, only just resisting a fist-pump. I smiled. 'Thank you, we'll pop up and have a word with him.'

Chapter Fourteen

PC David Trelawney, or Old Davey as he was locally known, had been another one of my dad's recruits. Son of one of the local pub landlords, he'd been fond of a drink and had spent a good few nights in the cells drunk before my dad had told him that if he liked the station that much, maybe he should work there. Except, of course, he doubted that Davey had it in him to pass the physical fitness test.

Local legend had it that that had been like a red rag to a bull, which Davey resembled in terms of his build, and had made him challenge my dad to a race along Penstowan beach.

Dad had beaten him easily. In front of most of the town.

Davey had not been happy, but instead of going off

and getting drunk again on the local scrumpy (which had been rumoured to cause blindness in large doses), he went into training. Davey challenged him to another race … which Dad also won, but only just.

That still wasn't good enough for Davey. He gave up the booze completely and started running every morning and using the beer barrels at his dad's pub as weights. He challenged Dad to another race, this time along the beach carrying a barrel over his head.

Dad lost – he could barely lift the barrel over his head, let alone run with it – and turned up at the pub the next morning (where Davey was nursing a very bad victory hangover) clutching an application for police college with his name on it. And the rest, as they say, was history. Old Davey had a been a copper rather than an alcoholic (although the two are by no means mutually exclusive) ever since.

Davey was loyal, built like an ox on steroids, and just about the straightest cop you could hope to meet. One thing he wasn't was particularly old, even now.

We turned into the corridor where Cheryl's room was and stopped as we saw the uniformed slab of muscle standing outside. He must've been approaching sixty but you could tell he was still impressively ripped under that uniform, and you'd certainly think twice before mentioning retirement to him. Debbie looked at me in surprise and whispered, 'Why's he called Old Davey? I was expecting some doddery old fella...'

'Morning,' said Old Davey. 'Gonna have to stop you there, my lover. You can't go in.'

'Hi, Davey, remember me?' I said. He looked closely at me.

'Can't say as I do, me duck,' he said. Then suddenly his expression cleared. 'No! It ain't Little Jodie?' I smiled and nodded. I had been 'Little Jodie' among Dad's police colleagues for almost as long as he'd been Old Davey, despite not having been little for years.

'It is. How're you doing? Can't believe they haven't put you out to pasture yet...'

He laughed. 'She's proper cheeky, this un! Always has been. I heard you were back. What you doing here, though?'

'Terrible business, innit?' I said, and he nodded.

'Aye, it is that.'

'And they think Tony Penhaligon did it!'

He looked uncomfortable. 'Yeah, well, he had a motive all right, didn't he? Still, I wouldn't have thought he had it in him to do that. Not kill someone.'

'No, me neither. So we were hoping to get Cheryl's stuff. The hotel's got more guests coming and they need the room...'

Old Davey shook his head. 'No, they haven't. What are you up to?' He grinned. 'You wouldn't be the bloody irritating, nosey woman the guvnor's been moaning about, would you?'

'Oh yes, that's me,' I said, brightly. 'You going to let us in or what?'

'What,' he said. 'I can't, as much as I'd like to.'

'Oh, come on…' I smiled at him but it didn't work. It always works in movies.

'What you hoping to find?' he asked, suspiciously. Debbie and I exchanged looks and she shrugged. Might as well tell him.

'Cheryl's disappeared, yeah? The happy couple were meant to be going away on honeymoon and we thought, if she's left her passport behind in the room, or in the car, then that shows she wasn't planning to disappear, 'cos you'd take something important like that, wouldn't you? And credit cards, and all that. So that could mean that maybe she was murdered too. Which is what DCI Withers thinks, isn't it?' Davey didn't speak, so I carried on. 'But of course, if we search everywhere and we *can't* find her passport and purse, then she must've had them on her, which makes it more likely that she planned her disappearance and is still alive. And therefore Tony didn't kill her.'

Davey looked at us thoughtfully. 'You know of course that I can't give you any information on this case? Seeing as you ain't a member of the local constabulary or Mr Penhaligon's legal counsel?'

'I know that. But maybe...'

'I wouldn't be able to tell you if we'd already thought of that, and had searched Miss Laity's belongings both here and in the car.' He looked at me meaningfully. So they'd already done that. Withers was so convinced of Tony's guilt that he was looking for evidence to prove it was him, instead of looking for evidence to find Mel's killer – a subtle difference, but a difference nonetheless. 'Of course, if we had already searched her stuff, the last thing you'd want to hear is that we'd found Miss Laity's passport, because that would make it look like something nasty's happened to her. You understand I can't do that, right?'

'Yes,' I said. 'I understand. Is there anything else you can't tell me?'

Davey looked confused. 'No, when I said I *can't* tell you, I actually meant—'

'Yeah, yeah, I know what you meant!' I said quickly. Davey was a nice bloke but he was definitely more brawn than brain, and this was akin to doing mental gymnastics for him. 'Look, if I ask you some questions you can just say yes or no if you like, but if you did decide to tell me anything I won't let on it was you. Withers will never know, okay?'

Old Davey hesitated.

'Eddie was really proud of you, you know,' I said,

shamelessly playing on his loyalty to my dad. *Sorry, Dad, but it's for a good cause.*

Old Davey smiled, with a hint of resignation. 'Go on then, but only 'cos I owed your dad.'

'Cool. Okay … what about time of death?'

'Now that's a tricky one, I heard. It's all because of the dog.'

It was my turn to look confused. 'Germaine? Mel's dog?'

'Aye. The lady on reception said when she got to work at 6am the dog was barking. There were no reports or complaints of a dog barking before that.'

'So you think Mel could have been killed in the morning? What would she have been doing here that early?'

Davey shook his head slowly. 'We don't know. Maybe she could have come back to have another go at stopping the wedding. But the DCI still thinks she was killed the night before, during the party. The doc said he'd normally be able to go by body temperature versus ambient temperature—'

Debbie looked at me; now *she* was confused. It was catching.

'Human body temperature is normally roughly thirty-seven and a half degrees,' I explained. 'After death the body loses heat at the rate of around one and a half degrees an hour until it reaches ambient temperature – the temperature of the environment around it. So you can normally work out fairly accurately how long someone's been dead.'

She still looked bewildered but said, 'Oh. Right…'

I turned to Davey. 'So what's the problem?'

'If the body had been left outside overnight, like the guvnor thinks, it would have been pretty cold, and that would have slowed down the rate of heat loss. But by the time it was found it was a hot day, plus the dog had been sitting on her chest, guarding her and keeping her warm for God knows how long.'

'Meaning the rate of heat loss would have been all over the place, and really buggering up time of death.'

Davey nodded.

'But if she'd been killed at night, surely someone would have heard the dog barking well before 6am? There's a hotel full of people; some of them must have been light sleepers,' said Debbie.

'Yes,' I said. 'Which suggests *the dog* wasn't there all night, but Mel still could have been. She told me herself that the dog is basically Houdini. She's always escaping, so Mel could only leave the window open a tiny bit when she left her in the car, otherwise she'd wriggle through the gap. When I picked the dog up yesterday I noticed the window of Mel's car was open more than when I last saw it. So maybe she was killed the night before, but the dog was in the car and only got out and went to find her the next morning?'

Davey shrugged. 'Could be. I'll mention it to the guvnor. I won't say where it came from. Don't know how much difference that will make to the case, though.'

I thought hard. 'When I left Mel, she said she was going to give the dog a walk round the grounds as she'd been shut up in the car for too long. I went back to the party for about fifteen minutes, then I went to see Cheryl. Tony left soon after me. He says he went out to talk to Mel after seeing her through the window, walking the dog. There are witnesses who saw him leave the party then, and that's one of the things Withers is basing his evidence on. It's not unreasonable to believe that she was walking the dog for fifteen minutes, is it? But she can't have been killed then because if she'd been killed in front of the dog it would have barked and it would have carried on barking all night. And as we've established, no one heard it until 6am. The dog must've been in the car when she was killed.'

'Yes...' Davey looked doubtful. 'That don't mean he didn't sneak out and kill her later on.'

I sighed. 'No, I know. But there are no witnesses that say they saw him leave the hotel again later, are there?'

'No.' Davey shifted uncomfortably. 'Look, I can't really tell you anything else. I don't know much else for a start, but I do know that Withers'd have my guts for garters if he knew I'd been talking to you.'

'It's all right,' I said. 'And thank you. I really appreciate it.'

'I've got a question,' said Debbie. I glanced at her in surprise. 'Why are you called Old Davey when you're not that old?'

He laughed. 'Truth is, I been called Old Davey most of my life, on account of my grandpa. He was a Davey too. My dad was the youngest of six children, and I was the youngest of *his* children, so by the time I came along Grandpa Davey was pretty old. They called him Young Davey for a joke, you know, like they call big blokes 'Titch' or something. So of course they had to call me Old Davey, so they knew which one of us they was talking about.'

'Of course,' said Debbie. 'That makes perfect sense…'

'It does if you're Cornish,' I said.

Chapter Fifteen

W e left the hotel and went outside. I tried not to look at Mel's car in the car park, surrounded by police tape, and now Cheryl's was cordoned off, too.

We sat in Debbie's car.

'So what have we learnt?' I asked.

'Bugger all?' suggested Debbie. I shook my head.

'No. We've learnt roughly what time Mel was killed.'

She looked amazed. 'We have?'

'Yes. Tony saw her at 9.30pm. It sounds like they must have had quite a chat, if they made up enough to have a hug, and then she would have put the dog back in the car, so say that took half an hour? At least. So it was after 10pm and before 6am, when the dog started barking.' I looked at her thoughtfully. 'I went and talked to Cheryl at about the same time, and she was still in her room. As far as I can make out, I was the last person to see her, as everyone thought she was having an early night before her big day. Tony sent her a text when he went to bed, about midnight, but she never replied. So she could easily have done it between, say, 10pm and midnight – assuming she murdered Mel and then did a runner – otherwise why not answer her phone?'

Debbie looked at me in complete astonishment. 'You think Cheryl murdered Mel? Why would she do that?'

'Why not? If Mel knew about her affair, Cheryl would have had just as much motive to shut her up as Tony – more, in fact. Tony only really has a motive if Cheryl's dead and he killed her too.'

'But we don't know if Cheryl *is* dead.'

'Exactly! Withers is acting like she is, even without a body. It's the only way Tony being the murderer makes sense.'

Debbie thought about it. 'Okay … but like we said earlier, why would Cheryl leave her passport and all her stuff behind? Unless she wanted it to look like she'd been bumped off, too… Do we know for certain that Mel even knew about the affair? She didn't tell you she did, did she?'

'No, she— Oh, bugger!'

A black car had just pulled into the hotel car park: Withers. I glanced at Debbie and slid down in my seat, and she followed suit.

'Who are we hiding from?' she whispered.

'DCI Withers,' I said, and she grinned at me. I ignored it. 'He's already told me off twice today; I don't want him to see me here again.'

'Okay… I'm sure I've seen people do this in movies though, and just when they think they've got away with it—'

A tap on the window next to me made us both jump. I sighed; I knew who it was before I looked up.

'Yep,' I said. 'I think I've seen those movies too.'

I sat up and wound down the window. Withers bent down and stuck his gorgeous, irritating face level with mine.

'Ah, DCI—'

'Out of the car, please, Jodie.'

'Actually, we were leaving; I just came back to get my sausages…' I could feel my cheeks burning. Why the hell was I burbling on about sausages to this man?

'Ms Parker, please.' He gave me a please-don't-demean-yourself-by-trying-to-wriggle-out-of-it look. I looked at Debbie, then opened the car door.

Debbie started to get out too.

'No, not you, Mrs … Ms…' DCI Withers shot me the tiniest of glances before he could stop himself, as if my presence had reminded him not to just assume someone's title (something we'd been taught in the Met, which clearly hadn't caught on here yet).

'Debbie Roberts,' said Debbie, giving him a dazzling smile. *Hang on*, I thought, *you're married to the man of my teenage dreams. Don't you start flirting with this one!*

Withers smiled back, showing off his white teeth and rugged jawline. Oh, he was so smooth. 'Debbie. I need to have a word with Ms Parker here, but you can leave.'

'She's my lift,' I said weakly.

'Not anymore she isn't,' he said. Debbie gave me an apologetic look and got back in the car. Withers waited for her to leave, giving her a cheerful but firm wave when she hesitated at the exit and looked back. Then he turned to me with a sigh.

'What part of "butt out" do you not understand?' he said.

'I dunno, probably the same part of "innocent until proven guilty" that *you* don't understand,' I said.

He raised his eyebrows. 'And how exactly am I not understanding that?' he said.

I shrugged. 'I dunno. Lack of training?'

I thought it was quite a witty comeback under the circumstances but he obviously didn't. He grabbed my arm and marched me away from the hotel, into another part of the grounds. There was an old folly or pagoda thing, painted white with lilac wisteria and pink rambling roses growing over it. It was beautiful and romantic and just the sort of place I wouldn't normally mind a bloke leading me off to for some privacy, only not this bloke, and not under these circumstances.

He led me up the steps and sat me down firmly on a bench, then stood in front of me.

'Why are you causing me so much trouble? What exactly are you accusing me of, Ms Parker?' he said. He seemed a bit miffed. *Good*, I thought.

'Why do you care what I think?' I asked. He just stared at me. 'Let me guess, you haven't been here very long and you're feeling a bit insecure about your position. I'm assuming Penstowan's not like anywhere you've worked before?'

He smiled thinly – he was a world-class thin-smiler – but I got the feeling I'd touched a nerve.

'You could say that.'

'This is your first major case here – definitely your first murder case; we don't get a lot of those down this way – and you want to make a good impression by solving it quickly. But this is Cornwall. We don't do things quickly here, and we don't expect you to, either. We just want you to do it properly.'

'I *am* doing it properly.'

'No, you're not,' I said. 'You've already decided that Tony Penhaligon is the murderer.' He opened his mouth to speak but I held up my hand to stop him. 'Yes, I know he has the most obvious motive, and the most obvious explanation is normally the right one. But—'

'But you know Tony,' he interrupted, sarcastically.

'Yes, I do. And you've got a theory and you're trying to find the evidence to back it up, instead of looking at the evidence and coming up with a theory from that.'

'I can assure you I'm not,' he said, but he didn't look that assured himself.

'I get it,' I said. 'Your theory is completely plausible; it even sounds likely. But only if Cheryl's dead, and we don't know that she is. There's no body. *If* Mel knew she was having an affair, and *if* Cheryl decided to leave because Mel threatened to expose her, and *if* Tony found out anyway and lost his temper with Cheryl and *if* he knew that Mel knew ... that's a lot of ifs.'

Withers sat down next to me. To my amazement, he actually looked likegiven him food for thought.

'Melissa Penhaligon had absolutely no enemies,' he said. 'I've asked around, and everyone liked her, even after she dumped Tony. They all seem to think she got her comeuppance when her lover dumped her. The only person who had any reason to bear her a grudge was Tony.'

'And Cheryl, if she threatened to expose her affair to Tony.'

'Yeah...' Withers couldn't really deny it. 'But if she was going to go to the trouble of murdering Mel to save her relationship with Tony, why wouldn't she stick around and go through with the wedding? Why kill someone to protect something that you then give up anyway?'

We stared at each other, then both turned away and looked at the flowers growing over the pagoda, thinking deeply.

'There's always Roger Laity,' I said, as a thought occurred to me.

Withers looked at me sharply. 'What makes you say that?'

'Mel said that Cheryl was after Tony's shop,' I said. He nodded.

'Yeah, you told me that. But Mr Penhaligon – the older Mr Penhaligon – told me it was in a family trust. It wasn't Tony's to give away.'

'I know that, and so did Cheryl. But apparently Roger Laity had been implicated in some dodgy dealings at the council. Nothing illegal, by the sounds of it, but definitely unethical.' I tried to remember exactly what Mel had said. 'Mel said her cousin worked there and had heard something. She said the Laity family have plans for Penstowan that not everyone would agree with.'

'What the hell does that even mean?' he asked, a little exasperated.

'I don't know,' I admitted. 'But maybe it was to do with the shop. The first thing Mel did when she saw me was ask if I was investigating the Laitys.'

'Hmmm...' Withers took out his phone and looked up

a message. 'I thought so. I had a message earlier saying Roger Laity had been here, asking to take Cheryl's belongings home.'

I know, I thought, but I knew better than to mention it. Plus, I'd forgotten that the receptionist had even mentioned it once I'd got talking to Old Davey.

Withers grinned. 'I also got a garbled message about a dog escaping from a car from PC Trelawney, and I thought for a moment he must have eaten a dodgy pasty and been hallucinating. And then I thought, who just inherited a dog they can't control and keeps popping up at my crime scene?'

'I have no idea what you're talking about...' I said, making a point of studying a rose very carefully, but I could see the look of amusement on his face. He looked nice when he smiled properly. I sniffed at the rose then looked back at Withers, but he'd turned away. 'So why would Roger Laity want Cheryl's things? I know he was her guardian, but she didn't live with him anymore. Apart from the fact it would probably be down to Tony to collect her things, what's the hurry? She's been missing less than forty-eight hours.'

'Yeah...' Withers looked thoughtful for a moment, then came to a decision. He stood up. 'Right, I'd better take you home.'

I stood up, disappointed to be dismissed again so easily, and followed him down the steps to his car. He held the door open for me, then got in and started the engine. He sat for a moment, letting it idle, then turned slightly to me.

'If you don't mind, I need to take a bit of a detour first.'

Chapter Sixteen

We drove out of the car park and along the avenue of trees that led out of the hotel grounds and to the road. But instead of turning left to Penstowan, he turned right, then right again onto the A39 heading south.

'Where are we going?' I asked.

'You'll see,' he said. 'I'm only doing this to shut you up.'

'Doing what?'

He kept his eyes on the road. 'Stop talking before I change my mind.'

I looked out of the window and watched the countryside flash past. It was quiet and it started to feel a bit awkward, not like the comfortable, companionable silences I shared with Tony. *Oh God, please put the radio on or something*, I thought, and to my surprise he did. It was tuned to a local station which played innocuous chart hits, most of which I didn't know, each sounding much the same as the one preceding it. *I must be getting old*, I thought.

'This music! It all sounds the same to me,' said DCI Withers, making me start in surprise. He was reading my mind.

'You do know that's a sign of getting old?' I said, and he laughed.

'Yup.'

We were headed towards a bend in the road, one I knew only too well. I tensed as we approached it, just as I'd always done since the crash – not that I'd driven along here much in the last few years.

Withers noticed. 'What's the matter? I'm a safe driver.'

'I'm sure you are. I just know someone who had an accident here, that's all.' I wasn't going to tell him about it. We passed a signpost for Crackington Haven.

'Now *that* is a fantastic place name,' he said. He was actually trying to lighten the mood. Wonders would never cease.

'Have you been there? It's a great place for a walk, really rugged.'

'Yeah, and a nice pub there too.'

'Are we popping in for a pint?'

He laughed. 'Much as I could do with one, no. We're going to Boscastle.'

'Boscastle?'

'Home of one Roger Laity.'

'You're taking me to see Roger Laity?'

'No, I'm taking you to sit quietly in the car while I talk to him. Don't make me regret this.'

'My lips are sealed,' I said, and he gave me what could only be described as 'a look'.

'I'll believe that when it happens…'

The Laity family home was on the outskirts of Boscastle. It perched high up on the hillside, overlooking the pretty town and harbour. A sweeping gravel drive led through manicured lawns and flower beds bursting with colour to an imposing stone-built Georgian mansion. It was the sort of place wealthy middle-class incomers from up country would call a 'cottage in the country', and everyone else would call a 'bleeding massive house'. It *was* bleeding massive. There was a stone outbuilding next to the house, whitewashed and converted into a garage or workshop, by the looks of it. It was about the same size as my actual house. The door was shut, its frosted glass panels giving nothing away about its contents.

There was a newish Range Rover, de rigueur for the wealthy man-about-countryside, parked in front. Unlike in London, where cars like this were really only used for handling the rough terrain of Kensington and Chelsea or the frozen wastes of Islington, this one looked like it had actually been taken off-road, as nature intended; the wheels were muddy, and there were even a few weeds with yellow flowers sticking incongruously out of one of the grills at the front. As DCI Withers pulled up next to it, Roger Laity came out of the house. He was carrying a sports bag and looked surprised to see us.

Withers looked at me. 'Stay here,' he said.

'Why did you bring me, if I can't get out?' I said.

'Buggered if I know,' muttered Withers. 'I brought you so you can see that I *am* following all lines of enquiry, and then you'll leave me alone, yes?'

'Mmm,' I said. I wasn't going to commit myself. He rolled his eyes, then pressed the button to wind down my window.

'You can listen in, but that's it.' He opened the door and as he got out I heard him say, 'I'm going to regret this…'

Roger Laity approached the car, a fake smile composed of one hundred per cent pure bullshit on his face. He wasn't just surprised to see us, I thought; he was unhappy about it too. He held out his hand to shake

Withers's warmly, but that warmth did not extend to his eyes.

'DCI … Withers, isn't it? I never forget a name,' he said, bending down slightly to get a look at me inside the car. 'And that's the young lady who leapt into action so spectacularly the other night. What brings you here?' He quickly put on a sincere face. 'Is there some news of my niece?'

'I'm afraid not,' said Withers. 'We were just passing and I thought we'd drop by and go over a few things, see if there's something we missed.'

Laity's smile became even more fake. It was impossible to be 'just passing' Boscastle unless you were actually heading there, so he knew that Withers's visit was not quite as casual as the DCI would have him believe. He shifted the bag in his hand. Withers looked at it.

'Sorry, you were just off out somewhere,' he said.

'No,' said Laity. 'Only to see a friend.'

'I won't keep you long. So it's just you and your wife living here? And your son? Are they around?'

'No,' said Roger. 'My wife's gone to stay with her mother for a few days, down in Helston. She's not well at the best of times and this whole business has really upset her nerves.'

'Sorry to hear that,' said Withers. 'And your son…?'

'Craig?' said Laity. 'No, he moved out a couple of

months ago. He went home this morning. Work tomorrow.'

'I see. Where does he live?'

'Oxfordshire,' said Laity. 'I believe he made a statement yesterday, not that he saw anything.'

'That's absolutely fine.' Withers had a soothing voice. 'Now, of course we're concerned about Cheryl's whereabouts, but what I'd really like to talk to you about is the murder. How well did you know the victim?'

Laity briefly looked surprised, but he hadn't become a successful businessman (with a bleeding massive house) by letting his emotions get the better of him. His expression turned thoughtful. 'Hmm, let me think… You know, I honestly don't think we ever met?'

'She didn't work for you at any point, or have anything to do with your business? What was your business again?'

Laity definitely looked a little uncomfortable. 'I own a string of campsites along this coast. Very successful campsites. I do employ quite a few people, mostly seasonal of course, but I don't recall ever hiring her.'

'Oh. That's strange…' Withers shook his head. 'Never mind.'

Laity looked alarmed. 'What's strange?'

Inside the car, I was hopping around in my seat in frustration. *Let me talk to him!* But I had to admit that Withers was doing a pretty good job, especially as we didn't even really know what we were accusing Roger Laity of, if anything.

Withers looked bemused. 'I don't suppose it's anything, really. Only the victim apparently made some allegations about your business dealings with the local council. Do you have any idea what she was talking about?'

Laity no longer looked alarmed, just annoyed.

'My dealings with the council are my own business,' he said.

'That depends on what they are, really,' said Withers. 'Not to worry, I'll have a word with them tomorrow and see if I can get to the bottom of it. Thank you for your time, Mr Laity.' And with that he turned away, leaving Roger Laity looking after him in angry astonishment. *Oh, that was good*, I thought. He'd definitely been up to something, and it was looking like maybe Mel *had* had an enemy after all.

Withers went to open the car door and winked at me, then turned back to Laity, which I was glad about because my stupid cheeks stupidly went all hot and red and stupid.

'Oh yeah, you were at the hotel earlier asking about Cheryl's belongings? They're part of the crime scene so we'd like to keep hold of them for the moment, but if there was something in particular you were after…?'

Laity shook his head. 'No. I just wanted to have them

near me. I'm still clinging to the hope that she's alive and has just seen sense and left that … that idiot Tony, and I'd like to have them here for her, in case she comes back.'

'I see. We'll need them for a while longer but I'll let you know when we release them. Thanks again.'

He got in the car but didn't turn on the engine. I opened my mouth.

'Not yet,' he said.

Roger Laity looked at us awkwardly, obviously waiting for us to leave. Withers picked up his phone and put it to his ear, making it look like he was taking a call.

'Is he watching?' he asked. I discreetly peered at Laity.

'Yes,' I said. 'He looks really uncomfortable.'

'Good,' said Withers, putting down the phone with a grin and starting the engine.

We drove away from the house. In the rearview mirror I saw Laity take out his phone and go back into the house. I caught Withers's eye in the mirror; he'd seen it too.

'So he doesn't look at all guilty of anything, does he?' I said, and he laughed.

'A fine upstanding citizen, if ever I saw one.'

Chapter Seventeen

We drove the rest of the way back to Penstowan in a slightly less awkward silence than we'd left it in. A couple of times I tried to make conversation, but Withers appeared to be deep in thought and, although he answered pleasantly enough, he wasn't to be drawn any further. I was dying to ask him what conclusions (if any) he'd come to after our visit to Roger Laity, but I thought better of it; he'd taken quite a big and unexpected step, letting me go along with him, and if I wanted to stay in his confidence I was probably best off waiting for him to share things with me rather than badgering him.

We turned into my road and he pulled up outside my house.

'So...' I said, not entirely sure what to say. 'What happens now?'

'What happens now is you let me get on with my job.'

I looked at him in surprise. 'But I thought— What was that all about? Taking me to see Laity?'

'That was about showing you that I *am* following all lines of investigation, regardless of what you may think.' Withers looked amused. 'What, did you think we were partners or something now?'

'Of course not,' I said, flustered, because, ridiculous as it was, that kind of was what I'd thought. Of course we weren't partners. I was a chef, not a police officer. 'But what are you going to do about Roger Laity?'

'What do you want me to do?'

'Well, he's proper shifty, isn't he?'

Withers sighed and turned to look me in the eye. 'Jodie. Stop it. Yes, he did look guilty, but guilty of what? Not of murder.'

'You can't be sure of that,' I said stubbornly, but I knew he was right.

'Yes, I can. You saw him when I mentioned Mel; he was completely taken by surprise. I'm sure he's guilty of something – people like him usually are – but you could tell that was the first he'd heard of Mel's allegations.'

'But can't we – I mean, *you* – at least find out what he's up to?'

'No, not really.' Withers was starting to get irritated. 'Not unless his dodgy business dealings with the council are directly linked to Mel's death, and I don't see how they can be. He runs campsites, for God's sake.'

I stared out of the window. I hated to admit it, but he was right. Which didn't help Tony. He must've known what I was thinking because his tone softened.

'Look, I know you're trying to help your friend, but I've followed up the lead you gave me and it's a dead end. There's no real motive for Roger Laity to kill Mel, and there's nothing to implicate him in Cheryl's disappearance. We've searched her belongings and as far as I can tell there's nothing there that could embarrass him or get him into trouble. He's just a concerned uncle.'

'I know…' I said. But there had to be something.

'Tony is still our chief suspect as far as I'm concerned,' said Withers gently. 'I'm sorry, but there's still so much more that points to him than to anyone else. And the information you gave us about the dog, well, that just makes it more likely that Mel was killed on Friday night, around the time we've got witnesses seeing him go outside.'

'I know he didn't do it,' I said firmly. He sighed and shook his head.

'If he didn't do it then he's got nothing to worry about, has he? I'm not trying to fit him up; I'm trying to find the truth. The evidence is there that will either put him in the clear or convict him, and either way I will find it. But you have to leave me and my officers alone to get on with it. You're not a cop anymore, Jodie. Get used to it.'

———————

Get used to it. That was easier said than done while Tony sat in a police holding cell. I watched Withers drive away, then went indoors.

'Where have you been?' Daisy was on me the minute I walked through the door and I immediately felt awful.

'Sorry, darling, isn't Nana here?'

'Yes, she is,' said Mum, bustling into the hall. 'But I should probably go home…'

'At least stay for dinner,' I said. 'It's getting a bit late.'

'Okay,' she said, and Daisy and I exchanged glances; we both had the feeling that Mum was actually really enjoying having company again.

I walked into the kitchen and began to look through the fridge.

'Sorry about being out so long,' I said, pulling out some chicken breasts that only had one day left before they went out of date, and some cauliflower and various other veggies that needed using up. 'DCI Withers wanted a chat with me.'

Mum looked smug. 'I told you he was her type,' she said to Daisy.

'Erm, I am here, you know,' I said, getting out a

chopping board and beginning to chop up veg. 'It wasn't a social visit; it was about the case. Can you get me some garlic and olive oil?'

I set them to work, and soon the three of us were crushing garlic, tossing vegetables in olive oil, and bunging them in the oven to roast. I took another chopping board, cut the chicken breasts into chunks, and sprinkled them with ground cumin and coriander, then Daisy threaded them onto skewers with hunks of mushroom and red onion. I smiled, the stress of the last couple of days fading away; cooking always did that to me. It took me to my happy place.

I'd always enjoyed cooking – if, like me, you enjoy eating, it pays to know how to cook – but it had really come into its own after a few years in the force. I'd started to get more responsibility and with it, more stress. I'd found that the simple act of preparing a meal – a proper meal, not just piercing the film on a microwave lasagne – did wonders for my mental health. Putting on some music, dancing around the kitchen and following a recipe, even one that you knew off by heart and didn't have to read anymore, helped to clear the mind.

We sat down forty minutes later to eat a delicious meal of Moroccan chicken kebabs, roasted vegetables, through which I'd then mixed a spoonful of spicy harissa paste, and the Israeli couscous that I'd not used at the wedding. Mum tried at first to ask me about DCI

Withers, but eventually she gave up and just enjoyed her meal. I even opened a bottle of wine, given to me by the estate agent when we'd moved in, and it wasn't half bad.

It was exactly what I needed – a good meal with the people I loved best in the world, in our new home. Germaine sat under the table, whining occasionally for scraps, and despite all of us saying we wouldn't give in to her emotional blackmail as it would only encourage her, she seemed to be very well fed by the end of it.

We sat and watched the telly afterwards, some comedy movie on Netflix that we all enjoyed at the time, although the next day I'd have been hard pushed to tell you what it was called or who was in it. I made some hot chocolate and Daisy snuggled up to me on the sofa, which hadn't happened for some time. I knew as she got older these snuggles would get less and less frequent, so I made sure to enjoy this one.

Mum hadn't mentioned going home again. I was quite happy for her to stay the night again, but I made a mental note that tomorrow I should take her home, if only for her to get some more clothes if she wanted to stay longer.

She took a sip of her cocoa and raised the subject I'd been avoiding even thinking about all evening.

'So why are you so set on clearing Tony's name?' she said.

'Because he didn't do it, of course!' I said, thinking, *Let's not talk about this now...*

'But why does it have to be you?' said Daisy. 'We moved down here to get away from all this police stuff.'

I reached out and took her hand. 'It's not like that, darling. I'm not about to do anything dangerous or risky. I promised you I wouldn't, didn't I? I'm just helping out an old friend. It feels like the right thing to do.'

Mum shook her head. 'We get that, but even so ... why not leave it to that dishy policeman?'

'He might be dishy but he's convinced Tony's guilty,' I said.

'But if he's innocent, they won't be able to charge him, will they? I know there's all these things on the telly where they convict the wrong man and then he gets out and he's out for revenge and it's a bloodbath' – I tried to think what Mum could possibly have been watching – 'but you told me yourself, even in the Met stuff like that doesn't really happen. Guilty people are more likely to get away with it than innocent ones are to get sent down.'

That was true, but it was no consolation when it was one of your friends who was in danger of being the exception to the rule. Not when it was on my manor...

Maybe that was it. Who was I kidding? That was *definitely* it. Except it wasn't my manor; it was my dad's.

I sighed. 'I never noticed it before, but there are

echoes of Dad everywhere in this town.' Mum didn't speak, but she nodded. 'I mean, at the station, there are still some of his recruits there. I thought they'd all have retired. Even Withers has heard of him. If Dad was still here, *he'd* be helping Tony, *he'd* know he was innocent. It feels like I need to make sure there's no miscarriage of justice on his patch.'

Mum shook her head. 'You don't have to prove anything to Dad, sweetheart.'

'I kind of do,' I said. 'I always wanted to be just like him, but I wasn't, was I? I left the job. I didn't get as far as him. The whole point of going to London was to make something of myself, to make him proud of me, but I was in the Met for seventeen years and I never got past sergeant.'

'I didn't think you wanted to,' said Mum, and I was momentarily irritated because that was true and I just wanted a good wallow. 'You told me you liked being out on the beat too much. I remember you moaning about having more paperwork and less legwork even when you made sergeant. Exactly like Dad, in fact. He enjoyed his job but he did get frustrated being stuck behind a desk.'

'Yeah, but...'

'Grandad was well proud of you,' said Daisy. I looked at her in surprise.

'He was?'

'Yes. We came down here the Christmas before he died, do you remember? He read me a bedtime story and I don't know why we started talking about it but I told him you put bad people in prison, and he said he knew and he was very proud of you. I was only little but I always remember him saying that because he made me feel proud of you too.' She looked at me warily. 'You're not going to cry, are you?'

'No,' I lied, sniffing furiously. I hugged her tightly, and then Mum came and sat next to me and joined in, and then the dog decided she didn't want to be left out and jumped up and joined in too, and I thanked my lucky stars that Tony had delivered me a sofa that was big enough for a family love-in.

Chapter Eighteen

I woke up the next morning feeling ... well, I wasn't entirely sure how I was feeling. Part of me felt a little happier about DCI Withers; he *had* taken my lead about Roger Laity seriously enough to go and see him, and I couldn't really deny that it seemed unlikely Laity had killed Mel, whom, as far as anyone knew, he'd never even met. His surprise upon hearing that she'd made allegations about his business also seemed more and more genuine, the more I thought about it. And yet...

Roger Laity was definitely hiding *something*, and without investigating it, was there any way of knowing for sure that it *hadn't* somehow contributed to Mel's death and Cheryl's disappearance? He'd also looked really uncomfortable throughout our visit, and that sports bag... I wasn't sure if I was imagining it now because (like Withers) I was trying to wrangle the evidence into fitting some kind of theory, but he'd subconsciously shifted the bag around in his hands the whole time they spoke. I knew from my experiences on the beat that if someone was carrying something they didn't want you to know about, or if they'd hidden drugs or illegal goods in their home, at least seventy-five per cent of the time they would inadvertently give it away by a tell-tale flick of their eyes, or by standing in front of it or something. The trick was in being able to spot it. What was in the bag? Where had he been going?

Of course, I was probably reading far too much into all this. His wife was away, and he probably was genuinely going to see a friend, or even a mistress; maybe his bag had been full of saucy underwear! I shuddered at the thought of Roger Laity in a pair of budgie smugglers. Maybe the guy I'd bought my van from should've opened his fetish shop in Boscastle instead.

You're not a cop anymore; get used to it, I told myself. I should just let Withers get on with it. He knew what he was doing. He wasn't out to get Tony; he was just using his own experience to go with the most likely suspect first. And when they couldn't find enough evidence to charge him (because he didn't do it), they would have to let Tony go. I hoped to God they didn't have enough evidence, because although I had told my mum in the past that innocent people don't tend to get put away, it did happen. Not often – although prisons are notoriously full of 'innocent' people, and maybe more of them than we realise actually are – but it did.

But, assuming they did let Tony go, would they ever find out who the real murderer was? The longer an investigation goes on, the less likely it is to be solved. There's a 'golden hour' in any investigation when the evidence is fresh, the crime scene uncontaminated, and potential witnesses and suspects haven't had a chance to forget things, concoct alibis or generally make stuff up. The police had moved quickly once Mel's body was found; they'd protected the scene, done forensics, taken DNA samples, got statements from everyone at the hotel, and taken someone into custody. But it was now forty-eight hours since she'd been discovered, longer than that since she'd been killed, and with Withers still convinced Tony was the murderer, to my mind they were looking in the wrong place. By the time they started looking in the right place, the trail would have gone cold. And then there would be no justice for Mel, or Cheryl if she actually was dead, about which my mind changed almost on the hour. I couldn't see how she could be alive and not contact Tony or her uncle and aunty to let them know she was okay, but then, if she was dead, who had killed her and where was the body? And without finding the killer, the shadow of suspicion would forever be upon Tony. There's that old saying, 'There's no smoke without fire', which is absolute rubbish – you only had to witness some of my cheating ex-husband's attempts at cooking to realise that – but people still believe it.

I should leave the police to investigate. It wasn't my job anymore. That little voice in my head – the one that had gone *oooohhhh* when Withers winked at me or flexed his muscles, and was therefore not really to be trusted – said, *Yeah yeah, we both know you're not really going to leave this alone*. And this time it was right.

I dropped Mum off at her house. She'd not been back for about three days and had run out of clean undies, and she had stuff to do, so Daisy and I left her to it with instructions to call us if she wanted some company.

I took Daisy and Germaine into Penstowan. The holiday season was just kicking off, which made it difficult to park, and I knew that the locals would soon be moaning about all the 'emmets' who had flocked to our little town from all over the country, getting in the way, leaving their cars in stupid places, dropping their litter… They would moan quietly, though, as half the town's residents were originally from places other than Cornwall (it had grown massively over the last twenty years, as people got sick of high house prices in other parts of the South), and, of course, the tourists had plenty of money and were happy to spend it on beach inflatables, ice-creams, and fish and chips on sunny days, and in the tiny local cinema and the bowling alley on rainy ones. For many of the local shops and businesses, a good summer season meant they could relax through the winter. A bad summer season meant sampling the delights of the local dole office and surviving on baked beans from Lidl. I knew plenty of people who had done it.

We walked along Fore Street, Germaine stopping to sniff every now and again. I couldn't blame her. The street outside Rowe's Bakery smelt delicious; they made the best pasties anywhere, ever, and I really would fight anyone who said otherwise. We looked in the window at the saffron buns and the different types of pies and pasties, and wondered if it was too early for lunch. It was a bit, but we could always come back this way...

We passed Penhaligon's. The store was open as usual, as if nothing had happened. If everything had gone as planned on Saturday, they wouldn't have been expecting the new Mr and Mrs Penhaligon at work anyway; they would have been off on their honeymoon. I felt a protective wave sweep over me at the thought of Tony at the police station. Withers would have been questioning him relentlessly, trying to get a confession out of him if possible (always the easiest way to secure a conviction). I looked at my watch; Tony had been arrested yesterday afternoon at around 1pm, and the police could only hold him for twenty-four hours before either charging him or letting him go. So Withers only had three hours to come up with something that would make the charge stick. Unfortunately, I didn't put it past him. And of course there was nothing stopping them extending those twenty-four hours or even re-arresting him at a later date if new evidence came to light...

I put it out of my mind and laughed as Germaine got herself and Daisy tangled up in the lead. Daisy squatted down and lifted her paws (the dog's, not my daughter's) through the madly woven web of nylon leash, and I thought, *Oh, what a tangled web we weave, when first we practise to deceive...* This case was a tangled web indeed.

It might be too early for a pasty, but it's never too early for an ice-cream, so I bought us both a double scoop from a local ice-cream maker (forest fruits made with clotted cream for me, and chocolate fudge brownie swirl for Daisy) and we sat on a bench, away from the madness of the street and overlooking the sea. I looked at my beautiful daughter as we both slurped indelicately at our ice-creams, and my heart did a big happy flip at the look of pure and unadulterated joy on her face. I knew it had been a big wrench, leaving London; she had friends, and her waste-of-space dad, back there. But we'd lived in a cramped and ridiculously expensive two-up, two-down terraced house with just a tiny patch of grass for outside space, and she'd always been an outdoorsy type. We'd gone on day trips out to the countryside, or to the coast, and even as a toddler she'd loved to walk through the woods and chase squirrels (at one point she'd wanted to be a dog). It wasn't as if she didn't know Penstowan; we'd visited her grandparents as often as we could, whenever I could get away from work. But despite being convinced that this was a much better environment for her to grow up in, I'd still worried. Ninety per cent of parenting seems to be worrying about how much you're screwing up your kids, but today, looking at her expression, watching her laughing as the dog licked ice-cream off her leg where it had dripped, I thought maybe I was doing a pretty good job after all.

Daisy waved to a couple of kids walking towards us – a blonde girl of about her age and a boy of about seven or eight, who looked like your typical younger brother, tagging along and being just about tolerated.

'You know them?' I asked. They looked vaguely familiar.

'They live in our road,' said Daisy. 'I spoke to them yesterday when I was walking Germaine. They seem nice.'

The kids reached us.

'Hello!' The girl had an open, friendly face with a smile that made you want to smile back. She squatted down and stroked Germaine. 'Aww, she's so cute! We're going to the beach. Do you want to come?'

Daisy looked at me, unsure. We were having a nice time, just the two of us, but she needed some friends of her own age and, with any luck, this girl might go to the same school she was due to start in September.

'Fine by me,' I said, and she smiled. After making her promise to phone me if she needed anything, and slipping her a £10 note so she could buy herself and her new friends a pasty or a bag of chips for lunch, I watched the three of them head down onto the sand, the little brother running ahead while the two girls chatted. Germaine whined and strained at her leash. I bent down to pat her, almost head-butting her as she stood on her hind legs to try and lick my face.

'Sorry, old girl,' I said. 'No dogs allowed on the beach. You'll have to stick with me.'

But what was I going to do now, left to my own devices? That little voice in my head piped up again, asking, *Aren't the council offices two streets away…?*

The Penstowan Municipal Building was one of those fine examples of civic architecture from the 1970s. It had taken all the lessons learnt from the brutalist buildings of the 1960s and completely ignored them, sticking with the tried and tested concrete box design, lined with rows and rows of windows which made them really uncomfortable to work in, whatever the weather – like a greenhouse in the summer and an icebox full of whistling draughts in the winter. At six storeys high, it was one of the tallest buildings in Penstowan. Outside, there was a weird bronze sculpture that was meant to represent a lifeboat in a third-rate Henry Moore kind of way, now green with verdigris and splodged white with seagull droppings. It stood on a short plinth in the middle of a concrete pool. It was supposed to have water in it but I could only remember it being full once, when it had been topped up for the Queen's fiftieth anniversary in 2002, just before I'd moved to London. There had been a big street party in the town, and by the end of the night I think half the partygoers (who had fully enjoyed the cheap 'Golden Jubilee' scrumpy laid on by a local brewery in honour of Her Maj) had peed in it. It had been drained the next day and left empty, save for the cigarette butts, chip wrappers, and beer cans that inevitably gathered there until periodically removed by street cleaners.

I ignored the 'No Dogs' sign (I still felt like I was just looking after Germaine for Mel, and I didn't want to risk anything happening to her; Mel would never forgive me) and went inside.

The reception area was high-ceilinged and my footsteps echoed on the tiled floor as I approached the desk. The woman behind the desk was deep in concentration, looking at something on her computer, and did not look up as I reached her. I cleared my throat.

'Hello,' I began, then stopped because I realised I didn't know the name of the person I was after. The woman behind the desk looked up, frowning, but her face suddenly cleared when she saw me.

'Nosey Parker!' she said, smiling. 'I heard you were back.'

'That's me,' I said, trying not to give away the fact that I had no idea who she was. 'Nice to see you.'

She laughed. 'You have no idea who I am, do you? Nina—'

'Nina Falconer! Oh my God!' I was relieved when her name suddenly popped into my head. She'd been in my year at school, and had been goal attack in the netball team (I'd been wing defence and had hated it).

'Nina Matthews now,' she said, smiling.

'No! Not you and Liam?' Liam Matthews had been a Fifth Year bad boy when we'd been gormless Third Years, suspended numerous times for smoking in the toilets and fighting.

She nodded. 'Yep. I tamed him,' she said proudly. 'I heard you were back, I ran into Louise Gifford—'

'How did *she* know? I haven't seen Louise for about ten years.'

'She said her mum had heard it from your mum.'

'Of course. The OAPs' coffee morning has a lot to answer for...' Germaine tugged at the leash and I nudged her with my foot, hoping to keep her quiet. Of course, it didn't work. Nina raised her eyebrows and stood up, looking down at the carpet where Germaine was doing her best to look cute but inconspicuous.

'Isn't that poor Mel's dog?' asked Nina.

I nodded. 'Yeah, there was no one else to take her. Terrible business, innit?'

'Yeah, terrible business. You think Tony did it?'

'Tony? Ha! We're talking about the boy who passed out when we dissected a frog in Biology. I don't think so, do you?'

Nina looked doubtful. 'I dunno. I heard the police arrested him...'

'He's helping them with their enquiries; he's not been charged,' I said firmly. 'Anyway, that's kind of why I'm here...'

Mel's cousin Trish worked in the Planning Department. They hadn't expected her to work that day, not after such a tragic family event, but she was diligent and, as she had told Nina that morning, the Machiavellian workings and twisted logic of the local council planning regulations were just about the only things in the world able to take her mind off it.

Trish came down to the foyer and took me into a nearby side office. She was pale and she had dark shadows under her eyes, but her face lit up at the sight of Germaine, who gave a little bark and jumped up at her. I felt a pang; Trish had a much more legitimate claim to Mel's dog than I did, and if she decided she wanted her I could hardly refuse.

'Hello, Germaine! Who's a lovely girl?' Trish fussed over the Pomeranian, smoothing her fluffy white hair and gazing into her eyes.

'You're obviously old friends,' I said, and she nodded.

'She's a lovely dog,' she said. 'Thank you so much for taking her in. Is that why you're here? I would love to take her for poor Mel' – her voice choked a little, and I could feel my own throat constrict at the thought of telling Daisy I'd given the dog away — 'but I've already got two of my own, and I just don't have room.'

Sweet Jesus, thank the Lord, I thought, relaxing. 'No, no, we love having her! She and my daughter are best friends already. No, I wanted to talk to you about Mel.'

She looked at me, warily. 'You're not police, though? This isn't official?'

'No,' I said. 'I'm a private investigator. Well, sort of. I'm a caterer. But I'm also ex-police, and I was there, and I don't believe for a second that Tony did it.'

She smiled sadly. 'I don't know what to believe. But no, Tony would not be the first person that sprang to mind as a … a murderer. Even after what she did to him – which she really regretted, by the way.'

'I know, she told me. She told me several things, actually, just before she was murdered. And that's what I'd like to ask you about.'

Chapter Nineteen

I left the council buildings feeling slightly more confused than when I'd entered them. Trish had given me a lot to think about. Whether it had any bearing on Mel's murder was anyone's guess, but it could have been used to put pressure on Cheryl. Roger Laity had made it perfectly clear that he had not been keen on her marrying 'that idiot' Tony (I bristled indignantly on Tony's behalf), but maybe he'd found a way to turn the undesirable match to his advantage.

Whatever, from what Trish had told me, Roger Laity's dealings with the council had not been illegal as such, but they'd sailed close enough to the wind to draw attention and been subjected to something of a cover-up. At the very least he was guilty of being unethical, but then it seemed to me many successful business people were.

My phone pinged with a text message from Daisy. She was having a great time with her new friends and she'd see me at home. I smiled and went to put the phone back in my bag, when it rang.

'Oh dear, *that* didn't last long, did it?' I said to Germaine, who looked at me as if to say, *You do realise I don't speak English, right?* I laughed and went to answer the phone, and was surprised to see that it wasn't Daisy. It was a local number I didn't recognise.

'Hello?'

'Jodie, it's Brenda.'

I looked at my watch. Almost 1pm. They'd be releasing Tony soon, I thought.

'Have you heard from the police?' I asked her. 'I'm just down the road, if you want me to pick him up?'

Brenda sounded distraught. 'No, Tony's solicitor just rang me. They're holding him for another twenty-four hours...'

I strode along Fore Street and turned into Orchard Lane, no longer home to any orchards but the location of Penstowan Police Station. There was an exhausted bark behind me and I slowed down, guiltily; Germaine was game for a run, but she had shorter (and rather hairier) legs than me, and she was finding it hard to keep up.

'Sorry, sweetie,' I said, but I didn't stop. My blood was up.

I bounded up the ramp to the door of the police station just as DCI Withers came out. He put out both hands to stop himself knocking me over, steadying me as my momentum came to an abrupt halt against his (muscular) frame. I couldn't help noticing that he had quite large hands and a reassuringly firm grip, before pulling myself together and glaring at him.

'What the hell are you playing at?' I said.

He smiled arrogantly. 'I'm off to get some lunch. Wanna come?'

'No, I don't bloody want to come! Why aren't you releasing Tony? If you don't have enough to charge him then you have to let him go.' I realised he still had hold of me and I shrugged him off.

He did that irritating thin-lipped smiley thing again. By now it was starting to make me want to slap him.

'New evidence has come to light,' he said shortly.

'What new evidence?'

'You do realise I'm not obliged to tell you everything, don't you?' He looked at me and I got the feeling that I kind of amused him at the moment, but it wouldn't take much to change that to irritation. Did I care?

'You do realise I won't stop pestering you until you do?' I said, and he sighed. He looked at his watch.

'I really don't have long and I need some food. Come and have lunch with me.'

And that was how one minute I was glaring at Withers in front of the police station, and the next I was sitting outside the Kings Arms with a glass of wine and a ploughman's lunch while he sat opposite me tucking into a prawn baguette and a pint of lemonade. Germaine sat under the table with a bowl of water, looking up hopefully now and then in case any scraps were forthcoming. She'd already had a go at a pickled onion that had resisted my attempts to spear it and shot off my plate, and her face when she bit into it had made both my lunch companion and me laugh.

'Come on, then,' I said, slightly bewildered at the turn events were taking. He was (I told myself) the last person I wanted to have lunch with. I wondered how many times I would have to tell myself that before I believed it. 'Spill.'

Withers chewed and swallowed a mouthful of baguette. 'All in good time. I've been hearing a lot around the station about your dad since you came back. Why did you move away?'

'A lot of people who grow up in places like this can't wait to leave,' I said evasively. 'It's so quiet.'

'You wanted to go where the action was?' He sipped

his drink, regarding me closely over the rim of his glass. I shifted uncomfortably.

'Something like that…'

'Didn't you get on with your dad?'

'Oh, was your nickname at school "Nosey" as well?' I asked sarcastically.

He laughed. 'I'm just interested.' He took another bite of food, still watching me.

I sighed. 'Okay, if you must know, it's hard when everyone thinks your dad's a hero. I mean, he was – to me, as much as to everyone else. He made a difference to a lot of people's lives round here. Anything I did was bound to suffer by comparison.' I toyed with my food, remembering the argument we'd had when I told him I was joining the Met. 'I told him he was a big fish in a small pond, and I wanted to be a big fish in a bigger one.'

'Oh…'

'Yeah, "Oh." And then when I got to London I realised that little fish actually achieve more.' He raised his eyebrows. 'The big fish spend all their time fending off the sharks. The little ones just swim about undetected and unbothered, getting on with the job. I liked being left to get on with it. And that's when I understood why my dad had never left Penstowan. They wanted him to move up the ranks, but that would have meant being tied to a desk in Exeter or somewhere, and he just wanted to stay here and look after the place.'

'But of course you couldn't come back and do the same, because you'd have been admitting he was right.' I was surprised to see sympathy on Withers's face, and felt tears spring to my eyes. I'd missed my dad (and my mum, of course) when I'd been in London, but now I was back – properly back, not just for a visit – and I was walking the streets that he used to walk, and sitting in the pub where we used to come for the occasional Sunday lunch, and driving the road where ... well, anyway, I had been getting ridiculously emotional and I really needed to pull myself together. He'd been gone for seven years, for goodness' sake. Why the hell was I telling DCI Withers all this? This man with his sardonic eyebrows and his chiselled abs and his nice hair—

'Anyway, that's all water under the bridge. You said new evidence had come to light?' I said firmly. The subject of me and my dad was closed. End of.

Withers nodded and swallowed a mouthful of prawns. 'We've pinned down the exact time of death.'

'I thought the doc was struggling with that?'

'She was. But Mel was wearing one of those.' He inclined his head towards the fitness tracker on my wrist. 'It tracked her heartrate.'

I looked down at my tracker. My heart was beating slightly faster than it should have been. I put it down to my speedy march to the station earlier, rather than my close proximity to Withers.

'It tracks your heartrate and sends it to an app on your phone,' I said.

He nodded. 'The information also goes into the cloud,' he said. 'Of course, the companies who make these trackers have all these privacy policies in place to reassure you they're not going to sell your information to a third party, which makes it a pain in the posterior for us, but eventually they were able to look at Mel's stats and tell us when her tracker stopped reading a heartrate.'

I was impressed that he'd thought of that, but I didn't want him to know. 'Oh, right. But how does that strengthen the case against Tony?'

'Mel's heart rate spiked at 10.27pm, which we assume is when she was attacked, then slowed down and stopped at 10.42pm, when she…' His voice trailed off; he didn't need to finish that sentence.

'But Tony said he only spoke to her for half an hour, which puts him back at the party around 10pm.'

Withers shook his head. 'Only it doesn't. We have witnesses who saw him leave around 9.30, but he didn't come back until 10.45pm. And when he did, he was wearing different trousers.'

That threw me for a minute. But I was still convinced of his innocence. 'So he was off changing his pants, not murdering Mel. But you're implying that he changed them because they were covered in Mel's blood or something.'

Withers looked at me steadily. 'We found Mel's DNA on Tony's shirt, but the lab thought it was weird that it just kind of stopped at his trousers. Malcolm Penhaligon took some photographs earlier on in the evening, and it was only when we saw those that we realised the trousers Tony gave us for forensics weren't the ones he had on in the photos. We went back to his house and found *them* in the washing basket. There doesn't appear to be any sign of blood on them, but why would he change them?'

It didn't look good, I had to admit that.

'What does Tony say about it?'

'He hasn't said anything yet. He's talking to his solicitor.' Withers took another big bite of baguette. 'We also got hold of Cheryl's phone records for the evening. She sent him a text message telling him they needed to talk at 9.37pm, which is around about the time he left the party.'

'And just after I spoke to her,' I said. 'Oh...'

'Oh what?'

'I told her that Tony was a good bloke, and if she had any doubts...'

'And then she immediately got on the blower to him. Sounds like she *did* have doubts. No one actually saw him in the garden with Mel. Hegone up to Cheryl's room and heard she was dumping him, then gone straight outside to find Mel and kill her for stirring up trouble.'

He smiled grimly. 'Except by the sounds of it, it was you that stirred up trouble...'

I didn't want to think about that. 'Tony did tell me she'd texted him, but he said he didn't see it until later, by which time she'd sent him another one saying not to worry about it and she was going to bed.'

Withers nodded. 'Yes, but that wasn't until 11.20pm. Maybe she had already left, and she wanted to stop him discovering she'd gone. Or maybe he sent it to himself after disposing of her to stop himself looking guilty.'

I sighed wearily. 'You're doing it again. There's no body; this is not a double murder investigation—'

'Not yet it isn't,' he said. 'Come on, Jodie, what else can have happened to her? Where is she? She left everything behind, her money, her passport, everything, in fact, except her phone. Even if she'd left Tony, why wouldn't she be in touch with her uncle and aunty to let them know she was all right?'

I thought about telling him everything I'd learnt from Trish today but decided against it. I didn't know myself yet what it could mean, and when he found out I'd been investigating Roger Laity he would go ballistic.

'Why are you telling me all this?' I asked him, keen to get him away from the subject of the Laity family. 'I mean, I know I said I'd pester you into submission, but...'

He laughed softly. 'You know the saying, pick your

battles? Well, you're a battle I'd rather not have. I can shut you out of this case and then have to put up with you stalking me and demanding answers, or I can let you know what's going on and' – he gave me a cheeky grin which literally made me go hot all over; I didn't know it was possible for your toes to blush, but mine did at that moment – 'and have you stalking me for entirely different reasons...' I pulled a face and threw the half-dog-eaten pickled onion at him. He dodged it easily and I was mortified to see it land in someone's beer two tables away.

Germaine sighed and shifted under the table, resting her head on my feet. I knew that within a matter of seconds my trainers would be covered in dog hair.

Withers smiled. 'Was that the dog sighing or you?'

'The dog,' I said. 'But I know how she feels.'

Withers bent down and made a fuss of Germaine, then sat up. The flirting was over and it was back to business. 'Anyway, that's why we're keeping Tony in custody for the moment. I'm not charging him yet, but I do think we've got enough.'

'Then why *aren't* you charging him?'

'Because I don't want to send this case to the CPS before it's watertight.'

I looked at him, amazed. 'You've got doubts, haven't you?'

He looked at me seriously. 'No, I don't. But believe it

or not, I don't want to charge the wrong person. I want to be sure.'

'And you're not sure.'

'Try and remember that I'm not the enemy here, Jodie. I'm not so desperate for a conviction that I'll send down the first likely-looking bloke for it. I'm a good copper. I want to know what happened. In an ideal world I'd want a confession.'

'You won't get one,' I said.

He gave an exasperated groan. 'I know. Are the Cornish all this bloody-minded and stubborn?'

I thought about it. 'Yeah, last time I looked...'

Chapter Twenty

It had just gone 2pm by the time I finished my lunch. Withers had gulped the rest of his baguette and left about twenty minutes earlier, apologising for leaving me to eat on my own. I really didn't know how to feel about him. He was a right cocky bugger, but then that kind of came with the territory; you can't show indecision or uncertainty when you're a police officer because criminals (or more accurately their lawyers) will spot it a mile off and use it to their advantage.

But he'd also seemed completely sincere about his reasons for keeping Tony in custody, rather than charging him. I had known detectives who were under so much pressure to get a collar that they really would have moulded the evidence to fit the suspect, just as I had initially accused Withers of doing. The top brass sometimes became so obsessed with crime figures and statistics that it felt like all they were interested in was getting the numbers up, of putting someone, *anyone*, away, regardless of whether or not they were guilty. Most people, it seemed to me, measured a police force solely by the number of crimes they had solved, which was dangerous; but then, how else were you supposed to do it? Things like people feeling safe in their neighbourhoods? Like kids who might otherwise have turned to crime being steered away from it by community policing? Getting the *right* people behind bars, even if that meant fewer arrests? To me (and to my dad), these things mattered just as much. How many crimes did we manage to prevent, either by making people aware of keeping themselves and their possessions safe, or by being a visible presence, or by running initiatives that channelled bored kids into productive pastimes rather than leaving them to hang around and fall into trouble? These were just as important, but almost impossible to track.

I smiled to myself. Rant over. Withers was a good guy, if a little arrogant. But he was still more or less convinced of Tony's guilt. More or less. I had to work on that 'more or less' and give him a few more doubts.

I was about to leave the pub when the phone rang. Mum.

'Hello, love,' she said. 'I've done all my chores and I'm at a bit of a loose end. What are you up to?'

I thought for a moment. I *should* leave the investigating to DCI Withers. But we all know the difference between *should* and *would*, don't we?

'Fancy a drive out to Boscastle?' I said.

It's only about forty minutes from Penstowan to Boscastle, but if you don't have a car, it might just as well be on another planet. There are no trains in that part of Cornwall – the nearest station is in Exeter, an hour's car drive away. I'd made the mistake once of coming down to see my parents on the train, and had just missed the bus that left Exeter St Davids once every two hours and which took nearly that long to get to Penstowan. I'd got a cab instead, which had cost me an eye-watering £85 and been worth every penny. There are buses, except rural buses are like honest politicians (they're out there, but they are few and far between) and the quickest you could get to Boscastle using public transport was about two and a half hours.

Mum didn't drive and consequently she hadn't been to Boscastle since my dad had died seven years ago. She looked out of the window, enjoying the countryside and pointing out any pretty cottages and gardens we passed, and I realised with a pang just how small her world had become. She had lots of friends – she always had done – but since she'd been on her own she'd made more of an effort to join clubs and community groups and she now had a better social life than me. But it all revolved around Penstowan. Would that happen to me too, now I'd moved back? It was one of the fears that had made me leave home in the first place.

'So,' she said, as we approached the town. 'Why this sudden urge to visit Boscastle?'

'I just thought it would be nice—' I started, but she interrupted me.

'Rubbish,' she said. 'Yes, it *would* be nice to come here for a cream tea one day, the three of us, but a spontaneous drive at three o'clock in the afternoon? Hmm. That Roger Laity lives near here, doesn't he?'

'Does he?' I said innocently. I hadn't told her that Withers had brought me here yesterday. She was already a bit too keen to set me up with 'that nice young detective' (or anyone else who had good hair, all their own teeth, and lived locally, probably to make sure I didn't move away again) and I didn't want her reading anything into it.

'I told you he did,' she said, twisting in her seat to look at me. 'Have you found something out?'

I thought about denying it for a second, but she was my mum and as such she had an uncanny knack of knowing when I was lying. I'm not sure how it works but I have a pretty good bullshit detector when it comes to Daisy, and my mum has the same with me. We came to a lay-by just before the fork in the road that would either take us down into the town or up towards the Laity house. I pulled in and switched off the car engine.

'Okay. I found some stuff out this morning about Roger Laity's council dealings. The stuff I'm assuming Mel was talking about.' I drummed my fingers on the steering wheel, thinking out loud. 'I can't see it being a motive to kill Mel in itself, but I reckon it could have put pressure on Cheryl to stay with Tony, so her family wouldn't have wanted him to find out about her affair.'

'Ooh, it sounds proper juicy,' said Mum, taking a packet of wine gums from her handbag and offering me one. 'Go on.'

'Apparently, one of the councillors was asked to resign as there had been complaints that their relationship with Roger Laity was a bit … close.'

'Ooh, you mean they were doing the horizontal foxtrot?' Mum's eyes were wide. I tutted.

'No, they weren't doing the … what are you like, woman? I mean, ol' Roger the dodger was taking them out for expensive lunches, buying them tickets for the theatre, treating them. Not quite manila envelopes full of cash, although some of the other councillors did accuse them of it, but there wasn't any proof.'

'Oh,' said Mum, looking slightly disappointed. She carefully selected a red wine gum and began to suck it. 'Bit of a shame. That Roger Laity was a right looker in his younger days.'

I shuddered, imagining him carrying that sports bag full of saucy undies, and started the engine again.

'Anyway, I don't know how relevant any of it is, but if the police aren't going to question him about it then I feel like I should...'

We drove along the narrow lane towards the Laity family home. I wasn't entirely sure what I was going to say to him but I'd always been pretty good at winging it.

Just as we reached the driveway into the house, the Range Rover I'd spotted parked outside yesterday pulled out onto the road, with Roger Laity behind the wheel. I quickly passed him – he was going the other way, into Boscastle itself – and drove on, hoping he hadn't seen me.

'Wasn't that him?' said Mum. I nodded. 'What are we going to do now?'

I pulled into the driveway of another massive house and did a U-turn.

'I'm going for a nose around.'

I drove back to the turning and hesitated. If I drove down there and parked, and he came back, my car would be instantly noticeable and I'd have no way of sneaking away. Then again, if he found me wandering around his house, miles from anywhere with apparently no car, I'd look like a spy or something. Best to look completely innocent and open. I turned down the driveway, Mum oohing and aahing at the lovely garden, and parked next to the garage.

I got out and Mum followed me.

'What are we looking for?' she asked, and I had to admit I had no idea.

'Suspicious stuff.'

'Like what? Plastic flamingos? Dodgy garden gnomes?'

'Just stay by the car and let me know if you hear him coming back.' I wandered over to the house and knocked. I didn't expect anyone to be there; he'd said only yesterday that his wife was away and his stepson had gone home, but with a house this size there was every possibility he had a housekeeper, or at least a cleaner, and I didn't want them looking out of the window and spotting some strange woman sneaking around the shrubbery.

There was no answer. Good. I stepped back and looked up at the house. I wasn't sure what I was expecting, but ... nothing. I looked down at my feet, the gravel crunching as I stepped back further onto the driveway.

There was a dark patch on the gravel, a stain where yesterday the Range Rover had been parked. It looked like an oil stain or something, and it looked relatively fresh. Hmm. Where had I seen a stain like that recently?

'Curiouser and curiouser,' I said to myself. I walked back over to the garage and peered in through the frosted-glass window in the door. I rubbed at the dirty glass with my hand, but still all I could make out was the vague suggestion of a car.

I looked around, then down at the door knob. It was an old wooden stable door. Underneath the relatively fresh coat of white paint I could see that the wood was old and splintered. It was, I thought, like the family who lived here; everything looked nice and respectable on the outside, but underneath it was rotten. Hark at me, getting poetic or philosophical or whatever in my old age.

I put my hand on the door knob, expecting it to be locked, but it moved easily. I looked back at Mum, who was still happily eating wine gums like she was watching something exciting at the cinema, gave her a cheesy thumbs-up, and went inside.

Inside the garage it was dark, but clean and tidy. There was a work bench along one side, with an array of suspiciously clean and shiny tools, lined up and kept in

order of size: secateurs, shears, tree lopper, chainsaw...
Either these tools had never been used, or their gardener
had OCD, or Roger Laity was a serial killer who was
very good at cleaning up the evidence after he'd
dismembered his victims. I shuddered, and this time it
had nothing to do with the image of him in his pants.
Cheryl *had* disappeared off the face of the earth. What the
hell had been in that sports bag yesterday?

I shook my head, dismissing such ridiculous
fantasies. Old Roger liked to style himself as a ruthless
and successful businessman, but this was Boscastle, not
American Psycho. I turned my attention to the car, which
was under a tarpaulin. Like everything else, the tarpaulin
was free of dust, spiders, or any of the other detritus that
normally finds its way into a garage. So either the car
hadn't been in here for very long, or the gardener with
OCD had been at work again.

I lifted the tarpaulin, expecting to see the sort of car
that someone like Roger would have put to bed so
carefully – a Mercedes, or maybe a red open-top midlife-
crisis-mobile, the type of car that would be his pride and
joy. But it was an old banger, a beaten-up Peugeot 205
that was probably about twenty years old. I could not
imagine Roger driving a car like this, or letting his wife
drive it either; it wouldn't have fit the image.

I lifted the tarpaulin further. In the front passenger
footwell of the car lay a mobile phone.

'Curiouser and curiouser,' I said again. I tried the car door. It was locked, but on the work bench was a set of keys with a Peugeot key ring.

I opened the car and picked up the phone (taking care to use the edge of my T-shirt to cover my hand, so as not to leave any fingerprints) and the screen sprang to life; it still had some charge in it, so it couldn't have been in here long.

The police hadn't found Cheryl's phone...

Trembling with – nerves? excitement? I'm not sure which – I took out my own phone. I had Cheryl's number because she had called me several times in the week leading up to the wedding, usually to complain about something on the menu, until Tony had put a stop to it. I dialled her number and looked expectantly at the phone in my other hand.

It didn't ring. It wasn't Cheryl's. Dammit.

'Ca-caw, ca-caw!' Mum made a ridiculous bird noise outside. It sounded urgent. Either she was being attacked by seagulls (Cornish ones have a reputation for being badass) or Roger Laity was coming back...

Chapter Twenty-One

I threw the keys back on the counter, pulled the tarpaulin over the car, and shot out of the garage, closing the door behind me and joining Mum with an innocent smile on my face just as the Range Rover pulled up by the front door. *That was too close*, I thought, but I had to admit I liked the thrill of nearly getting caught.

Roger Laity got out of the car, looking a little flustered at the sight of us. A quick flick of his eyes over to the garage door behind us betrayed his alarm, but he seemed to relax slightly as he saw that the door was shut. The fake smile appeared.

'Afternoon, ladies,' he said. 'I didn't expect to see you here again so soon.' Mum half turned to me in surprise but didn't say anything.

'I'm sorry to just turn up like this, Mr Laity, sir,' I said, in my best, most ingratiating voice. I debated tugging at my forelock but dismissed it; that might be going too far. 'I just wondered if I could have a word with you?'

A look of annoyance fleetingly crossed his face, but then he gave a strained smile.

'I am rather busy…' he started.

'I appreciate that. I won't take much of your time. I just wondered if you'd heard from Cheryl? I don't know if you're aware, but she hired me to do the catering for the wedding.'

He looked at me in surprise. It was obviously the last thing he'd been expecting me to talk about.

'Oh, I see,' he said, although he clearly didn't. 'So what can I do for you? Did she not pay you? It's down to Tony to pay you, not me.'

'Oh no, no,' I said quickly. 'No, that's all sorted. It's a bit delicate, really. Cheryl mentioned that you were hoping to open a hotel in Penstowan, and she said she would talk to you about me running the kitchen. She said the wedding was kind of like an audition.'

Roger pursued his lips. He seemed unsure of how to react.

'I don't know where you heard that—' he began, but I interrupted him.

'I heard it from a friend at the council, same place Mel heard about it. So it's not true you bought the two buildings next to Penhaligon's, hoping to turn them into a hotel, but the council refused you permission?'

Roger was on the back foot, and he reacted defensively. 'I own those buildings, yes. I rent them out—'

'You mean the shop that mad hippie woman sells her crystals in?' said Mum conversationally. 'I can't see her lasting past the summer season.'

'That one and the book shop,' I said. 'But he's put in a planning application to knock them down and turn them into a car park. I heard it was to service the boutique hotel he wanted Cheryl to persuade Tony to open in the Penhaligons' building.'

'Malcolm would never go for that,' said Mum, shocked.

'Not coming from Roger here, no,' I said. 'But if it was coming from Cheryl, Tony probably would have done it eventually, and he might have been able to persuade his dad to go into business with the Laitys. And then of course Roger would do what he's done in the past – find some way of muscling his partners out of the business.'

'I want you off my property right now!' Roger was so furious he almost spat the words into my face . I'd hit a nerve.

'There was that guy down Newquay way, wasn't there, who let you use some of his land for a campsite and suddenly found that he no longer owned it. And the one in Truro with the mobile home park—'

'I want you off my property now, before I call the police!' Roger took out his phone.

'Cheryl disappearing like that really put a spanner in the works, didn't it?' I said. 'Whoever killed Mel didn't do it quickly enough to stop Cheryl running away. That's really mucked up your plans, hasn't it? And left you with two useless shops that probably cost you more in mortgage repayments and maintenance than they get you in rent.'

'I'm dialling them!' said Roger, holding up his phone. I doubted he'd actually call the police but I thought it would be best if we left, just in case.

'Don't worry, we're going,' I said, ushering Mum into the car. I opened the car door but stopped before I got in to look back at him. 'I know you're involved in this, Mr Laity. I know you're hiding a lot more than the stuff I uncovered at the council today. The police will find out. Best come clean before they do.'

I got in the car, started the engine, and drove away, and it was only then that I noticed how much I was shaking. Mum looked at me.

'Are you all right, love?' she said, offering me a wine gum before adding with typical Cornish understatement, 'That were a bit intense, weren't it?'

'You did WHAT?'

Daisy stared at me, furious, incredulous. We were sitting at the kitchen table eating our dinner and Mum had just spilled her guts about what we'd been up to. *Thanks, Mum.*

'Mum, you're not a copper anymore!' said Daisy. She seemed really upset and I felt a huge pang of guilt. 'You can't go around doing stuff like that. You could get hurt!'

'I'm sorry, sweetheart, but there was never any danger,' I said, reaching across the table to squeeze her hand. 'I had Nana with me. I would never put her or you in harm's way.'

'He'd have had me to deal with if he'd tried anything,' said Mum militantly. 'I did a self-defence course for older ladies down the community centre. I'd have hit him with my handbag, jabbed him in the particulars with my elbow, and poked him in the eye with my keys.'

Daisy and I looked at her fierce expression and immediately got the giggles. She looked a little bit offended but it served her right for dobbing me in to my daughter.

I stood up to clear the plates, still giggling.

'I'm sorry, darling. I promised you I would never do anything dangerous again, and I meant it. But I can't promise not to get involved. I'm worried about Tony,' I said. That made me stop laughing. 'It feels like no one else is fighting his corner. Poor Brenda and Malcolm must be so worried. And Mel's mum… I want to find out what really happened for her, too.'

'But what if he *did* do it?' asked Daisy, and I didn't really know what to say. Why was I so sure Tony was innocent?

I was saved from having to reply by the sound of a car pulling up outside.

'Who's that at this time of day?' asked Mum, although obviously we were at my house and there was no reason why she should have any idea who it was.

I looked out of the window to see Withers get out of his car and stride up the path.

'Oh, crap…'

———————

I opened the front door as he was still raising his hand to knock.

'DCI Wi—' I began, but I didn't get any further.

'What the actual bloody hell are you playing at?' Withers looked at me in angry exasperation. 'I put my job on the line today, letting you know what's going on with the case, and this is how you repay me?'

'What's happened?' I asked innocently, but we both knew that I knew what he was talking about.

'There's been a complaint made about you.'

I gritted my teeth. I had naively thought Roger Laity would stop short of reporting me, what with him so obviously hiding something. 'Son of a...'

'Oh, what, did you think Laity would let it go?' He shook his head in disbelief. 'You think he was happy about you turning up on his doorstep and accusing him of ... well, actually, I'm not even sure *what* you were accusing him of—'

'Evening, detective!' Mum appeared next to me, a big smile on her face. 'Would you like a cup of tea?'

'No, I would *not* like a—' Withers forced himself to calm down and smile at my mum. 'Good evening, Mrs Parker. Thank you but no; I just need to talk to Jodie.'

'Okay then.' But she didn't move. I rolled my eyes.

'He means *alone*, Mum. Never mind.' I stood back to let him in, and opened the door into the living room.

He followed me in and sat on the sofa, while I sat in the armchair opposite him.

'What am I going to do with you, Jodie?' he said, shaking his head. He'd calmed down but it didn't take a genius to work out that he was still utterly infuriated with me.

'Look, I'm sorry, but I found out all about Roger's

dodgy dealings at the council this morning, and I thought—'

'This morning? You mean before you had lunch with me? And it didn't cross your mind to mention it to me before you went blundering in and upset him?' He glared at me in between rhetorical questions. *So many* rhetorical questions. 'Does it give him a motive for killing Mel? I mean, a proper one?' he said, as I opened my mouth. I shut it again. 'No, I thought not.'

'It *sort of* does,' I said. 'He definitely had very good reasons for wanting the wedding to go ahead, despite the fact he clearly wasn't that impressed with Tony.'

'Wanting the wedding to go ahead and killing someone who, as far as we can tell, he'd never even met before are two very different things,' Withers said patiently.

'I know, but...' I shook my head. 'There's something not right there. I found this car hidden away in the garage—'

'Listen to yourself! "Hidden away in the garage"? What do you normally keep in a garage?'

I looked at him, perplexed. 'Well, most people I know keep boxes and lawn mowers and stuff in them. I don't know anyone who actually puts their *car* in there. But that's not what I mean. Look, Roger has this expensive Range Rover thing, which he parks outside. I'm assuming Mrs Laity also has a nice car, but of course she's conveniently' – Withers rolled his eyes – she's conveniently in Helston at the moment, despite the fact that her niece, her adopted daughter whom she's brought up since she was fifteen, has disappeared. So I would expect the Laitys to put one of their fancy top-of-the-range cars in the garage. But no, there's some old banger in there – not the sort of old banger you might want to restore, not a classic or anything, just an old Peugeot 205. And there was a phone in the footwell, which obviously hasn't been in there very long because it still had some juice in it and I dunno about you, but my phone needs charging at least every other day.'

Withers held up his hand. 'Right, stop there. You broke into his garage and had a poke around? For God's sake, you know you can't even do that as a police officer, let alone a private citizen!'

'I didn't break in; it was unlocked. But it's weird though, don't you think?'

'Not really. So he's got an old car. So what?'

'Can you at least run the licence plate? I wrote it down when I got home. Here.' I reached into my pocket and pulled out a scrap of paper with the number on it. 'I've got a good memory for car registrations, so I'm certain the first bit's right, but I might have got the last couple of digits round the wrong way.'

Withers took the bit of paper and looked at it, with

the air of a man who wasn't quite sure how he'd ended up here.

'I dunno. I came here to have a go at you and now you think I'm going to run a plate for you?' he said, shaking his head.

'You are going to though, aren't you?'

He sighed. 'Yes, I am. But only to prove to you that there's nothing sinister about it.' He took out his phone and called the station. 'Good, you're still there. Can you run a number plate for me?' He gave them the number and waited. 'No, a Peugeot. Try the last two digits round the other … you found it? Who's it registered to?' He turned to look at me as he spoke. 'Craig Laity. No, that's fine…'

'Are there any other cars registered to Craig?' I asked.

'Hang on. Are there any other cars registered to that owner? … None. No, that's fine. See you in the morning.' He disconnected the call. 'Mystery over. It's Craig's car.'

I shook my head vehemently. 'No, it's not mystery over at all. Craig's gone home to … where was it? Oxford? How did he get there if his one and only car is in the garage?'

Withers rolled his eyes. 'I don't know if you've heard of them, but there are these things called trains. If you can imagine a big iron horse that runs on rails…'

'Oh, ha ha. You're so funny. Where's the nearest train station?'

He shrugged. 'I dunno. Bude?'

I tutted. 'Bude? Get outta here. Exeter, more like. Getting anywhere on the train from down here is a nightmare. Why would you use the train if you had a car? It's not like he can just pop back and pick it up later. And whose phone was that? It wasn't Cheryl's. I tried calling her and it didn't ring.'

'All right then, Sherlock, *you* tell *me*. Why does Roger Laity have his son's car in the garage?'

'*Hidden* in the garage.'

'It's not hidden. You found it so it can't be.'

I thought about it, then … a eureka moment.

'I know why. It's obvious, innit?' Withers looked like it was anything but obvious. I smiled. 'We've accepted that Cheryl was having an affair, right? But we haven't tried to work out who she was having it with.'

Withers looked at me, then pulled a face. 'Craig? Eww. He's her cousin.'

'Not really. He's Roger's stepson. They're only related by marriage.'

'And by the fact that they grew up together after Cheryl's parents died. Eww. Again.'

I shook my head. 'She was fifteen. He must have been about the same age as her. Think of all those raging teenage hormones, thrust together under the same roof. Obviously she's an adult in those photos, so maybe they only gave in to it when they were older. Maybe it's been going on for years!' I was getting a bit overexcited now. 'They're not really related, but growing up in the same family does make it a bit yucky. No wonder they kept it a secret. Forbidden lust! In Boscastle!'

Withers laughed. 'Yeah, all right, there's no need to go all *Fifty Shades* on me.' We looked at each other and I was surprised to see him turn slightly crimson. I could feel my own cheeks going the same way. He laughed again and stood up, striding over to the window so he didn't have to look at me, which was a relief. 'So if they were having an affair, then what? Are you saying you think they've run away together or something?'

I nodded. 'They left everything behind so they can start all over again in another part of the country, as two completely different people.' I sighed before I could stop myself. 'That's kind of romantic, really.'

'Er, yeah, if you say so,' said Withers, pragmatically. 'Because starting from absolute scratch is really easy, isn't it? A new name means you need to get hold of fake ID, you need fake references so you can get a job… It takes a lot of money to start over, and neither of them had any as far as I can tell.'

'Then there's a less romantic explanation,' I said. 'Craig killed Mel for threatening to spill the beans, and he killed Cheryl for … some reason, and now Roger Laity is hiding him somewhere.Or maybe he's in Helston with his mum, and that's why he left his car in Boscastle.

Roger is up here trying to get him a fake passport or something so he can leave the country. I bet that's what was in the sports bag yesterday!'

The DCI looked at me almost admiringly. 'Oh, you noticed that too, did you? Yes, I wondered about the sports bag. I thought maybe he was off to see his mistress and it was full of ... toys.' We looked at each other and shuddered. 'But it could have been everything Craig needs to start over somewhere else.' I nodded.

'Craig Laity killed Cheryl. Maybe Mel came across him moving her body, so he killed her too.' I looked at Withers. 'Roger Laity is sheltering a murderer.'

I accompanied Withers to the front door where he stopped and turned to me with a smile.

'You're a regular Columbo, aren't you?' he said.

'I thought I was Magnum P.I.?' I said. He laughed.

'Yeah, sorry about that. I didn't quite know what I was dealing with at the time...' He looked at me with a frank expression on his face. 'Look, I'm going to be honest here. Tony is *still* the most obvious suspect. You know that. But I promise you, I am taking your theory seriously. I'll put some feelers out about Craig Laity and see if the police in Oxfordshire can track him down.'

'Was he at the hotel on Saturday when Mel was

discovered?' I asked. 'It would be interesting to see his statement.'

Withers shook his head. 'I have no idea,' he said. 'There were nearly a hundred guests there plus staff.' He grinned. 'And caterers. My DS went through all the statements. I'll have a look.'

We both jumped as a furry white cannonball smacked excitedly into our legs, almost knocking me off my feet. Withers caught and steadied me, then bent down to stroke Germaine, who had got fed up with being cooped up in the kitchen with Mum and Daisy and come to see who our visitor was. She immediately jumped up and put her paws on his leg, smothering his black trousers in her white hair.

'Sorry,' I said, as he brushed at his hairy legs. 'I'm still getting used to finding dog hair everywhere.'

'Everywhere?' he said, raising an eyebrow.

'Cheeky! Not quite everywhere... That reminds me, I worked out why Tony changed his trousers. They had dog hair on them, didn't they? He changed them because Cheryl had sent him that text asking him to go and see her after the party, and I remember him telling me she was allergic to dogs, so he put clean ones on. And then when you asked him for the clothes he was wearing that night he just gave you the ones he had on when he went to bed without thinking.' I grinned at his incredulous face. 'Am I right?'

Chapter Twenty-Two

I woke the next morning feeling restless. It was only 6am but the sun was already shining through the gap in the curtains, and I could tell it was going to be a lovely day. Weather-wise, at least.

I leapt out of bed (not literally) and made some tea. Daisy normally woke early too, but during the holidays she often stayed in bed reading for a while. Mum was in the spare room again, where she'd finally got out of the habit, ingrained over her and Dad's working lives, of getting up at the crack of dawn. I probably had the house to myself for a couple of hours. Germaine nuzzled my hand. Apart from the dog, of course.

I opened the back door and let her out into the garden. She was very well house-trained but even after taking her out for a walk round the block before bedtime she would still be waiting by the door with her paws crossed, desperate for a pee first thing in the morning. I was forty years old. I knew how she felt.

I took my tea outside and sat on the wall that separated the garden from the field behind it and, beyond that, the cliffs. Even though there were about ten houses on this street, half of them backing onto the same field, it was always quiet and peaceful out here, even later on in the day, save for the occasional baaing noises of the sheep who were our mutual neighbours. The view was beautiful, but I sat facing the other way – into my garden – and imagined what I could do with the currently uninspiring patch of lawn. I love flowers, but I have a tendency to forget about watering, and then I try to make up for weeks of neglect by drowning them in gallons of the stuff. Surprisingly enough, this never works. I needed to find plants that were hard to kill…

Had Mel been hard to kill?

I didn't know why that popped into my mind, but it wasn't a very welcome thought on such a sunny morning. I sipped my tea. It had looked (from my cursory examination of the crime scene anyway, which had been less an examination and more of a quick nosey whilst trying to keep people back until the police arrived) as if Mel had fallen and hit the back of her head on the bench, which I thought would be enough to knock you out. So that could've been an accident. But the gash on her forehead told us otherwise. Had someone hit her first, which had made her fall, or had they bashed her in the head while she was down to finish her off? I shivered, despite the sunshine; I could only imagine the fury someone would have to feel to kneel down next to an unconscious or at least incapacitated woman and smash her in the head with … with what? There had been no murder weapon at the scene, but it was obviously some kind of heavy, blunt object. Maybe a rock? There were a few arranged decoratively around the nearby pond. The murderer could have grabbed one as the nearest thing to hand, which would point to it being spontaneous and unplanned. And then maybe they'd thrown the rock back in the water?

Germaine meanwhile was having a grand old time, barking at a straggly yellow plant that had had the temerity to grow in the damp shady spot by the side fence. The nerve of it. She tugged at it, but it sprang back and whacked her in the face so she decided to let it go with just a warning. It knew she was watching it now.

I laughed as I brushed yellow petals off her snout.

'Leave it alone,' I said. 'If it's misguided enough to want to grow in this garden then it needs help, not digging up.'

I went back inside the house and rewarded Germaine for guarding the house against threatening-looking weeds with a bowl of doggy biscuits. I made myself some toast and listened to her crunching her way through her breakfast, then turned on the TV. But I couldn't concentrate; I had metaphorical ants in my pants and couldn't sit still. I finished eating and jumped in the shower (again, not literally; safety first), then as soon as I heard movement from Daisy's room I stuck my head around the door and told her I was off to the hotel. I *still* hadn't picked up the food left over from the Wedding That Never Was, and I didn't want that surly hotel chef getting his hands on my organic bangers, so I needed to get over there sharpish.

I left Daisy lying in bed, reading one of Mum's old Agatha Christie novels to Germaine (who seemed to be enjoying it), and headed to Parkview Manor.

———

There was no one around when I got to the hotel. It was a bit early for guests to be up and about, if there were any still staying there after the discovery of Mel's body, which hadn't been in any of their glossy marketing brochures. I smiled at the receptionist – the same receptionist who had been there on my previous visits – and headed into the kitchen. The chef, Serge, a pale-skinned, dark-haired guy in his early sixties with a completely unplaceable but vaguely Eastern European accent, was just starting to prepare the breakfast buffet.

As I entered he glared at me and brandished his spatula in an unsettling manner, but didn't say anything.

'I'm just getting my sausages,' I said placatingly. 'And the desserts. Give me ten minutes and you'll never know I was here.'

Serge sniffed (I wasn't sure if that was meant to suggest that it would take a lot longer than ten minutes for him to forget me and would probably involve counselling, or that I was so insignificant he would have already banished me from his thoughts, had he even bothered to spare me any in the first place) and turned back to his streaky bacon.

I loaded everything back into the plastic crates I'd brought it in just four days ago and staggered back to the Gimpmobile, which was parked and lowering the tone right in front of the steps into the hotel. It took two trips to carry everything, and I wasn't convinced that I had all the desserts – there seemed to be at least one of each missing, and I suspected that Serge had taken it upon himself to check out the competition and taste them – but that was it. Done. I didn't need to come back to this blasted hotel ever again.

So if you want to look at the crime scene again you'd better do it now. There was that little voice again, getting me into trouble. But I had to admit it had a point. I shut the back of the van, looked around, and then headed over to the crime scene.

The tent was gone, although there was still police tape around the bench area. That was all that was left to show that poor Mel's life had ended here. I looked around at the ornamental pond; there were some big, heavy rocks, just as I'd remembered, and they were scattered around the edge of the pool to make it look less formal, more natural. It was hard to tell if any had been moved; they'd been placed quite randomly. But when I looked closer, there was an indentation in the mud. Something heavy *had* been here until recently. I squatted on my heels and peered into the pond; I suspected it wasn't particularly deep, but with the waterlilies and some kind of pond weed growing in it, giving the koi carp who lived there shade and something to nibble at, it was dark and shadowy and impossible to see the bottom. I was sure all of this had occurred to Withers anyway; as much as his insistence on seeing Tony as the only possible suspect (until I had hopefully inserted a few doubts in his mind) had irritated me, I had to admit that from what I'd seen, he was a good copper and he knew what he was doing. Not good enough that I would step back and let him get on with it, of course...

I stood up and looked over at the faint pathway in the grass Germaine had led me down the other day. The days of summer sunshine and the heavy dew in the mornings meant that the tall grasses and sedges had already sprung back to life and the pathway had all but disappeared. The only way I could tell where it had been was from the two metal stakes that had been shoved into the ground and wound around with more of the police incident tape. I skirted them and trailed through the long grass, some of it tall and wispy enough to tickle my hands, which hung by my side.

The rest of the grounds were perfectly manicured, Mother Nature teased and combed and styled to within an inch of her life, but this corner of the garden had been left as a wildflower meadow. In amongst the long, fluffy white tufts of the grass seed heads wove deep purply-blue cornflowers, sunny yellow marsh marigolds, and the tiny palest pink, almost heart-shaped flowers of enchanter's nightshade. Bees buzzed in and out of the undergrowth, at this time of day not yet having to compete with the constant hum of summer holiday traffic from the A39 that by midday would penetrate even here. It really was idyllic, if you blanked out the fact it was the scene of at least one murder. The trail had, I'd thought, been created by someone dragging a body; but could something else have caused it? Maybe a suitcase on wheels, being tugged along the uneven ground? Cheryl had left a suitcase in her car, but maybe that had been a decoy, a stunt suitcase, designed to throw people off the scent. Tony had said she'd been selling possessions; maybe she really had been putting together an escape fund, and had brought a second piece of luggage – an escape kit – with her? A really large suitcase could possibly have made the trail. And yet…

I didn't believe it. Someone had dragged a body along here. Whether it had been a dead body, or an injured one, or even a drugged one, I had no idea. It all just felt *wrong*. The murders I'd been involved in during my time in the Met (only on guard or escort duties; I'd been uniform, not a detective) had all been straightforward. Nine times out of ten it was an ex-husband or partner killing a woman who had had the nerve to leave them. Depressing, but simple. Occasionally we'd had gang killings, but they were simple enough too – a drug dealer getting greedy and being taught a lesson by the boss, or someone trying to muscle in on a territory. But this one made my head hurt. And my heart.

I walked to the end of the trail, listening to the birds singing. I had no idea what birds they were, but I liked to hear them anyway. I stopped at the wooden fence and looked over at the lay-by beyond, not wanting to touch the rotting wood and get another splinter.

Holy moly. The tarmacked lay-by was clean(ish) now, but I suddenly remembered where I'd seen an oil stain like the one outside Roger Laity's house…

Chapter Twenty-Three

I couldn't stand around there all day cogitating, not with a Gimpmobile full of organic sausage waiting for me (not a euphemism), so I walked thoughtfully back to the van. I was so deep in thought that I didn't notice the black car parked nearby.

'Oh my God, you just can't leave it alone, can you?' Withers's voice brought me out of my trance. He was standing on the hotel steps with his hands on his (snake-like) hips.

'I've got a genuine reason to be here today!' I protested. 'I came back to get my' – for some reason, saying the word *sausage* in front of this man made me feel intensely uncomfortable, a situation which could only be made even more mortifying by adding the word *organic* –

'organic sausages,' I finished, failing miserably to avoid saying either word. He grinned.

'You and your sausages. Are they real sausages or are you using imaginary ones as an excuse to come back here, hoping to bump into me?'

'You're very sure of yourself,' I said. 'I'm sorry to disappoint you, Detective Chief Inspector Withers, but if you'd care to mount an interior inspection of my vehicle you'll find it's practically wall-to-wall pork.'

He laughed loudly at that. 'I can honestly say that's the least enticing invitation I've had in a long time.' He walked alongside the van, studying the decals. 'Interesting artwork for a caterer…'

'I thought so at first, but it's growing on me. Not literally, obviously,' I said. 'That would be anatomically difficult.'

'It certainly makes you easy to spot and hard to forget.' He leant against the bonnet of the van. 'Not that I ever get a chance to forget you, because every time I turn around you're at my crime scene.'

I sighed and sat on the hotel steps. 'I'm not doing it on purpose.' He raised an eyebrow. 'Well, all right, I am. I can't help it. I guess I'm just…'

'Nosey?'

I laughed. 'That was my nickname at school. Nosey Parker. I wasn't then but I have to admit I probably am now.'

Withers sat down next to me. '*Something* we can agree on, anyway. So, Nosey Parker, do you want to know what I just discovered?'

'What?'

'I just spoke to the staff member who was behind the bar and he said that after you broke up the bitch fight – which I would really like to have seen, by the way – and the party got started again, Cheryl and Craig Laity had words.'

'What sort of words?'

He smiled ruefully. 'That would've been nice to know, wouldn't it? Unfortunately he didn't hear what they were talking about. He said they weren't exactly arguing, but they didn't want anyone else hearing because as soon as Tony joined them, Craig walked away. And there's more.'

'Go on...'

'Craig left the party early. He didn't see when exactly, but he thinks Craig and Roger had both left by half ten, quarter to eleven, whereas most of the guests didn't leave until closer to midnight.'

'Hmm...'

'What does "hmm" mean? Come on, Parker, out with it.'

'The lay-by, near where Cheryl's earring was found. There was an oil stain there.'

He shrugged. 'It's a lay-by. Cars break down and pull

over, they have leaks, oil, brake fluid, all sorts.' He grinned. 'Bodily fluids sometimes, too.'

'Eww, eww, eww. Anyway, it wasn't some historical whatever-it-was stain, because it was there on Saturday and it's not there now. It was fresh and now it's dried up.'

'You went and looked at the lay-by? Just now? You need a hobby.'

'I've got a hobby: interfering in police investigations. There was a similar stain on Roger Laity's driveway, right where his car was parked when we went there on Sunday.'

'And you saw this during your unofficial visit yesterday?'

'Yeah.'

'Hmm…'

'That's what I said.'

Withers looked at me thoughtfully. 'I'll have to check that scene of crime took photos of the lay-by, not just where the earring was found. I don't know that it could be used as evidence, but…'

'But it gives you something to think about.'

He nodded.

'So does this mean you finally accept that Tony didn't do it?'

Withers looked at me steadily. 'No. But I do accept that he's not the only one with a possible motive, and he's not the only one who had opportunity. That's the best I can say at the moment.'

I smiled. 'Then that'll have to do.'

I left Withers talking to the hotel receptionist – whom I could see, through the hotel doors, looking at in him in doe-eyed adoration as she answered his questions – and drove home. I unloaded everything, leaving Mum and Daisy to work out the logistics of how to get a hundred or so vanilla panna cottas and chocolate tortes in the fridge (I suspected that their solution would involve eating several of them), not to mention those blasted sausages, which were in danger of becoming the bane of my life. Then I headed straight back out again. I had an appointment.

'So this is the famous van?' Rob Trevarrow wiped his hands on an oily rag in the gesture beloved of all small-town mechanics since time immemorial – it was probably part of the City and Guilds Car Mechanics course – and inspected the Gimpmobile. I'd been to school with Rob, who, at the age of six, had wanted to be an astronaut but at the age of sixteen had realised he was probably more likely to succeed in life if he just went and worked in the family garage. Luckily, he'd always been good with his hands (certainly according to my friend Helen, who had gone out with him in the sixth form) and he soon discovered that being able to fix just about anything with a motor would stand him in good stead down here, where people tended to hold on to their old bangers (and tractors and muck spreaders) pretty much until they fell apart. 'Yeah, I can see why you might want a re-spray...'

I laughed. 'I quite like it, but I think it might give clients the wrong impression.'

He nodded. 'The MOT's still got a while on it, so I reckon if we give it a service and a general check over we can let you know if there's anything on the way out, and then we'll get Gary in the body shop to take all the decals off and spray it. It'll be good as new. Do you want to leave it now? I've got a few things booked in over the next week, but I can do the service in between them if you like. You'll probably get it back quicker that way, to be honest.'

I decided to leave the Gimpmobile in Rob's capable hands. I could walk home from here and I still had my car. He showed me where to park so it was out of the way.

I walked over to his office to hand over the keys but then stopped. There was a familiar looking Range Rover parked in a bay. I found Rob.

'Here you go,' I said, handing him the keys to the Gimpmobile. 'Is that Roger Laity's Range Rover?'

'Yeah,' said Rob. 'I didn't realise you knew him.'

'Yes,' I said. 'I was talking to him the other day.' That much was true. 'He said he was after a mechanic, because he had a leak or something…'

'In the radiator, yeah,' said Rob.

'I mentioned it to him because I saw there was, like, an oil stain or something where he'd been parked,' I said, screwing up my face as if I was trying to remember our conversation.

'Yeah, probably. It's leaking anti-freeze. I expect one of the hoses has split. It happens a lot round here, with all the pot holes and untarmacked roads.'

'Does that stain? I remember I had an oil leak once and it really stained the concrete in my garage.'

'Nah, it normally dries up and goes away.' *Like the stain in the lay-by*, I thought. Interesting.

I left the garage and walked through Penstowan. It was almost midday and I thought about picking up some pasties for me, Daisy, and Mum for lunch, but I'd eaten rather a lot of them since moving back and I had the feeling I'd look like one if I carried on at this rate. And it wasn't like I didn't have a fridge full of food at home, even if it was just as fattening and unhealthy as a pasty.

I had just reached the end of Fore Street when I got a phone call from possibly the last person I was expecting: Tony.

'Tony? Are you all right? Where are you? Have they let you go?'

'If you stop asking questions for a moment I might be able to tell you,' he said. He sounded exhausted. 'I'm at home. You busy?'

Tony opened the front door of his house, stared at me for a second, and then pulled me into a massive bearhug. I was surprised, but at the same time I rather liked it.

I finally pulled away and followed him inside.

'How come you're out?' I said. 'I thought they had until one o'clock?'

'So did I,' he said. 'But DCI Withers said they didn't have enough to charge me and that I was lucky to have such loyal friends.' He turned to look at me. 'I take it he meant you?'

I shrugged. 'Not just me. Callum and Debbie, and your parents…'

'But mostly you.' He smiled. 'I heard Old Davey talking to one of the older blokes – the desk sergeant? – and he said Withers had been dead certain it was me to start off with, but he seemed to have had a change of heart. And that he'd been seen in the company of a certain person who had just come back to Penstowan…'

'He might've been…'

Tony looked serious. 'If it *was* something you did, I can't thank you enough. Sitting in that interview room,

Withers got me so confused I almost started to think I *had* done it.' He sat down on the sofa and put his head in his hands. I sat down next to him and put my arm around his shoulders. 'My head's all over the place. I don't understand how any of this happened. I keep thinking I'll wake up in a minute and everything will be okay.'

''Fraid not, my lover,' I said, in my best Cornish accent. I'd kind of lost it over the years. I heard him laugh gently.

'Spoken like a true local.' He sat up. 'I know you didn't like Cheryl…'

I shook my head. 'That's not true. I didn't know her well enough. You liked her, and that's the only thing that matters.'

'Well, it isn't, because if I ever do get married again I want all my friends to like her, but anyway … I met Cheryl when she came to work at the shop. She was very polite, good at her job and that, but a bit aloof. I thought she was a snooty cow at first, to be honest. But then I saw her one day, when she thought no one was looking, and it was like her mask had slipped. And underneath it she was a bit sad, a bit lonely.' He turned to me. 'I just wanted to stop her feeling sad, and make her realise she didn't need a mask.' That was typical Tony. He looked like your average scrumpy-swilling pasty-eating football-watching Cornishman (except, actually, he didn't anymore; I had to admit he was pretty fit in both senses of the word these days), but inside he was much deeper and more sensitive than you'd think. A big softy, in fact. I couldn't for the life of me remember why we'd only gone out with each other for two weeks.

There was a knock on the door. We looked at each other, both remembering the last time we'd sat here and there'd been a knock. It had been Withers, coming to arrest him.

But it wasn't this time. There was another knock and a 'Cooee, love, are you in there?' It was Brenda.

Tony got up and answered the door. I smiled as I heard muffled voices; there was obviously another big bearhug going on.

Brenda and Malcolm came in, all relieved smiles, followed by Callum and Debbie. Tony looked happy, but a bit overwhelmed, to see them all.

'Tea,' I said firmly. 'Let's have some tea.' I left them all to sit down and talk while I went into the kitchen.

My phone pinged as I picked up the kettle. Withers.

Tony's trousers covered in dog hair (like you said). No sign of blood so not enough forensic evidence to charge him or keep him in custody. Happy now?? NW.

I felt a little surge of triumph. Withers had actually admitted I was right, and I had it in writing, and I was never going to delete that text. And NW? *I wonder what his first name is? Neil? Nigel? Please don't be a Nigel.*

I looked up to see Tony looking at me curiously. I put my phone away. 'It's nothing. I was going to make some tea.'

He smiled. 'I'll do it. I just wanted to get out of everyone's way. It's nice of them to come round, but…'

'A little bit too much all in one go.'

He nodded. 'Exactly.'

He took the kettle from my hands and filled it at the kitchen sink. He looked completely washed out and swayed for a moment, so I reached out and put a hand on his arm to steady him.

'You look done in,' I said. 'When did you last eat something?'

'I dunno. They did feed me in there but I couldn't make myself touch it.' His stomach rumbled.

'If only I'd known, I'd have brought you a sausage,' I said. He looked at me and we both began to giggle uncontrollably.

'I bet you say that to all the boys,' he said, gasping for breath. 'I've seen your van.' That started me off as well, and pretty soon we were clutching each other for support.

'Oh, stop, stop!' I cried, still laughing. 'Ooh, my pelvic floor muscles…'

'Everything all right?' Brenda stood in the doorway

watching us, smiling. Tony nodded but he was in no position to actually speak.

We finally got ourselves under control, although every now and then we'd catch a glimpse of each other and start giggling hysterically again. Brenda and I carried the tea out to the living room and Tony got out a packet of biscuits, which he demolished almost singlehandedly.

'So what now?' he said. He had shadows under his eyes and he needed a shave, but he was looking more awake.

'What now?' said Brenda. 'Now you sit here and wait for the police to find the real killer.'

'And for Cheryl to turn up,' said Callum.

'You look like you need a kip,' said Debbie. Tony shook his head.

'I'll be all right after I have a shower. I just feel like I need to *do* something.'

I could hardly argue with that; I'd felt the same when he'd been languishing in police custody. But I wasn't sure if I should share all my deductions – okay, suspicions and wild conjecture – with him. Would that make him feel better or worse?

As if he was reading my mind he said, 'The worst thing is not knowing. I don't know if Cheryl's dead or alive. I don't know if she left me or someone took her away. I don't know if I should be angry, or hurt, or grieving. I just want to know how I should feel.'

I had to tell him everything I knew, or everything I thought I knew, anyway. But not yet.

'How about you go and have a shower,' I said, 'and then we'll have another Council of War.'

Fifteen minutes later he was sitting in front of us, clean-shaven, smelling a *lot* better than he had earlier, wearing a clean T-shirt and cargo shorts, and clutching another mug of tea. He was starting to look like his old self again. Did I really want to upset him?

But I didn't get the chance to, because he started to speak before I did. He pulled some thin sheets of paper from his pocket and put them on the coffee table between us.

'I just found these,' he said. 'I looked through Cheryl's bedside drawer as I was getting dressed, just in case … I dunno … and they were tucked down the back.'

I looked at them. They were receipts, headed *Nancarrow Cash Exchange*.

'That's the pawn shop on Nancarrow Street,' said Malcolm.

'Yeah.' Tony looked at me. 'So I was right. She did sell all that stuff.'

'What stuff?' Brenda looked confused. He handed her the wad of papers and she began to sift through them. I leaned over and read them as best as I could as they were upside down to me.

'These are the tickets you need to get your stuff back, aren't they?' I said.

'Yeah.'

'So she didn't actually sell anything,' I said. I had the feeling this changed everything. 'She pawned them. She kept the pawn tickets. Why would she keep them?'

He shrugged. 'I dunno.'

'It's all here: the laptop, the figurine, even the kitchen stuff.' I was getting a crick in my neck trying to read it all. Debbie leaned over and took a receipt from Brenda's hand.

'Flipping 'eck! She got a grand for a ring?'

'Yeah, the day before the party, going by the date on the receipt. I know which one it was and all. Her mum left her an engagement ring. She was going to wear it at the wedding as "something old", you know? But you remember, Mum, you said you'd lend her the pearl necklace you wore to your wedding? Cheryl said that would take care of something borrowed *and* something old.' He fingered the flimsy slip of pale-yellow paper. 'I didn't think anything of it at the time, although I was surprised she weren't wearing her mum's ring. But so what? How does this change anything?"

'Because she kept the pawn tickets. It means she wanted to get her stuff back, don't you see?' I leaned forward and grabbed his hand. 'You know what this means? She planned to still be around to go down the pawn shop and get what she could back. Certainly her laptop and her ring. She wasn't planning to leave you! She must've needed money quickly.'

'But she could've just asked me—'

'Not if she needed it for summat she didn't want you to know about,' said Debbie.

He sighed and ran his fingers through his hair. 'I'm starting to think I didn't know her at all. What with the affair, and now this. I just don't get any of it.'

'Of course!' I said, sitting bolt upright and spilling my tea. 'The affair! Those pictures you got. How closely did you look at them?'

The others all looked at me like I was mad or at least completely insensitive.

'Believe or not, I didn't want to study them too closely,' Tony said, sourly.

'No, no, I know, but what I mean is, how can you tell when they were taken? Did her hair look different, or…'

He rolled his eyes. 'Again, believe it or not, her hair was the last thing I noticed. And anyway, she's had it in the same style for years.'

'Since about 1987 by the looks of it,' muttered Debbie under her breath, and Callum nudged her hard.

'So they could have been taken a while ago, before you were even together? When did you meet?'

'Two years ago.' Tony looked thoughtful. 'Yeah, they could have been taken before then, I suppose…'

'So she wasn't having an affair after all,' I said. 'Think about it. She's getting married to the man of her dreams' – Tony smiled sadly at me – 'and suddenly someone from her past pops up.'

'Poor choice of words, given what was happening in those photos, but yeah.'

'He shows up, with proof, threatening to ruin her wedding day. Tony, she wasn't raising money to escape you, she was being blackmailed!'

Chapter Twenty-Four

Tony looked at me steadily for a moment, then shook his head.

'No. No, I don't get that. Why would I care what she got up to before we got together? It's not like she'd told me she was a nun or something. I knew she had a past, just like I do.'

'Did she tell you about it?'

He shook his head again. 'No. I've never got this whole thing about telling your partner about all your exes or the number of people you've slept with. Why do I need to know that? She did start to tell me once, before we moved in together, but I told her I honestly didn't care if she'd had one boyfriend before me or a hundred. Don't look at me like that, I mean it.'

'No, I believe you, it's very … Tony. I was just thinking about Richard—'

'Dick,' he interrupted. He'd never liked my ex.

'He hated having his name shortened—' I saw Tony raise an eyebrow. 'Oh, right, you weren't referring to his name. Anyway, *Dick* went on and on at me when we started seeing each other, wanting to know how many men I'd slept with and saying it didn't matter, and when I gave in and told him he got all moody.' I laughed. 'God knows what he would've done if I'd told him the real number.'

Debbie laughed. 'I know what you mean…' She noticed Callum looking at her anxiously and smiled brightly and insincerely. 'Of course, I didn't need to lie to Callum because I really was a virgin when we met…'

I sniggered.

Brenda laughed as well. 'Oh, yes, they don't always get that what's sauce for the goose is sauce for the gander,' she said. Malcolm looked at her, mildly horrified, but didn't say anything. I didn't think he dared.

Tony smiled and stirred his tea with a finger; a thin film of milk fat had started to form on top of it (and this is why I hate full fat milk). 'So how could this guy be blackmailing her, if she knew I didn't care about that? She was thirty-one years old; she was always going to have a past.'

I thought about the car hidden in Roger Laity's garage, and the tell-tale anti-freeze, or whatever it was, stain in the lay-by the day Mel was found, which matched the one outside the Laitys' house.

'I suppose it wasn't so much what she'd done as who she'd done it with,' I said carefully. He looked at me, not understanding.

'What, like she was with a married man, or another woman or something?' said Callum.

'But I wouldn't have cared,' protested Tony. I waited for him to say something like, *I'd have wanted to see a few more pictures if she was with another woman, hehehe*, and was quietly gratified when he didn't. Although, given that Mel had left him for her female driving instructor, maybe that wasn't surprising. Still, Richard/Dick/that cheating swine would never have let an opportunity to be both crass *and* sexist – or basically just an idiot – pass him by. God, I'd had bad taste in men back then.

'No, but someone else, like … her brother?'

'She didn't have a brother,' said Malcolm, but Tony and Callum exchanged looks and I knew I'd hit a nerve.

'Craig.' Tony laughed bitterly. 'Bloody Craig.'

'Do you think that might be possible? I mean, I know *technically* he wasn't actually her brother, but her uncle and aunty wouldn't have been pleased, would they? They did bring them up together, like siblings, so it does feel a bit…' The only word I could think of was the one DCI Withers had used last night. 'Ewww.'

'Oh yeah, it sounds plausible all right,' said Tony. 'He was always sniffing around her. They were really close before she moved in here, then he got a big old strop on and we hardly saw him again, which was fine by me. When we first met, she took me round to meet her uncle and aunty and he was there, and he and Roger spent the whole night belittling me, about Mel leaving me for a woman, about the shop, about everything really. Pauline, her aunty, she was all right, but she was a bit of mouse. Barely said anything. You could tell that Craig had her wound around his little finger. Yeah, Craig is just about the only person in the world I would really have been upset about her being with. But even then, I'd have been upset, but I'd have got over it! Did she not realise that?'

I reached out and touched his hand. He really was one of the good guys and he deserved so much better than this.

'Maybe it wasn't just you she was hiding it from. I'm not the only one who thinks it's a bit yucky,' I began, but then stopped as I realised what I was saying. He probably wouldn't want the affair or whatever it was broadcast all over town. I backpedalled madly. 'I mean, you lot think it's wrong as well, don't you?'

The others nodded, but Tony knew that wasn't what I'd meant.

'Bloody hell, Jodie, who else knows? Who have you been speaking to?'

'Just DCI Withers,' I said. I tried not to notice the way Debbie's eyebrows rose at his name. God, she was worse than my mum. 'Sorry, I saw him last night and I told him what I suspected. I didn't know about the blackmail though; I thought maybe they'd run off together or something...' I didn't need to tell them what I meant by the 'or something': that Cheryl was dead.

Tony took a deep breath to calm himself down. 'So what makes you think Craig has anything to do with this? I hate the bloke, but as far as I know he doesn't – didn't – even know Mel.'

'I know he was there at the party on Friday night,' I said. 'I don't remember seeing him in the bar when I left but, to be fair, I wasn't looking. Was he there on Saturday? I don't remember seeing any of the Laitys.'

'Roger was there,' said Callum. 'I was doing my best-man duties, trying to herd the early arrivals into the bar for a welcome drink. He said Craig was running late but he'd be there for the reception.'

'Except Roger knew he wouldn't be, because...'

'Because what? What do you know?' Tony leaned forward. 'Jodie, you have to tell me. I'm going mad here.'

'Okay, first of all I don't *know* anything. This is just what I think might have happened.' I took a breath, giving myself a moment to get it straight in my head.

'Okay, you know the police found Cheryl's earring?' They all nodded. 'Well, actually, it was me that found it. There was a trail in the grass, leading through the grounds to a lay-by on the A39. Her earring was not far from the fence. Do you remember what Craig was wearing on Friday?'

Tony looked mystified. 'Not a clue.' But Malcolm reached into his pocket and took out his phone.

'I took some photos,' he said. 'I think Craig and Roger were standing near us at the time. Here, I can't see. I left my glasses at home...'

Malcolm handed me his phone and I looked at the pictures on his camera roll. There were several of someone's feet (presumably Malcolm's) and, for some reason, a random photo of Brenda's back, but I finally found one of the party. A group of men standing by the bar, Tony in the centre laughing at something Callum (who had been there, and I hadn't even recognised him) had just said, and behind them, scowling, Craig Laity in a white shirt with a thin blue or grey stripe running through it. Just like the scrap of material that had been caught on the fence.

'Oh, Tony,' I said, my voice starting to wobble. 'I'm beginning to think I'm right. I think he might have killed Cheryl.'

I told the assembled Council of War about the trail through the grass, which *might* have been caused by a suitcase but I thought was more likely to have been the result of someone dragging a body through the undergrowth. I told them about the unidentified stain, and the stain which *might* be a complete coincidence but which suggested to me that Roger Laity's Range Rover, with its anti-freeze-leaking hose, had been parked there recently. I told them about Craig's car, parked (hidden) in a garage in Boscastle when he was apparently back in Oxfordshire (to which everyone agreed there was no way you'd choose to get the train from down here when you had your own transport), with his mum conveniently out of the way in Helston. I told them about Roger Laity and his sports bag, which *might* have just contained saucy pants and the odd battery-powered toy (the thought of which was apparently even more *ewww* than Craig and Cheryl getting it on), but could equally have contained clothes and money for Craig, to help him get away.

'You think Craig' – Tony swallowed hard, unable to say it – 'you think he did something stupid and then he told Roger and asked for help?'

'Wouldn't he have rung his mum, rather than Roger?' asked Brenda. To be fair, had Tony been in that position, he *definitely* would have rung her rather than his dad, who was lovely but who embodied the laidback Cornish temperament too much to be of any use in such circumstances.

'I thought about that,' I said. 'Out of the two of them, who would be more likely to come up with the goods? Who would have the contacts, who would know how to get hold of cash in a hurry without drawing attention to themselves, and who would know how to get a false passport or ID?'

'Roger.' Tony nodded. 'Yeah, you're right. Pauline would do anything for him, but in reality, she wouldn't be able to help him.'

'So, what?' said Debbie. 'You reckon he's done a runner?'

I shook my head. 'I think it would be a bit quick. I think it would take a good few days to come up with fake ID. Unless he had it all planned, and I don't think he would've planned to kill Mel. Why would he? He didn't even know her. All I can guess is she came across him with Cheryl and tried to stop whatever was happening. No, I think he's lying low somewhere.'

'Roger's hiding him.' Debbie looked militant.

'Yeah.'

'He's got him holed up in a caravan on one of his campsites,' said Callum.

'It's possible,' I said. 'But which one? He's got a whole chain of them.'

Tony suddenly looked down, then around the room. 'Where's the dog?'

'Germaine? She's at home, why?'

He grinned at me, a mad gleam in his eye. 'Fancy taking her for a walk?'

I wasn't entirely convinced that taking Tony on a trek around the various Laity-owned campsites was a brilliant idea – God knows what he would do if we actually found Craig – but he was in a restless, slightly manic mood brought on by being stuck in a cell, aware that the real killer was out there somewhere, and I had the feeling that if I didn't go with him he'd venture out on his own and do something reckless. Even more reckless than I was likely to.

We googled the Laitys' camping empire and made a list of the ones within a fifteen-mile radius of Boscastle, for the simple reason that we couldn't search all of them in one afternoon. We discounted the ones that were tents only – in a hurry to hide from the police, who stops to put up a tent? – and concentrated on the ones that had static caravans already on site.

That left us with four campsites, all of which had public footpaths crossing or running alongside them.

'We'll do the one at Trebarwith,' said Debbie. 'We want to take the kids to Tintagel anyway.'

'We'll look at the one at St Juliot,' said Brenda. 'We can stop for a cream tea at that nice pub on the way back.'

'You and I can handle the last two,' said Tony.

I still had my doubts, but everyone was hellbent on finding Craig now I'd let the cat out of the bag with my suspicions, and there was no way I could stop them.

'All right,' I said. 'But remember, you're not there to make a citizen's arrest; you're just there to have a look around. Be discreet and don't put yourself in any danger.' I looked at my troops: two old-age pensioners, a fat bald guy and a mouthy Northerner, all of whom were treating this as a bit of a jolly. I suddenly missed my old colleagues at the Met very much. I sighed. 'Just be careful.'

Tony drove us back to my house to pick up the dog. Mum and Daisy both wanted to come with us, which I at first had my doubts about. But the sight of the two of them, and the dog, seemed to calm Tony down a bit, and I thought that their presence might help him control his behaviour. I didn't think we'd actually find Craig, to be honest – there were too many places for him to be hidden and, despite my gut instinct that he would still be holed up, there was always the possibility that Roger would have made him move on after my visit yesterday. I began

Murder on the Menu

to realise that just blundering in without thinking it through properly might not always be the best course of action. Not that I would ever admit that to DCI Withers, even under torture.

'Let's go to Millook Haven,' said Tony, as if he'd spontaneously thought of it. Mum looked at him, then at me, curiously; she might be daft but she certainly wasn't stupid, and she knew we were up to something. But she let it go.

It was a beautiful day. We walked along the cliff path and, for the first time since I'd seen him in the shop that day, Tony seemed to relax. Although he'd been excited about the wedding, I could imagine that Cheryl had been wound up about it (I could understand why now, if she was worrying about Craig turning up and ruining everything) and that would have made Tony stressed too. He was such an easy-going person normally.

Germaine ran ahead, sniffing out rabbits, although I suspected she wouldn't know what to do if she actually came across one. Daisy chased her, laughing, while Mum, whose knees were a little on the arthritic side these days, accompanied us as far as a big, flat boulder overlooking the sea, plonked herself down and announced she'd wait there for us.

Tony and I walked on. I watched him breathing the sea air deeply, colour returning to his cheeks. He almost looked happy. Almost.

He saw me watching him and laughed. 'What?'

'Nothing. It's just good to see you looking more like your old self.'

He grinned. 'If you're waiting for me to wipe my nose on my sleeve…'

'Yeah, not *that* much like your old self would be best.'

We walked on. The sea shimmered turquoise in the heat, sunlight glinting off the ripples. I looked at them, eyes squinting against the glare.

'You see the way the sun makes the waves go all twinkly?' I said. 'I thought about that when I was in labour with Daisy. I was trying not to have any pain relief—'

'Why on earth not?' Tony was incredulous. 'I'd have wanted every drug going. Actually, I'd have wanted to be unconscious.'

I laughed. 'Yeah, I did change my mind halfway through and get an epidural. Blow all that natural-childbirth nonsense. Anyway, it'd been going on for hours and I was exhausted, and the midwife told me to think about my happy place, to visualise something that made me feel good, and that's what I thought of. The sea off the North Cornwall coast. You and me and the old gang, swimming that day off Widemouth beach when we saw the dolphins, do you remember? I've been to places where the ocean's a lot warmer, but it's not the same colour as it is here on a sunny day. This place never leaves you, even if you leave it.'

Tony smiled at me. 'Of course I remember that. Does that mean you're back for good?'

'Never say never and all that, but yeah, that's the plan.'

'Your mum will be happy to hear that. So am I.'

We stopped and turned to face the sea. Behind us, on top of the hill, stood the Laity camp site.

'Do you still want to do this?' I asked him.

'Find Craig? Too right. Although, thinking about it, we could have just had a stakeout at Roger's house and followed him when he went out.'

I thought about how angry DCI Withers had been when he'd come round last night, after Laity had made a complaint about me.

'Yeah, not really. I think old Rog is already this close to getting a restraining order on me and if he'd spotted us following him…' I smiled ruefully. 'Okay, let's do this. But don't go blundering in there. That's my job.'

We walked up the hill and followed the footpath into the campsite. It was the first week of the summer holidays; the whole of Cornwall – apart from the beautiful but slightly bleak and family-unfriendly clifftop we'd just come from – was rammed, and the campsite was no exception. We wandered through the camp, past the caravans, towards the small shop and site office, being careful to look out for Roger Laity; I really did not want him to see us. But there was no sign of him.

Every single caravan showed signs of being occupied. There were children playing, beach towels hanging up outside, sandy flip-flops on the door steps – all the signs of a Great British seaside holiday. None of them looked like they were harbouring a fugitive, but then, what would that look like anyway?

Tony looked at me. 'On to the next one, then.'

We traipsed back down the hill, collecting dog, child, and mother on the way, then drove a few miles up the coast towards Bude. We stopped on the way to have lunch at a café overlooking a pond and wildlife reserve, and I almost forgot that we were not just having a nice family day out. But one look at Tony – who sat restlessly pushing his food around the plate, not able to eat more than a mouthful – was enough to remind me that we were searching for a murderer, in the unlikeliest of places.

Chapter Twenty-Five

W e finished lunch – a mackerel salad with fish so fresh it was practically still swimming – and ordered another pot of tea, with a chocolate milkshake for Daisy that looked so good that even Germaine – whose breath was suspiciously fishy, despite the fact we had all agreed not to give her any scraps – licked her lips.

Tony's phone made a *blip* noise, and he picked it up.

'Message from my mum,' he said. 'They've had a lovely cream tea at St Juliot.' He gave me a meaningful look, which I took to mean, *Nothing else to report.*

'The Bude campsite next then, I reckon,' said Mum. Tony and I exchanged guilty glances, and she laughed. 'I'm not quite the daft old biddy you think I am, you know.' She looked at Tony's plate. 'You not eating that?'

He shook his head. 'No, I'm just not that hungry...' His

voice trailed off and we watched in a mixture of embarrassment, disgust, and a smidgen of pride – because, after all, we had paid for it – as she wrapped up his fish in a serviette and put it in her handbag. I was just glad that Daisy was too busy fussing over the dog to notice, because at the age of twelve that would have made me die of shame.

'The campsite backs on to the marshes,' I said. 'We could walk along by the canal and then cut across, if Mum's feeling fit enough.'

'It's nice and flat,' said Tony. Mum rolled her eyes.

'I told you, I'm not an old biddy. I can walk, you know.'

'We know,' I said, grinning. 'And you can always stop and eat your fish if you get tired...'

We set off. The café was popular with walkers, and the canal path that wound its way alongside the water often got busy, particularly later in the season when the families had gone home. Today though it was fairly quiet, most of the holidaymakers enjoying themselves on the sandy beaches at Widemouth Bay and Summerleaze.

Daisy proudly held Germaine's lead – we couldn't let her off the leash here, in case she decided to follow a duck into the reeds and ended up in the canal – and chatted happily to Tony as I walked behind with Mum, who, despite her fighting talk, was puffing and panting a bit.

'We can always go back to the car and drive there,' I said, but she shook her head.

'No, it does me good to go out and get some exercise.' She smiled and nodded towards our faster walking companions. 'Look at them. Getting on like a house on fire.' She looked at me slyly. 'You see? You could've done worse.'

'Stop it, woman,' I growled, although my heart did do a little flippy thing as I saw them getting along so well. It was more to do with the fact that my beautiful daughter hadn't had much chance to spend time with her actual father, just hanging out and talking, going for a walk, laughing, like she was doing with Tony. We'd never had a proper family holiday. Even when we'd come down here to see my parents, most of the time it had just been the two of us. When we'd got married, the brass weren't too keen on couples working at the same nick, so I'd moved (because I was always the one to make any sacrifices), so Richard had been able to say that he couldn't get time off or swap shifts and I'd been none the wiser. It was only when I bumped into my old sergeant from that station and mentioned it to him that I discovered it was all lies and that he was getting time off after all, only he chose to spend it with his girlfriend and not his own daughter.

We walked on, smiling hello at other walkers as they passed us, most of them heading for the café we'd just left and looking forward to a cream tea. We crossed a small, quiet road and went over a bridge onto the other side of the canal. Here the waterway began to widen, and mirrored the river Strat on our right. In between them were the fields that would eventually lead into the marshes and, beyond that, the town itself.

I'd thought the walk across the clifftops had been good for Tony, but here he was so relaxed I almost expected him to break out into a happy whistle. He pointed out different plants to Daisy who, bless her, probably wasn't that interested but she did a good impression of it. She stopped while Germaine cocked her leg against a tree stump and we caught up with them.

'Enjoying yourself?' I asked, and they both smiled.

'Yes! Tony was telling me about birdwatching,' said Daisy. I looked at him in mild surprise; I couldn't imagine him coming out with a pair of binoculars. He laughed.

'Don't look at me like that! I used to come here with my grandpa. All sorts of birds round here, not just seagulls. Black kites, reed buntings, even the odd kingfisher. I used to love coming here with him. I haven't been for ages.'

We walked on, passing a group of kids kayaking, then turned off, away from the town and over the Strat, with the marshes on our left. Germaine gave a joyful bark and threw herself at a bird (I didn't know what it was, although Tony might have) which was minding its own business on an old fence post surrounded by straggly loosestrife, almost hidden by the purple flower spikes. The bird, of course, flew away from the fluffy white miscreant with something of a disdainful look, and the daft dog got her lead tangled around the old misshapen post.

'Oh, you berk,' I said, wading into the undergrowth and fighting with the leash. It took a while – during which time the others were no use at all, and just stood there laughing as the dog re-tangled the bits I'd untangled – but eventually we climbed back onto the path, both somewhat dishevelled and out of breath. Tony reached out and picked something out of my hair, and then held it out to me.

'A flower, milady,' he said, smiling. I took it from him. 'Hang on, there's another one; you've got it all over you...'

I dropped the stem he'd given me and flapped at my hair and back. 'What? Where?'

He gently slapped my hand away. 'If you stand still, I'll get it off you.' He held up a flower spike and examined it with interest. It had a slightly sticky, hairy stem, with lots of tiny yellow flowers and acid-green leaves clambering up it. 'You've actually chosen a very rare plant to fall into. Yellow crosswort. This is the only place in Cornwall it grows.'

'Thank you, David Attenborough,' I said, then stopped. I reached out and took the plant from him again, looking at it more closely this time.

'It doesn't grow anywhere else? Only here?' I asked.

He nodded. 'Down here, yeah. It mostly grows up North.'

I looked at it again to make sure; but I *was* sure. 'Roger's Range Rover had this sticking out of the grill when DCI Withers and I went to see him on Sunday.'

'What? Are you sure?' I nodded. 'Then that means he was here, on the marshes.'

'But there's nowhere to hide out on the marshes,' I said. 'And there's no reason to drive through here to get onto the campsite.'

'No...' Tony and I looked at each other thoughtfully. Without speaking, we turned to look at the path that led across the marsh to the hide, where local birdwatchers could sit and watch the Canada geese that migrated here. There was a gate at the other end of the reserve, where the local wildlife rangers came in to do regular checks.

I turned to Mum. 'Why don't you and Daisy stay here and get your breath back?' I said. 'Tony and I want to have a quick look at the wetlands, and Germaine's not allowed in there because of the birds.'

Daisy began to protest but Mum leant heavily on her arm.

'Oh yes, you stay with me and help me find somewhere to sit; my knee's playing up,' she said, and gave me a wink. *Thanks, Mum.*

We climbed the stile into the reserve and walked along the path. It was still beautiful and sunny but for some reason I felt cold. Neither of us spoke.

We reached the hide. It was empty. We peered through the slats in the wood, looking out onto the reed beds, but could see nothing.

'It's so quiet,' I said. It was, eerily so. Tony reached out and took my hand, and we followed the path.

This area was out of bounds to the public. A rough driveway led from the lane down to the gate, and on the other side of that were piles of old wood and vegetation set up as insect and hedgehog habitats. We looked around, but it was deserted. We inspected the gate, expecting it to be locked; there was a chain wound around the gate post and part of the gate itself, but the padlock holding it in place was rusty and didn't close properly. Anyone could have unwound it and opened the gate to drive through.

We climbed over. Despite the hot sun, the ground here was always soft, and there were tyre tracks in the mud. We followed them. They stopped abruptly, not far from a small reed-filled patch of stagnant water.

I looked at Tony, not sure I wanted to go any further; and I could see that he didn't really want to either. But we had to. We walked on to the edge of the water, and all of a sudden everything seemed surreal: the glare of the afternoon sun on the still water, the buzzing of insects in the bushes and reeds, and the chirping of the birds ... and the two of us, standing here.

Blip. The not-very-loud sound of a text message reaching Tony's phone made us both jump.

'It's Callum,' he said. 'He says there's one caravan at the Trebarwith site that's a possibility. It's the only one that looks empty.'

'Craig could be lying low in there,' I said, but I doubted it.

'I don't think so. What's that?' said Tony, and his voice sounded husky and dry. I followed his pointing finger.

Amongst the reeds, something floated. Hunched, misshapen, swollen with moisture. The sun was so bright on the water that it took me a while to make out the dark hair and the white shirt. It was impossible to tell from here if it was striped through with grey or blue thread, but I already knew it was.

We'd found Craig Laity.

Chapter Twenty-Six

'I don't suppose there's any point in me asking you what you were doing here?' Withers looked at me, an eyebrow raised sardonically.

'Tony only wanted to show me his weedy wobbler,' I said, smiling innocently. Tony snorted, trying to suppress an hysterical laugh.

'Reed warbler,' he said, controlling himself. Just. 'It's a bird.'

'Yeah, I got that.' Withers rolled his eyes. 'And you just happened to come across the body of a possible suspect in your ex-wife's murder case?'

'Yeah,' said Tony. 'What are the chances?' The two men glared at each other. I flapped my hand in front of my face, as if trying to swat a pesky fly.

'Phew, there's a lot of testosterone flying around here,

isn't there?' I said. Tony dropped his gaze while Withers turned to me.

'So, come on then, Miss Marple,' he said, folding his arms. 'Tell me why you thought it was a good idea to bring the main suspect—'

'Main suspect?' Tony interrupted. 'You let me go, remember?'

'…Why you thought it was a good idea to bring the main suspect with you to find the only other possible suspect we've got at the moment? You didn't think it might look suspicious, the two of you leading us to Craig's body?' He put on a sarcastic voice. '"Oh, look, there he is, fell in the marsh and drowned, case closed." You didn't think it might look a bit convenient?'

'To be honest, Detective, no, I didn't,' I said. 'Because we weren't expecting to find him dead. We thought he was holed up in one of his dad's caravans.' I explained to Withers about noticing the yellow crosswort while we were having an innocent walk along the canal path; I didn't think he needed to know that we'd set out to search the Laitys' campsites, and had already come up empty-handed at three others further down the coast. I told him how I remembered seeing that same yellow flower on Roger's car, when he had taken me there. He looked thoughtful.

'I remember his car was pretty muddy,' he said. 'I

can't say I noticed any weeds sticking to it though. But anyway, you decided to walk across the marsh, why?'

'There's a campsite just the other side of the field,' I said. 'I think it's one of Roger Laity's.' I didn't tell him I knew full well it was, and I didn't doubt for a moment that he already knew I knew. 'We thought maybe some of his land encroached onto the marshes, and maybe he'd moved a caravan or tent or something down this way so Craig could lie low there. As we were already here, we thought we'd just have a quick look before we called you. I mean, we wouldn't want to call you out unnecessarily.'

'And how did you end up here? The campsite is right over there.'

'We saw something,' said Tony.

'From the footpath?'

'Yes.'

'The footpath over there? The one that's about four hundred metres away, through a load of reeds and with a birdwatching hut in between it and here?'

'Hide,' I said.

'What?'

'It's called a hide. And no, of course we didn't see the body, but there were a lot of birds swarming around here and we thought they were all over an animal carcass or something, and we just thought we'd look.'

'Sounds plausible,' said Withers. 'Complete rubbish, of course, but plausible. I suggest you go home, Mr Penhaligon, so we know where to find you.' Tony and I both opened our mouths to protest, but Withers carried on before we could say anything. 'You'll want to know if we get any news about Miss Laity, won't you?' He turned to me. 'And you, Jod— Ms Parker, please remember that your elderly mother and your teenage daughter are not exactly Doctor Watson material, so if you must go poking about where you're not supposed to be, at least leave them at home.' And with that he turned and walked away, leaving a uniformed officer – the nervous young guy I'd seen at the hotel – to escort us from the marshes.

As we walked away Tony muttered, 'That Withers is a right flash git. Fancies himself, don't he?' I shrugged. 'He fancies you, too. You can do better than him.'

The rest of the day passed quietly. Tony took us home then went home himself, despite Mum inviting him to stay for dinner. Finding Craig like that had shocked all of us, not least because we'd all been so certain that he'd been the killer and Roger had been hiding him somewhere. Tony had been very quiet on the short drive home, and I realised that, despite the fact he hated Craig, finding his dead body had not given him any satisfaction.

We spent what was left of the afternoon in the garden, Mum and I weeding (actually, me weeding, Mum pointing out where I'd missed them) while Daisy sat on the wall, legs dangling over the other side, talking to the sheep. Germaine lay in the shade behind her, tongue lolling out, hot but not wanting to leave her young mistress's side. It was so cute and just one more thing that made me think we'd made the right move. If you ignored the fact that the body count had shot up since we'd got here, Penstowan was a great place to raise your kids...

We had a leisurely dinner of pasta carbonara and salad – I did think about doing bangers and mash, but I felt like if I never saw another sausage in my life it would be too soon – then sat in front of the telly. At 9.30pm Daisy took herself up to bed; I went up and tucked her in, not that she needed it (I still needed it though, as well as really missing reading her a bedtime story; why do our children have to grow up so fast?), and then I took Germaine for a last quick walk around the block.

It was a lovely warm night still, and the sun had only just started to go down; it set later down in this southwest corner of the country than in London. I waited as Germaine sniffed around a lamppost, deciding whether or not this was the one she was going to grace with her wee or if we'd have to move on to the one further down, and drifted off into thought.

'Jodie.' His voice made me jump. I turned around to see Withers watching me. 'Sorry, I didn't mean to creep up on you. You busy?'

I gestured to Germaine, who had lifted her leg experimentally, obviously working out her angle of urination and, finding it wanting, put her leg down again and moved on. 'Not exactly. I'm waiting for *her* to get busy.'

He smiled and together we strolled along to the next lamppost.

'I thought you might want an update,' he said.

'I do, but...' I stopped and turned to him. 'Why are you telling me everything? You wouldn't give me the time of day before, but now...'

'Yeah, sorry about that...' He ran his fingers through his hair. It messed it up, but if anything it just made him look even hotter. *Damn.* 'It helps to talk it through with someone. In the past I'd have talked to my DSU or something, but there isn't one here. Most of the time I'm the highest-ranking officer at the station, unless I want to go to Barnstaple. And there's not really anyone else I can talk to.'

He must be single. Mum would be pleased to hear that. I didn't care in the least, of course.

'Then fire away.'

We walked on, letting Germaine run ahead, the lead spooling out behind her.

'I went to see Roger and Pauline Laity,' said Withers. 'Broke the bad news.'

'Pauline's back? How did she take it?'

'She's devastated, of course. It looked to me like she genuinely thought he'd gone back to Oxfordshire.'

'What about Roger? Did you get a warrant to look in the garage?'

'No, I didn't. I didn't want him to think we were onto him.' He sighed. 'If we *are* onto him. I don't know what to think. I asked him what happened when Craig left, what time he went, did he drive, what route he would've taken, did he mention stopping to see anyone.'

'And?' Germaine's ears pricked up as another dog walker turned into our road; I recognised one of our neighbours with their pet, an elderly Labrador who would bark furiously when you passed their house, but would go quiet and look a bit embarrassed if you stopped and walked up the path, as if they couldn't remember what they were supposed to do next.

'He said that Craig had left on Saturday, while they were at the hotel for the wedding. Pauline had been quite upset because he left without saying goodbye; he just left a note which they found on Saturday afternoon when they got home. I asked if they still had the note but Roger said no, he'd thrown it away before Pauline had seen it because she was already upset.' He looked at me. 'Seem legit to you?'

'Not even slightly, but then not everyone gets on with their parents, do they?' I said. 'Had they argued?'

'Pauline said no, but Roger admitted he'd had words with him the night before.'

'About what?'

'About him coming along to the wedding uninvited.'

I laughed shortly. 'He didn't care about Craig not being invited when they turned up at the party together on Friday. Tony was really embarrassed and Cheryl was obviously not very happy about it either. It was quite clear even to me how uncomfortable they both were, but Roger seemed to think it was hilarious. So, he basically said, as far as he knew, Craig had left and gone home, perfectly fine, on Saturday afternoon?'

'Not exactly. He said that Craig's car wouldn't start, so he left it behind.'

'Likely. *Not*.'

'I did ask him how Craig would have got home without it, and wouldn't he need it back in Oxfordshire, but he just said he'd promised to get it fixed and that Craig often used to hitchhike, so he'd probably planned to get to Exeter that way and then get the train.'

'The suggestion being, he'd accepted a lift from the wrong person?'

Withers nodded. 'I don't buy that for a second. But I

also don't buy that Roger killed him and then dumped his body in the marsh.'

'But he was *at* the marsh. The yellow cross-thingy, the flower, proves it.'

'But we don't have the yellow crosswort. Apart from anything else, his car wasn't there this afternoon for me to look at.'

'No, it's at Trevarrow's. The garage on Ghyll Street? I took my van in there earlier and it was there. Apparently it's got a leaky hose.'

Withers smiled. 'So you were right about the stain, then? Unfortunately, Scene of Crime didn't take a photo of the lay-by, just the fence Craig's shirt got caught on.'

'Bugger.'

'Yep. Bugger.'

We walked to the end of the road. Germaine finally cocked her leg and got on with the job in hand, while we discreetly averted our eyes. Withers turned to look at me.

'I do believe you, about the stain in the lay-by and how Roger's car could have made it, and about the flower too for that matter. And if you remember, when we went to see him on Sunday, Roger told me Craig had left that morning. So he was either lying then or he's lying now. But none of it proves he did anything wrong. He still has no motive for killing Mel, or Craig. And then there's Cheryl; if something's happened to her, what's his motive there? Like you said before, he had more to gain from the wedding going ahead than from stopping it, even if he didn't like Tony much. If he had plans that involved using the Penhaligons' shop then Cheryl was his best hope of influencing them to let him. There's still only one person who really had the motive and opportunity for all of that.'

'You can't still suspect Tony?'

'Look at it from my point of view. We know Cheryl was cheating on him—'

'We found pawn tickets belonging to her!' I realised I hadn't told him about our latest discovery. 'We think she was blackmailed, that someone – probably Craig himself – was threatening to show Tony the photos of their affair, and she was selling her stuff off to raise money in a hurry.'

'Who's to say it wasn't Mel blackmailing her? Cheryl doesn't come up with enough money to shut her up, so Mel tells Tony, who goes mad and kills Cheryl and Craig in a fit of jealous rage, and then has to kill Mel so she can't drop him in it. It makes perfect sense.'

'Not if you know Tony, it doesn't.'

'And that's what we come back to, isn't it? You know the people involved. I don't. I'm objective, you're not.'

I wasn't having that. 'My dad used to say that being a police officer somewhere like Penstowan was both a blessing and a curse, because you always knew the people you were investigating. He said it was a curse because sometimes you absolutely *knew* someone was guilty, because you knew what kind of a person they were, but you couldn't prove it so they would get away with it and it would drive you mad. And other times, with other people, you absolutely could not stop searching for a way to clear them, because you knew no matter how bad it looked, they were not capable of committing the crime.'

Withers raised his eyebrows. 'And when was it a blessing?'

'Blowed if I know. Why do you think I joined the Met? But the point is—'

'The point is, you don't think Tony's capable of one murder, let alone two or possibly even three, and to be honest, as clear-cut as it looks, neither do I.'

'You don't?'

'No. And that's your bloody fault. I'd have had him banged up by now if it wasn't for you.'

'Good job I'm here, then.' I grinned. 'I'd hate for you to be involved in a miscarriage of justice.' I glanced down at Germaine, who sat there next to her puddle looking very pleased with herself, and then back up at Withers. 'The question is, where do we – sorry, *you* – go from here?'

Where do we go from here?

That was the question. And it definitely *was* 'we', regardless of what I'd said to DCI Withers, because there was no way I was backing down now.

I lay in bed, listening to Germaine snore in Daisy's room next door. She had crept onto the foot of her bed, making her murmur and reach a sleepy hand down to pat her on the fluffy noggin. Now both of them were fast asleep, and at least one of them was dreaming about chasing rabbits, going by the restless paws.

'Where do we go from here?' To my mind there was only one place left to go: back to the beginning. Back to Saturday morning, before we'd even discovered Mel or Craig were dead. Back to Cheryl's disappearance. Where was she? And was she still alive?

Chapter Twenty-Seven

I woke up the next morning still asking myself that same question. Was Cheryl alive? Withers was convinced she was dead and that they were now looking for a body, rather than a missing person, a body they might never find. We were surrounded by sea and cliffs and moors – all kinds of remote places where a body could lie undiscovered for years, depending on the weather and the tides. I had asked him about it the night before, before we'd said goodnight.

'Do I think she's dead? Put it this way.' Withers held up a hand and ticked things off on his fingers as he spoke. 'One, she disappeared wearing a red silk cocktail dress and high heels; Tony wasn't able to identify any other items of clothing missing from her wardrobe and it wasn't in her suitcase or hotel room, so we're pretty certain that's what she was wearing. Not an outfit particularly suited to either murdering two people or doing a disappearing act in. Two, as far as we can work out, she took absolutely nothing with her, other than her phone. She left all her clothes, her purse with all her bank cards in it, and her passport. There's been no activity in her bank account and she's not taken any money out, so unless she had a completely separate, secret account somewhere else, she's penniless. Three, there's no CCTV of her anywhere nearby. There're no cameras at the hotel because it's a listed building and apparently that's more important than guests" safety' – we both rolled our eyes at that – 'but there are cameras in town, at cashpoints, at the train stations in Exeter and Barnstaple, a few at bus stops, and there's no sign of her.'

'And she'd show up in that dress,' I said.

He smiled. 'Yeah, not many people wandering around Penstowan in cocktail dresses. And four, we think she had her phone with her – we certainly haven't found it – and after that last text to Tony at around 11pm, nothing. It's been turned off, so we can't trace it. If she killed Mel and Craig in order to hide her affair from Tony, why run away? At the very least, if she was still alive, I would have expected her to let him know she was all right and then maybe bin the phone.'

So who did that leave as the murderer? I *knew* deep in my heart that it wasn't Tony. He was kind, and funny, and had a big heart; I'd seen him cry at movies, and he was a closet birdwatcher, for Christ's sake! But...

Who else had a motive to kill all three of those people? I would not trust Roger Laity as far as I could throw him; he'd lied to DCI Withers about when Craig had left to go home, and I was ninety-nine per cent certain he'd been in the lay-by on Friday night and on the marsh at some point too. But Withers was right; Tony was the only one with a motive. If I didn't know Tony, would I still believe he was innocent? And that voice in my head, the one that had been too preoccupied with noticing Withers's biceps and stubble and speculating about his marital status, finally asked, *Would I still think Tony was innocent if I'd spent the last twenty years in Penstowan rather than London?*

I ignored that voice as I made breakfast for me, Mum, and Daisy; I paid it no heed as I stood in the shower and I shoved it to the back of my mind as I got dressed. But I couldn't quite forget that it was there, and it was beginning to drive me mad.

I was surprised to discover that it was only Wednesday; it felt like weeks had passed since the Wedding That Never Was. So much had happened since I'd moved back from London, just three weeks ago. To think I'd been worried about being bored, about the pace of life down here being too slow!

Daisy wolfed down her toast. She was meeting up with her new pal Jade, and together with some of her friends they were getting one of the infrequent buses into Barnstaple. She would be out most of the day. I was pleased – she needed friends her own age, and it meant she would know some of the kids when she started her new school in September – but it left me with nothing much to do. I supposed that, technically, I *could* make a start on the Banquets and Bakes website, or make some flyers, or do something that might actually lead to me getting some more paying work. Technically, now would be the perfect time to do it. Technically.

'You can come to the coffee club with me,' said Mum. 'Come and meet the gang.'

The thought of sitting in a church hall drinking lukewarm instant coffee with a bunch of geriatrics did not exactly (for some reason) make me quiver with anticipation, but then maybe I'd had more than enough excitement over the last few days. Maybe a calm (boring*)* morning listening to my mum and her mates talk about varicose veins and avoiding anything that felt like work was just what I needed to clear my mind and make me see things more objectively. And maybe inane gossip was exactly what I needed to drown out that nagging little voice, trying to convince me of Tony's guilt.

It wasn't that long a walk to the church hall, but it was a bit too far for Mum after the exertions of the last couple of days so I drove us, Germaine sitting in the back seat with her head poking out of the window. I'd managed to squeeze in a visit to the local pet shop on Monday and had bought a special harness thingy that clipped onto the seat belt, so she couldn't indulge in her love of escapology while the car was moving. She had to settle for feeling the wind in her fur and tasting the sea salt on her tongue as it lolled out, dribbling slightly.

We parked up as close to the church hall as we could. The street outside was full of cars; this was obviously the place to be on a Wednesday morning. As I unclipped Germaine, I felt my phone vibrate. It was a text message from Tony:

Morning, how are you today?

I didn't reply. I just needed some time away from him, away from the investigation, and away from that traitorous little voice in my head.

'I didn't think this place was your style!' I looked up and saw Debbie grinning at me. Behind her, Callum wrangled the two kids, who were obviously sick of having to behave themselves, towards their car, which was parked nearby. She leaned in to hug me. 'I heard about yesterday. By 'eck, that must've been a shock, finding Craig like that! How you feeling?'

'I'm fine,' I said, and I almost was. It was hardly the first dead body I'd seen. It was the first one I'd had a personal interest in, though. 'I think it shook Tony a bit.'

'Yeah, I'll bet it did,' she said. 'Poor Tony. He's not having a good time of it. What did that dishy DCI of yours say about it?'

'He's not *my* DCI—'

'He's right dishy though, isn't he?'

I laughed. 'Well, yeah… I don't know. He says that Tony is still the most obvious suspect, but he can't prove it and he doesn't even know whether he believes it himself now.'

Callum joined us. 'All right, Jodie? We gotta go, my lover; he'll be waiting for us…'

'Ooh, that sounds intriguing!' Mum was openly eavesdropping on our conversation. 'Who's waiting?'

'I'm sorry about her,' I said. 'She has no concept of privacy or personal space.'

Debbie laughed and exchanged looks with Callum. 'It's fine. We're going to meet an estate agent.'

'Does that mean you're moving back down here?' I hoped it did. Having Debbie as a neighbour would be fun.

'It's early days yet, but … you never know. We're looking at a house out towards Widemouth Bay.'

'Let me know how it goes!' I called after her, as Callum steered her and the two kids away.

We went through the big glass doors into the church hall, paid our entry fee – £3, with all profits going to the church fund – and made our way into the main meeting room, where tables and chairs were set out. I followed Mum, feeling like a spare part as she spoke to everyone in passing, waved at people across the other side of the hall, and basically worked the room like a networking pro. Various people stopped me to pat Germaine, and a few mentioned Mel and the 'terrible business' that had led to me inheriting the dog.

'Cooee, Shirl, over here!' An elderly couple in matching jumpers waved to us from a table in the corner. Mum smiled and I trailed after her lamely.

'Here they are, the troublemakers!' she said, sitting down at their table. I vaguely recognised them – Les and Janet – and we all exchanged hellos and pleasantries: how was I settling in, what was my new house like, how was Daisy enjoying it. But there was really only one topic of conversation in the room, fragments of which I'd heard as we weaved in between tables.

'So how you holding up, love?' said Janet kindly. 'Terrible business to get caught up in.'

'Terrible business,' said Les, nodding, and I was forced to agree that yes, it was indeed a terrible business.

'Oh, you know,' I said vaguely, and they all nodded, even though they clearly couldn't have known.

An even more elderly lady wearing a lacy half-apron approached our table.

'Morning, Joanie!' said Les, his voice rising. Old Joanie was obviously hard of hearing. 'How are you today?'

'Yes, it is, isn't it,' said Joan, and everyone at the table shared amused but sympathetic smiles.

We put our orders in – tea for me and Les, coffee for Mum and Janet, and a plate of biscuits for all of us – and old Joanie shuffled off. More of Mum's friends joined us, people I hadn't seen before and whose names I had no hope of remembering, who had retired and moved down from up country. By the time Joanie came back with our drinks – she may have been old and a bit doddery-looking, but she had pretty steady hands and only a tiny bit of my tea ended up in the saucer – there were about nine of us around the table and the volume of chatter in the room had gone up noticeably. It was rammed.

I relaxed as I sipped my tea and nibbled on a Bourbon biscuit. Mum's new up-country friends were nice, and as much as I'd dismissed them as a bunch of geriatrics (mostly to wind Mum up), they weren't really that old. I wasn't very good at keeping track of Mum's age; I knew she was thirty when she had me (which in those days was considered quite late, but it had just taken that long for her to fall pregnant), so that only made her seventy, and I reckoned that her group were all around that age. Had my dad still been alive, he'd have been seventy-two, but he'd died, in the best traditions of a Hollywood cop movie, a couple of months away from retirement age.

The group had been chatting and laughing about people I didn't know, but I didn't mind being on the periphery and just listening. But then one of them whose name I'd forgotten turned to Mum and said, 'That poor Laity woman, she must be devastated! To lose her son and her adopted daughter all in one go.'

'Yes,' I said. 'She was already upset about Cheryl going missing; to get back and find out Craig was dead as well... Poor woman.'

'Get back? Where had she been? Funny business, going away when one of your kids is missing, even if she's not one of your own,' said Janet. 'She always was a bit funny, that Pauline, though.'

'I could understand Roger being upset about it, but not her...' said one of the other oldies.

'Why would Roger be more likely to be upset?' I asked. They all exchanged looks that were sort of guilty-but-dying-to-share. 'What have I missed?'

'You know that his brother Hamish and Donna left town in a hurry, all those years ago?'

'Who's Donna?'

'Cheryl's mum,' said Mum. *Donna, not Clare OR*

Eileen… I rolled my eyes and made a mental note to tell Daisy later. She would have hysterics.

'Donna was playing around with both of the Laity brothers…'

'That she was,' said Mum, with a note of admiration in her voice.

'The hussy,' said Janet.

'Yes, that's what I meant.' Mum changed her expression to one of disapproval, but I didn't believe it for a second.

'Anyway, they got married and moved to Bristol and five months later, Cheryl was born,' said Janet.

'What … so you think that Roger might be…' I turned to Mum. 'Why didn't you tell me that? I wonder if DCI Withers knows? That might change things.'

'I don't like to gossip,' said Mum piously, and I snorted.

'Ha! Since when?'

'Still, not very nice of Pauline to disappear if her husband was upset,' said Les.

'Roger said her nerves had been shot to pieces so she went and stayed with her mum for a couple of nights.' I reached for another biscuit – a Jammie Dodger – and dunked it in my tea.

Janet laughed and shook her head. 'Nerves? That one? I don't think so. And her mum died years ago.'

I sat upright, waking Germaine, who had fallen

asleep on my foot and was now covered in enough biscuit crumbs to make the base for a cheesecake.

'She hasn't got a mum? What about her dad, or any other family?' Roger had definitely said she was visiting her mum, but I already knew we couldn't exactly trust his words.

Janet shook her head again. 'Her dad's in a nursing home, or was anyway; I don't know if he's still alive. I think she's got a sister who lives in Reading, maybe some nieces or nephews there. I used to work in the office when she and her first husband Mark had a printing company. She never said much but she was the one who made all the business decisions. Mark used to go out and play golf with the clients, but she was in charge. Don't let the mousy act fool you.'

'She didn't hesitate to sell the company and make everyone redundant when Mark died and she set her sights on Roger,' said Les. 'Sixteen years Janet worked there, and then one day that was it, no more job.'

'So, let me get this straight. She doesn't have any family or anything in Cornwall? Not in, say, Helston?' My brain fog, brought on by exhaustion and by the shock of finding Craig yesterday, was beginning to lift.

'Helston? Wouldn't have thought so. Oh, yes, please, same again,' she said to Joanie, who had come round offering more drinks.

I declined another cup of tea and made an excuse

about taking Germaine out for a pee. Mum looked at me; I knew she could see the synapses in my head firing, but all she said was, 'If you want to go off and do what you need to do, don't worry about me; someone here will give me a lift home.' I nodded and left, my mind whirling.

Chapter Twenty-Eight

I led Germaine outside and let her sniff at a grass verge while I went over what I'd just learnt. So Roger – who may or may not have been Cheryl's father, rather than her uncle – wasn't the only member of the Laity family who was a liar. Wherever Pauline had been, it hadn't been to see her mum. Had she been to Helston or somewhere completely different?

I thought back over the list of campsites we'd found the day before. I was sure there was one near Helston, close to the Loe, the largest freshwater lake in Cornwall and a popular beauty spot. Images of Craig's body, face down in the stagnant marsh water, ran through my mind. Had Cheryl met a similar fate, in the Loe? Had Pauline been busy disposing of her body, while Roger disposed of Craig's?

I shook my head to dismiss that idea; it was ridiculous. This was the Laitys, not the Mansons. I could imagine Roger and Pauline defrauding someone of their life savings, but going on a killing spree of their own offspring together, not so much.

I had to go to Helston. I clipped Germaine into the back seat – she looked at me in much the same way Daisy used to when I strapped her into her car seat as a toddler, kind of *Oh Mum, you're spoiling my fun* – and jumped into the driver's seat. I turned on the engine, then hesitated; should I call Withers? I felt like I should let someone know where I was going, just in case, but at the same time, if I told him about it he'd stop me going to check it out, and I didn't know if he'd send anyone else down there for a look or just dismiss it as nonsense. No, I would go down there and very carefully check out the campsite, just as we had done yesterday, with no detours onto marshland or anything. I'd take Germaine for a quick walk around the lake if the campsite turned up blank, nothing more dangerous than that. And if I did spot anything untoward or suspicious, I wouldn't investigate it myself but I'd call Withers then and wait for him to turn up. I wasn't daft; I wasn't planning on doing anything dangerous or heroic. I'd promised Daisy I wouldn't. So why did I have a small knot of anxiety lying like a lead weight at the pit of my stomach?

Maybe I should call Tony. He could come with me.

Yes. I dialled his number, waited for him to pick up …
and got through to his voicemail. *Dammit.* I hung up and
tried again, but it went straight to messages again. I
waited for the beep and then told him all the stuff I'd just
discovered, and that I was going to Helston. Then I
set off.

It took me about an hour and a half to get to Helston,
during which time I began to relax. By the time I got past
that bend I hated on the A39, I was enjoying myself. This
was fun! I loved being back in Cornwall, and I was
excited about my new catering business (if I ever got to
do any flipping cooking), but this got my adrenaline
pumping in a way that making a *velouté* never could. I'd
never been a detective, as such, but I'd always been
nosey. I put on some music and wound down the
window, singing along at the top of my lungs. I felt
happy. I hadn't been *un*happy, not for a while; once I'd
got that cheating swine properly out of mine and Daisy's
lives, once I'd decided to go to catering college and get
my life onto a different, healthier track, I'd been fine. But
there's something about sunshine and sea air, about good
music played loud on a car stereo, and about having
things to look forward to (I wasn't sure what exactly, but
I suspected DCI Withers was lurking in there

somewhere), that takes being relatively content to the next level.

I drove through the town, heading towards Porthleven. I smiled as I saw the turning for the nearby theme park – it wasn't exactly Alton Towers, but it was quaint and fun, and I remembered Mum and Dad taking me there when I was little – and drove on towards the campsite.

The site was situated off a narrow country lane, with nowhere to park, so I drove into the camp and parked outside the small site office and shop. Thank God I was in my car, and not the Gimpmobile; if Roger or Pauline were here, they wouldn't recognise my Toyota but they sure as hell would've spotted the van. *Note to self: undertake all future detective work in the car, not the van*, I thought, then smiled. Future detective work? I had told Withers I was a private investigator, but I hadn't actually meant it; it was just something he'd annoyed me into saying. Maybe deep down I *had* meant it...

I unclipped Germaine and went to let her out, then stopped; there was a 'No Dogs' sign up outside the office. Did that apply to the whole camp? I wound the window down a little way and patted her on the head.

'Sorry, sweetie,' I said. 'I'm going to leave you in here for a moment. I'll take you for a lovely' – I nearly said the word, which would have sent her into a paroxysm of frenzied excitement and made it impossible to leave her – 'W.A.L.K. after this, I promise.'

I shut the door and then, on an impulse, went into the office. There was a young girl behind the desk, talking on the phone and looking bored, but she paused her conversation and smiled in a friendly way as I entered.

'Can I help you?'

'Hi,' I said. 'I'm looking to buy a holiday home down here and a friend of mine recommended this site. I don't know if you know her? Cheryl?'

The girl looked blank, then shook her head. 'No, I don't know her. Did you want to have a look at a caravan?'

'Is it okay if I just have a look around the site? I'd really like to check out the location and the facilities first.'

'Of course.' She handed me a leaflet with a map. 'The static caravans are all down here...' She very helpfully pointed out an area that backed onto woodland, which in turn led down to the lake. 'This one here – and these two next to each other – are actually for sale. I can't let you in without the owners being here but if you like the plot, come back and I'll take you round the show caravan, see what you think.'

'Thank you,' I said. 'You've been really helpful.' And she had, because hopefully if those caravans were for sale they wouldn't be occupied by holidaymakers and would make the perfect place to hide a body until the heat died down...

I left the office and followed the map, ignoring the pitiful whining coming from Germaine in the car. I felt bad but I would only be five minutes; the site wasn't that big, and there were only about thirty caravans in all. I would have a good nosey around the ones that were for sale, already having an excuse if anyone challenged me, and a slightly more discreet peep at the others.

I felt my phone vibrate in my pocket and took it out to look. I was surprised to see I had three missed calls from Tony, but then mobile phone coverage in this part of the country could be patchy, especially when you got out into the more rural areas. I still only had a couple of bars, but that was probably enough to get through. I'd call him when I got back to the car.

I wandered down the tarmac path, past rows of tents. Most of them were zipped up, the occupants out enjoying the delights of Porthleven (there was a pasty shop there I remembered from my childhood that was almost as good as Rowe's in Penstowan ... *almost*), or having fun on a sandy beach somewhere. Towards the edge of the camp was a row of trees and a toilet block. I turned left at the rubbish bins, and the caravans stood in front of me.

It was very quiet and this end of the site felt cool and shady. I'd had friends who had lived in caravans like this most of the year round – not everyone in Cornwall is lucky enough to be able to afford a quaint stone cottage with a view of the sea – and I knew these places could get absolutely boiling hot during the summer, so this would be a good spot for them. Not so great in the winter, though, when it would be cold and damp.

Like the tents, most of these caravans appeared to be occupied by families on holiday. There were swimming costumes and towels hanging outside to dry – maybe yesterday had been a beach day, and today they were off to see St Michael's Mount or battle the crowds in St Ives – but there was no sign of anyone being inside.

I walked up to the first van that was for sale. The curtains were open, and a couple of the windows were open a crack. The site's caravan cleaners were probably paid to pop in and air out the unoccupied caravans, even if no one had been staying there. The van next door was the same – empty, but with the curtains open. There were a couple of steps leading to French doors at the front of the caravan, so I strolled up casually and pressed my face against the glass. I could see into the kitchen and living room area; no sign of anyone. I wandered around the side of the van but the windows here were too high up to look into.

The next few caravans were occupied. I came to the last but one, which was also for sale. It stood a little apart from the row, set back under a tree, which on a hot day like today was lovely but would have been a nightmare on one of those grey winter days when a sea mist rolls in and stays there for the whole of January. It was so dark in the shadow of the tree, compared to the bright summer sunshine elsewhere, that it took me a moment to notice that the curtains were shut.

I stood for a moment, wondering what to do. Should I knock? But was I even expecting there to be anyone alive inside, or was it the temporary resting place of Cheryl's corpse? I shivered, and it wasn't just down to the shade.

This caravan, like many of the others, had those steps up to the French doors at the front. I climbed them nervously and pressed my face to the window. It must be really dark inside...

Was that a light on? Through the weave of the curtain material I thought I could perceive a faint glow, but it was difficult to tell with the way the branches above me diffused the sunlight, the odd ray penetrating and reflecting on the glass. Or maybe the door from the bedroom area was open, and light from a window there was showing through? I stood back, frustrated; I just didn't know. But it was telling (or at least, I thought it was) that the curtains in this caravan were shut.

If Cheryl's body really was hidden inside, it would be a few days old now. Cheryl would be starting to smell less like Calvin Klein's Obsession and more like the remains of his dinner from two weeks ago. I swallowed hard, put my nose against the glass and sniffed gingerly.

Nothing.

Corpses really do smell quite strongly, quite quickly, and if I'd thought about it properly instead of going off half-cocked (side note: what exactly does 'half-cocked' mean? Should we be aiming to only go off fully cocked or not cocked at all?) I should have realised this would not be such a great place to hide one. The neighbouring holidaymakers would be sure to spot the terrible odour. I was relieved; to nick a quote from Oscar Wilde, to find two dead bodies in one week may be regarded as a misfortune; to find three looks like—

But I never decided what three looks like, as the door in front of me suddenly opened a crack and a terrified voice said, 'Jodie?'

Chapter Twenty-Nine

O nce I'd recovered my wits and rearranged my underwear I stared into the pale face in front of me. She was nearly unrecognisable without the make-up and the big hair, but she was most definitely alive.

'Cheryl?' I knew it was her, of course, but I couldn't quite believe it. Withers had had me convinced she was dead.

'Come in, quick!' She pulled me inside and shut the door.

I looked around the room. It was nicely decorated, but it was so dark it felt cold and uninviting. A pile of magazines lay on the floor next to the sofa, and the TV was on, sound turned down low. Cheryl walked over to the kitchen area and stood behind the counter, a barrier between the two of us.

She did not look well. The immaculately groomed, confident-to-the-point-of-being-aloof young woman who had questioned every single menu choice I'd suggested, who had given my welcome-party outfit the side-eye, and who had taken the heart of my oldest friend in the world, had disappeared, replaced by the nervous, fidgety ghost of her former self. Her manicured nails, which I had once admired for their vice-like grip on Mel's throat, were ragged and chipped. The 80s power dressing had gone, and instead of that red silk cocktail dress that had boldly declared its own glamour and sophistication, she was clad in a scruffy black velour tracksuit, which quietly muttered 'supermarket own brand'.

There was still a hint of the old Cheryl there though, because she noticed my none-too-surreptitious once-over and rallied enough to say, 'Tea?'

I stared at her for a moment, mouth open in disbelief. She had ruined Tony's life and all she could do was stand there and offer me a mug of PG Tips? She held my gaze defiantly for a few seconds, but then her bottom lip trembled and her eyes filled with tears. *Here it comes*, I thought, and it did. Her whole face crumpled as she put her head in both hands and wept, hard. Despite my initial anger and disgust with her, I felt for her. She seemed lost and bewildered, not the Cheryl I had briefly known and disliked before all this. I walked over and pulled her into a hug. I expected her to resist and pull away, but she didn't, just buried her head in my shoulder and cried harder.

I led her over to the sofa and sat her down, fumbling in my pockets for a tissue. Then I sat next to her, put my arm around her, and waited for her sobs to subside.

She finally calmed down, the tears drying up even though her breath was still ragged and shuddery.

'So,' I said. 'What the bloody hell is going on?' She looked tearful again. 'I'm not going to have a go at you,' I said quickly, 'but I need to know what happened, so I can help.'

She took a deep breath and wiped her eyes, blew her nose and offered back the tissue. I waved it away.

'Nah, you keep it... Tell me what happened on Friday night.'

'I don't know where to start...'

'Okay, then let me tell you what we've worked out so far.'

'We?'

'The police. And me and Tony.' Her eyes welled up again at his name, and I felt a little lurch in my tummy. Maybe she genuinely did love him. 'He's fine, by the way. Worried about you, of course.' *And worried about going to prison for three murders he didn't commit*, I thought, but I didn't say it. I didn't want her crying again.

'We found your pawn tickets,' I said. 'You needed money fast. Someone was blackmailing you, weren't they?' She looked at me, amazed, and then nodded. 'You were having an affair—'

'No!' She shook her head vehemently. 'I wasn't. It wasn't like that...'

'Craig?'

She looked at me with something like shame, and then nodded. 'We ... we had a relationship. It was still going on when I met Tony, but as soon as I realised it was getting serious, I finished with him. It never felt *right*. I know we aren't really brother and sister, but we were brought up as if we were. When I moved in with my uncle and aunt I was fifteen and Craig was seventeen, and the minute I saw him I just wanted him so much, and he felt the same. We resisted but on my eighteenth birthday we...'

'It had been going on that long?' I was shocked. That was *years*.

'No, no. After that night we avoided being alone together, and for a while it was almost like we'd got it out of our systems. He went away for work and it was all forgotten. But then he came back. And it was like we were teenagers again.' She studied her nails. 'The stupid thing is, I didn't even like him by that point. He'd always had this cruel sense of humour, but it had got worse while he was away. He was cynical and bitter. But he just had this hold over me. I don't know why...'

'What happened when you finished with him?'

'He didn't seem to care at first; he just smirked and said I'd be back. But when he met Tony, he was furious. He said he couldn't believe I'd dumped him for someone like Tony.'

'You mean someone kind, funny, and decent?' I felt a rush of indignant fury on Tony's behalf. She nodded.

'Exactly. He pestered me for ages but I thought he'd finally accepted it. Then, when we decided to get married, he threatened to tell Tony and I panicked. I offered him money to leave us alone, and that was it.'

'So, Friday night. You obviously weren't expecting to see him there?'

She shook her head. 'No. I'd given him some money that day in exchange for him promising to stay away. And then he turned up...' She looked at me, a look of pleading on her face. 'It was like ... he'd come for me; I was never going to get away and maybe I should just give in and go with him. Do you understand?'

I did. I'd worked with enough abuse cases in my old life to recognise gaslighting when I saw it. 'He controlled you. He made you feel like you needed him.'

She looked almost relieved. 'Yes. What with Mel having a go at me – at first I thought she knew about him, and that she was going to tell Tony – and then Craig appearing, it all felt impossible. Even when I realised that Mel didn't know, it was like fate warning me it was just a matter of time.'

'When I came up and checked on you, were you planning to run away?'

She sighed and stood up, then walked over to the sink to get a glass of water. She cooled her forehead against the cold glass before speaking.

'I didn't know what to do. I decided to tell Tony after the party and see if he still wanted me. And then I thought I'd write him a letter, in case I couldn't bring myself to say it.'

'But you never got further than "Dear Tony",' I said, and she shook her head.

'I didn't get the chance to.' She gulped at her drink. 'Craig rang me and told me to meet him in the garden, otherwise he'd go straight back in the bar and show Tony a photo. And he sent me the photo. It was...'

'I think I can guess what it was,' I said. 'He sent a couple of A4 prints to your house and Tony got them the next day.'

'Oh God...' She looked away, but I could tell she was crying.

'Tony didn't care,' I said. 'Well, he was upset of course, but he wouldn't have cared if you'd told him.'

'I know.' She pulled herself together. 'I was so stupid. I should have gone straight back down to the bar and found Tony, but instead I went out into the garden to plead with Craig to leave me alone. Mel was putting the dog in the car so I sneaked past her.' She was trembling, so I went over and held her hand. I might not have liked her, but it was impossible not to feel some sympathy for her. 'When I told Craig I wasn't going with him he just snapped. He spat in my face and told me he wouldn't let anyone else have me. I thought he was going to kill me.'

'What did he do?'

She didn't speak, but she pulled at the neckline of her hoody, which was done up all the way to the top. There were bruises around her neck, distinct enough that I could actually make out the shape of Craig's fingers. She looked at me, her body trembling but her gaze steady.

'I tried to get away but I couldn't. I was starting to black out when all of a sudden, he let go.'

'He just let go?'

'It was Mel. She must've heard us. She had this big rock in her hand and she hit him on the head with it. But it wasn't hard enough to kill him.' I could see the panic and fear rising in her eyes as she remembered, and I squeezed her hand. She took a deep breath to calm herself. 'He turned around and grabbed the rock off her, and then smashed her in the head with it. The next thing I know, she's on the ground and he's on top of her, strangling her, although it looked to me like she was already dead. So I picked up the rock from where he'd dropped it, and hit him as hard as I could. And I killed him.' She swayed. I took the glass from her fingers before she dropped it and half-carried her back to the sofa.

'So it was self-defence,' I said, and she nodded.

'Poor Mel,' she said, starting to cry. 'She was just trying to help me...'

'So, what I don't get,' I said carefully (I didn't want her getting hysterical on me again), 'what I don't get is what happened next. Why did you move Craig's body? Why didn't you call the police?'

'I don't know. I panicked,' she cried. 'I called my uncle, but he didn't answer. I suppose he was in the bar and didn't hear his phone. So I rang Aunty Pauline instead. I just wanted someone to tell me what I should do.'

'Why on earth would she tell you to move the body? And why leave Mel's? I don't understand.'

'She said the police never believe women in cases like that. She said they'd see the photos Craig had taken of me and they'd know we were lovers, and they'd think I'd killed them both to stop them telling Tony.'

'That's rubbish. If you'd gone straight to the police and told them, they'd have believed you, especially with Craig's reputation. And what about Tony? You just left him, not knowing what'd happened to you.'

'Pauline says the police think I killed them both and they're looking for me. Tony must know he's better off without me. That's why I'm hiding here, until my uncle and aunty help me leave the country.'

I laughed scornfully. 'Pauline is off her trolley.

Everyone thinks you're dead. And the police have arrested Tony for the murders of all three of you.' I didn't mention that they'd let him go; apart from anything else, unless I could hand her in to the police, I wasn't entirely sure they wouldn't arrest him again.

'But that's … Tony would never hurt anyone!' Cheryl looked genuinely shocked. 'Why didn't Pauline tell me? I don't understand—'

'You don't understand what?' We both jumped and turned to see Pauline Laity standing in the side doorway. 'You! What in God's name are you doing here? You're just the caterer! Why is it you seem to do everything but bloody cook? Cheryl, sweetheart, I don't know what this woman has told you, but you have to ignore her. She's making a play for Tony and wants you out of the way.'

'That's rubbish!' I said. 'Cheryl, your aunty here is bonkers. If she's the one who told you to move Craig and dump him in the marsh, she's made everything a hundred times worse than it could have been.'

'You dumped him in the marsh?' Cheryl looked horrified. 'I thought… You said you'd bury him! He was your son! How could you…?'

'How could I help the woman who killed him?' sneered Pauline, and all of a sudden I wondered how anyone could think of this woman as mouse-like. She'd fooled Tony; she'd even fooled DCI Withers, who had fallen for her grieving mother act. 'How could I help the woman who broke his heart *and* took him away from me?'

'You're not helping her,' I said, realisation finally dawning. 'You're making her look guilty.'

'She *is* guilty! She killed him!'

'In self-defence,' I said calmly. 'You know that, otherwise why go to all this trouble to incriminate her and make it look like she'd planned it? Only we know she didn't plan it.'

'You don't know anything,' spat Pauline, but she was looking less sure.

'No? We know it was Roger's car that moved Craig's body. We know it was parked in the lay-by while the two of you dragged his body through the long grass and over the fence. We know it went onto the marsh. Whether it was you or him driving, I don't know. I'm thinking you roped Roger in to do it while you brought her down here. You knew he'd do anything to help her.'

Cheryl looked confused. 'What makes you say that?'

Pauline glared at me. 'Do you know how many years it took Roger to accept Craig as his son? He was only four when we married; he was just a little boy and he needed a daddy. Every time Roger introduced him as his 'stepson' it broke my heart. And then you came along, perfect little missy.'

'But Uncle Roger never—'

'But he's not her uncle, is he?' I said. Cheryl looked at

me, eyes wide, while Pauline looked at me in the same way a cat looks at a mouse just before it pounces. Nasty. She slowly walked over to the kitchen and opened a drawer, taking out a large knife and placing it on the counter. I watched her hands as she spoke.

'Men are so stupid. It took him a while to catch on, but I knew the minute she turned up,' said Pauline. 'That's why your mother ran away, dear ... because she knew the baby she was carrying wasn't her husband's but her brother-in-law's. I knew it, I just knew it. And then of course when Roger finally realised... You do know he changed his will? Everything that should have been Craig's is yours. And I just had to go along with it, treat you like you were my daughter. As if I hadn't already had to live with the knowledge that he would never love me the way he'd loved your mother.'

'Did you know about the relationship? Did you know what Craig was doing to her?'

She laughed again. 'What *he* was doing to *her*? She used him until she found someone else who she thought had more money than he did. She's just like her mother.'

Cheryl leapt to her feet and started towards Pauline, but I jumped up and grabbed her arm.

'No,' I said quietly. Pauline laughed and picked up the knife, studying the blade.

'I've never felt the slightest urge to kill anyone,' said

Pauline. 'I never planned to kill you, not even after you killed my lovely boy.'

'The lovely boy who was a nasty, gaslighting abuser? You did a great job there, Pauline. There must be some kind of Mother of the Year award with your name on it,' I said, taunting her. I wanted to get her out from behind the counter. I gently pushed Cheryl behind me, towards the French doors. Outside, a dog began to bark. I recognised that bark…

'You've made things worse for her by turning up,' said Pauline, still looking at the knife in her hand. 'I was just going to keep her here for as long as possible, locked up until she went mad, and then turn her over to the police, by which time she'd look so guilty she'd go down for both murders. Or maybe until she did herself in, I don't know. I hadn't really planned that far ahead.'

I stepped back, forcing Cheryl to step back too. Pauline came out from behind the counter.

'Oh no, you're not leaving so soon?' she said, advancing on us.

Outside, the barking got louder; Germaine had performed her escape act and was right outside the French doors. I half turned and pushed Cheryl towards them as Pauline came at me, knife raised—

And then everything happened at once. Cheryl had just stretched out her hand towards the French doors when they flew open to reveal Withers standing on the steps, with Tony right behind him. Germaine dashed in and launched herself at Pauline, who shrieked and turned towards her, knife beginning its descent...

'You leave my dog alone!' I shouted, swinging the fire extinguisher, which I'd spotted by the TV earlier, at her head. It connected with a loud *THUNK!* and left Pauline lying insensible on the floor of the caravan.

'Are you all right—?' Withers began, then stopped as he saw me standing over Pauline's prostrate body.

'Things were getting a little heated,' I said, waving the extinguisher. 'All sorted now.' I laughed weakly and sank to the floor, where Germaine overwhelmed me with excited doggy kisses.

Chapter Thirty

Pauline came round a few minutes later, much to my relief. I'd initially been aiming for her arm, intending to make her drop the knife rather than knock her out, but when she had turned on Germaine I'd just seen red. She looked like she regretted waking up, as she found herself handcuffed and under the watchful gaze of old Davey Trelawney. An ambulance arrived, and she was hauled to her feet and taken off to be checked over before being escorted back to Penstowan police station.

Cheryl flew into Tony's arms and sobbed all over him. Tony was clearly relieved that she was okay, but I couldn't help noticing that he seemed uncomfortable and maybe even a little distant towards her.

'You okay?' said Withers. I was sitting in the front seat of his car. I'd been wrapped up in a blanket – it was one of those things I'd always automatically done when dealing with someone in shock, without really knowing why, and it was actually quite comforting to start with but now it was making me hot (or was it just the presence of DCI Withers?). Someone had brought me a coffee and Germaine was lying at my feet. I got the feeling she might never let me out of her sight again and that Daisy would probably do the same once we got home. If I told her.

'I'm fine,' I said. 'But very, very glad to see you. You timed it just right.'

'That *was* a bit of a close call,' he said. 'I don't suppose that will persuade you to stick to cooking from now on?'

'Of course it will, DCI Withers,' I said with a grin. He laughed.

'Oh my God, you actually enjoyed that, didn't you?' He shook his head. 'I can see I'm going to have to keep you under surveillance in future.'

I shrugged off the blanket before I caught fire. I was sure it was just the sun making me hot, and not the thought of DCI Withers keeping a close eye on me…

'So how did you find me?' I asked. 'Did Tony call you?'

'God, no. I went round there to arrest him again and he was just on his way out.' He grinned at me, and I realised he was joking. 'He burst into the station babbling about some voicemail message you'd left him, so I thought I should come down here before you got yourself into trouble.'

'Too late,' I said lightly.

'As usual.' He gave a wry smile. 'I should have known you'd have solved the case by the time we got here. Your mad dog had just got herself out of the car as we arrived, so we followed her and she led us to the caravan.'

We watched as the paramedics finished checking Cheryl over and nodded to Withers, who in turn signalled another plain-clothes officer to take her away. She was gently put into a waiting police car and driven away.

'What'll happen to her now?' I asked. He shrugged.

'I'm not sure. It's pretty clear she killed Craig in self-defence, and that all this nonsense was orchestrated by Pauline Laity, not her. She'll go down, I reckon, but not for long. She's not a danger to anyone. Pauline, though ... she's scary.' I laughed, but he was right; she was bonkers. 'She and Roger will both go down for perverting the course of justice, being accessories to murder after the fact... It sounds like Roger would have done anything for his little girl.'

'Anything except tell her she was his.'

He nodded. 'Can't be an easy thing to tell someone, can it?'

I looked over towards the ambulance. The paramedic

closed the rear doors and drove off, leaving Tony standing there alone, looking lost. Withers followed my gaze.

'You'd better go and talk to him,' he said. 'If he hadn't come and found me, things could have turned out very differently. And he insisted on coming along to rescue you.'

I walked over to Tony on legs that had almost stopped shaking, the adrenaline that had carried me through beginning to subside.

'So…' I said.

'So…' he said, and we both laughed. 'I don't really know what to say. Are you okay? What you did there was amazing…'

'Why, thank you.'

'And stupid. Really, really stupid. If anything had happened to you—'

'But it didn't.'

'No. Thank God.' He took my hands and scanned my face. 'You really are all right? I'm so sorry I didn't get your call. I went in to work to try and take my mind off things and I just didn't hear the phone, and then I got your message and I was so worried about what you were getting yourself into—'

'I know, I've had the lecture from Withers already.'

Tony smiled. 'I went straight round to the station and

told him we had to come and find you. To be honest he didn't take much persuading…'

'Fancies me, like you said,' I said cockily.

He laughed. 'Yep.'

'So you and Cheryl…'

'I don't know. We'll have to see.'

Chapter Thirty-One

Two days later, I walked into Penstowan to collect my van. As I walked, I thought about the conversation I'd had with Daisy that morning over breakfast.

'So, all this investigating stuff...' she'd started, hesitantly. I felt a *huge* pang of guilt, although I couldn't honestly say that I regretted getting involved – I still thought it was more than likely that Tony would have been charged without me sticking my nose in – and I also couldn't really promise that I wouldn't do it again. But I wasn't sure if I was going to tell my daughter that.

'Sweetheart, I am so sorry,' I said. 'I made you a promise, and then the minute we came down here I got involved in this. I shouldn't have, I know, but I—'

'No, you were right to,' she said. She sighed, looking

older than her twelve, nearly thirteen years. 'You had to help Tony, and I'm glad you did.' She toyed with her spoon, stirring her bowl of granola. 'You really loved being in the police, didn't you? I didn't realise how much you'd miss it.'

I stared at her. 'It was my decision to leave.'

'You wouldn't have left if I hadn't asked, though, would you?' she said, and now she was the one looking guilty. I swept her up off her seat and into my arms, kissing the top of her head.

'I'm your mum; my main purpose in life now is to look after you and keep you happy.'

'I want *you* to be happy too,' she said. 'And you're not happy unless you're poking your nose into things.'

I laughed. 'That's a bit harsh. But accurate.' She pulled away and looked at me with a serious expression on her face. *She's been forced to grow up too quickly*, I thought.

'I won't ask you to make me any more promises you can't keep,' she said. 'Just promise me you won't put yourself in any danger.'

'I'll happily promise that,' I said.

It took me about thirty minutes to get to the garage, but Rob hadn't quite finished the van and told me to come back in an hour. I decided to make the most of this unaccustomed quiet time – with no Mum or Daisy, Tony or DCI Withers, not even the dog, competing for my attention and no murder investigation occupying my mind – and treat myself to a visit to Rowe's for a coffee and a cake.

'Jodie!'

I stopped and looked round in surprise. He was the last person I'd expected to see here, which was probably daft as he must live locally and he had to eat.

'DCI Withers,' I began.

'I'm off duty. If I have to call you Jodie, then the least you can do is call me Nathan.'

'Nathan...' So *that* was what the 'N' stood for. I tried it out. It felt weird, but I was kind of relieved it wasn't Nigel (no offence to any Nigels out there). He laughed.

'What, did you think my parents christened me "DCI" or sumthin'?' His accent, which he usually tried to hide, came out on that one word.

'Ah, I've been wondering what your accent was,' I said. 'I mean, in as much as I spare you any thought at all...'

'Yeah, I bet.' He held the door open and stepped aside so I could go in before him, then followed. 'Can I get you a coffee?'

'Okay ... *Nathan*.'

We sat down and didn't speak until the waitress had

come over and taken our orders – a latte for me, and a cappuccino and an apple muffin for him.

'You don't strike me as an apple-muffin guy,' I said.

'No?' He looked amused. 'Tell me, as you're a cook – sorry, a *chef* – if you were going to bake me a cake, what would you make?'

'I don't know,' I said. 'I've *gateaux* give it some thought.'

He groaned. 'That's a terrible joke.'

'I know. I do tend to *crumble* under pressure…'

'Does that count? Is that a cake or a dessert?'

'If you were a true *friand* you wouldn't ask.'

He laughed. 'I'm desperately trying to find a way of introducing a cream horn into the conversation,' he said. I willed my cheeks not to go red. *Please don't blush, please don't blush…*

'Cheeky! You're such a *tart*…'

The waitress came over with our drinks. The muffin looked delicious and I wished I'd ordered one; I'd intended to, but I hadn't wanted to look like a pig in front of With— *Nathan*. Ooh, that was going to take some getting used to. I didn't want to question exactly why I cared what I looked like in front of him.

'On second thoughts, can you bring another muffin?' he said to the waitress, smiling at me. *Cocky bugger*.

'No, no, I'm fine,' I said, and he pretended to be surprised.

'It wasn't for you; I want two,' he said, then laughed as I rolled my eyes at him. He added sugar then stirred his drink and said, 'Liverpool.'

'What?'

'My accent. That's where I come from. Well, Crosby. Liverpool-by-the-sea.'

'Oh. So what brings you down here?'

'My fiancée and I thought it would be a nice place to raise a family.' For some reason there was a slight sinking feeling in my stomach, but I didn't say anything. He sipped his coffee. 'She was dead keen, so I transferred here and bought a house, and then she decided she was staying in Crosby, so...'

'Oh no,' I said, hopefully sincerely, although amazingly my stomach suddenly felt better again. The waitress placed the other muffin in front of me and I tucked into it happily.

'Anyway, I just wanted to apologise for threatening to arrest you,' he said.

'Which time?' I asked.

'How many times did I do it?'

'At least three, if I remember right.'

He laughed. 'Okay, I apologise for however many times it was. But you don't give up, do you? You're tenacious. You must've been a good copper.'

I nearly choked. 'What about "Big shoes to fill"?' I asked him, a bit miffed. He looked genuinely surprised.

'You know, when you found out who my dad was, and you said, "Big shoes to fill," I thought you were implying—'

'I wasn't implying anything!' he protested. 'God, no, if anything I was thinking about me. Your dad was well loved, and I'm not even particularly well liked.'

'Can't think why,' I said, but I said it with a grin. He smiled ruefully.

'Yeah, right…'

We sat for a moment in silence, enjoying our coffee and muffins. Then he looked up and said, 'I mean it. You must've been a good copper. Why did you leave?'

And there it was. The million-dollar question. I was surprised that no one else had asked me; I knew there must be a few people round here – the people who thought I was getting too big for my boots by going off to the big city, as though Penstowan wasn't good enough for me – I knew they must've been speculating about why I was back.

'Do you know how my dad died?' I asked. He shook his head.

'Line of duty, that's all I know,' he said.

I nodded. 'Yeah. Well, sort of. He didn't really go out on the beat when he became Chief Inspector, it was mostly desk work. He was sixty-four years old when he died. He should've retired by then, only they let him stay because it was all admin so it wasn't physical work, and they were short of experienced officers. He only had another couple of months before his birthday, when they would have made him take compulsory retirement.' I remembered hearing the news. I'd left home by then, of course, and was in London, and it was the last thing I expected to hear. 'He was on his way home one night when he saw this car being driven by a couple of teenagers. He knew them, and he knew it wasn't their car, so he rang the station and said he was following them. But they got spooked and took off, and they crashed going round a bend on the A39. You know the one... And Dad crashed into them. Such a bloody stupid way to die, all because of a couple of bored teenagers.'

'I'm sorry,' said Nathan. 'But that's not when you left the force?'

'No,' I said. 'I don't know if you remember, it was just over a year ago now, there was a van attack in Central London? We had a phone call saying there was a bomb planted in a tube station, and when we started evacuating, this madman drove a van into the crowd of commuters.'

'I remember that; it was terrible. You were there?'

I nodded. 'Yeah. There were five of us evacuating the station when the van came up on the pavement and started hitting people. We didn't know what to do; we couldn't send everyone back down into the station in case the bomb went off, so we formed a human shield in front of them and sent everyone into a nearby department store, all the time watching the van get closer and wondering if the station behind us was going to explode.'

'Bloody hell, Jodie...' Nathan reached for my hand, then thought better of it. I was mildly disappointed.

'It could have been worse. The van hit a bus stop – thankfully there was no one still waiting there – and he got out, waving this big knife around, so we all ran at him and disarmed him. Gave him a bit of a kicking as well while we were at it, if I'm being totally honest. The bomb threat turned out to be a hoax, designed to get everyone out of the station.'

'That must have been terrifying. No wonder you left.'

I shook my head. 'I didn't lose my nerve, if that's what you think.'

'I didn't mean that.'

'I would have stayed on. Yeah, it shook me up, but you know what the job's like; you're all in it together, and you keep each other going, don't you?' I smiled as I remembered the camaraderie, the banter in the canteen. I'd loved it. 'I had counselling. But my daughter didn't.'

'Ah...' said Nathan.

'Everyone films everything these days, don't they? Bloody mobiles. And the TV news encourages the public by using their footage. She was only eleven, so she didn't see it on the telly at the time, but some of her schoolfriends did. They asked if she'd seen her mum being a hero, so she looked it up on the internet. She had nightmares for weeks. She cried every time I left the house. And I remembered how much I used to worry about my dad, out on the beat, when I was little. And all I had to contend with down here was housebreakers and joyriders. Daisy had so much more to worry about.'

'And that's why you left,' said Nathan.

'It is. And as much as I miss it, I don't regret leaving for a moment.'

We finished our coffees and said our goodbyes, which felt oddly … *odd*, almost formal. The investigation was over, but it wasn't as if our paths would never cross again, not while we were both living in Penstowan. Then I walked back to the garage to pick up the van.

The engine purred instead of coughed, and Rob was right; it looked and drove as good as new. Except when you looked at it in a certain light. In a certain light, even without the old fetish shop decals and with several new layers of paint, you could still see a faint outline.

And I knew my van was destined to be the Gimpmobile for ever. I drove home.

———

'Someone to see you,' said Mum, opening the back door behind me. I looked back and saw Tony.

'All right?' I said, budging up so he could sit on the garden wall next to me.

'Yeah. What're you doing?'

'Enjoying the view.'

He sat down and swung his legs around so we were facing the same way, his feet dangling over one of the many gorse bushes that dotted the Cornish countryside.

'Oh, wow.'

'It's why I bought the house,' I said, 'but I haven't had much time to sit and look at it.'

Most of the garden was to the side of the house, with just a small patch at the back, and the hillside made the stone wall low enough on this side to sit on but too high on the other for my ovine neighbours to jump over (I hoped). Beyond the field was the edge of the cliffs, and beyond that, the sea. The sun was starting to set, the sky turning from orange to red to purple to deep blue, reflected on the surface of the water.

'It's so peaceful,' said Tony.

'Yep.'

We sat in silence, watching the sun sink lower.

'You know, you've never asked me why I left the force,' I said. He smiled. 'Reckon I know why. I saw you on the telly.'

'I didn't lose my nerve—'

He laughed. 'I didn't say you did. I wouldn't dare! You left because of Daisy, didn't you? I remember how much you used to worry about your dad, and I reckon you didn't want her to worry about you.'

I turned to look at him in admiration.

'Tony Penhaligon, you are surprisingly emotionally literate.'

'I'm not sure what that means but I'll take it as a compliment.'

I turned my head as I felt Mum hovering behind us in the garden. She held out two mugs of tea.

'Thought you'd like a brew.'

'Thanks, Shirley,' said Tony. 'You joining us?'

'No, no, I'll leave you two to it...' She scuttled away with a knowing look on her face. I wondered if she'd look so smug if she knew I'd had coffee with the handsome DCI that afternoon.

'So, Cheryl got bail,' said Tony, his eyes on the vista in front of us.

'I heard,' I said. 'I saw Nathan Withers earlier.' I felt rather than saw him turn to me in surprised disapproval.

'Oh, it's Nathan now, is it?'

'He's all right,' I said, and Tony scoffed. 'He came through in the end, didn't he?'

'Eventually,' said Tony, grudgingly. 'I'd still be banged up if it wasn't for you.'

'Dunno about that.'

We sat quietly again, enjoying the view and each

other's company, even if we weren't in total agreement about our local DCI.

'She came to see me,' he said after a while.

'Cheryl?'

'Yeah.'

'Oh.' There were so many things I wanted to ask him, but I didn't.

'She asked me if we could try again,' he said, studying the view intently.

'Did she?' There went my stomach again, lurching. I wasn't entirely sure how I felt about him and Cheryl getting back together. Not that it was any of my business – I mean, it wasn't like I wanted Tony for myself or anything – but he was my oldest and, I realised with a shock, my closest friend. This unaccustomed emotional turmoil was too much for me. I was probably developing an ulcer. 'She might be going to jail, you know. I know it was self-defence, and I don't blame her, but even so—'

'I said no.' Tony reached out and plucked a flower from a group of pink sea thrift growing out of a crack in the wall. 'I told her I forgave her, but it's not enough. I said that if she really loved me she would've trusted me to help get her free of Craig. All she had to do was be honest with me, and she couldn't. And then to even think about disappearing without letting me know she was okay... I know Pauline confused her, but she didn't stop to think how it might affect me. It shouldn't have been down to you to prove my innocence. I'm just glad you did.'

He smiled and turned to me, holding out the flower. I took it.

'So how do you feel? Are you going to be okay?' I asked. He really did deserve to be happy.

'Yeah, I'll be fine. My only regret is I never got to try your cooking.'

I laughed. 'Well that's easily fixed. I've got two hundred pork sausages in my fridge.' I swung my legs back into the garden and stood up, holding out my hand as Tony followed suit. I pulled him onto his feet.

'Come on,' I said. 'Come with me and I'll make you the best sausage sandwich you've ever had.'

THE END

Jodie 'Nosey' Parker will return in
A Brush With Death...

Get your copy today!

Jodie's tried and tested recipes #1

'Bung it all in the oven' Cornish/Moroccan (Coroccan?)
chicken

This is a great recipe for using up any veg you've got
lying around. It's quick and tasty, and once you chop
everything up you just chuck it in the oven and wait,
giving you plenty of time to mull over your latest
murder case and work out how to prove your oldest
friend is innocent. Proper job!

1. Pre-heat the oven to 200°c. That's hot, but not
   as hot as a certain local DCI (my oven doesn't
   go up that high).
2. Dice **carrots**, **sweet potato**, **potatoes** and
   anything else you've got lying about into

chunks. Remember, the larger the chunk, the longer it'll take. This is true of so many things in life, not just in cooking. **Pumpkin** and **squash** work well in this recipe too. Chop **cauliflower** into florets. Cut a **red onion** into quarters and crush at least two cloves of **garlic** (never trust a recipe that calls for one clove. One clove isn't enough for anything, not even a recipe called One Clove of Garlic). Leave out the garlic if you're planning on playing Fu— Snog, Marry, Avoid with someone, otherwise you'll end up being the one they *avoid*. A **red pepper** goes nicely in this too; chop it into large chunks.

3. Toss everything in olive oil, season with salt and pepper, then put in an ovenproof dish and bake in the oven. It'll probably take about 30-40 minutes, depending on how big your chunks are. My chunks have definitely got bigger since I left the force. I should probably get an exercise bike. Or some control pants.

4. Take some **chicken breasts** (one per person). Sprinkle ground **cumin**, **coriander** and **chilli flakes** (if you like a bit of heat) onto a chopping board, then roll the chicken breasts in the spice mix, making sure to cover both sides thoroughly. If you're at catering college, you've

got no money, and you're trying to eke out a small amount of chicken, chop it into chunks and thread them onto skewers, alternating with pieces of **mushroom, red pepper,** and **onion**. I once tried replacing the chicken with frankfurter sausages from my local German discount supermarket – they were only 10p a tin – but it wasn't quite the same… Bung the chicken into the oven. Chicken breasts will be done dreckly (around 20 minutes, depending on the thickness) while kebabs will cook a bit quicker. Frankfurters will be the quickest of all to cook but they'll taste disgusting and end up in the dog.

5. Measure one cup of **Israeli couscous** into a pan and cover it with hot water. Crumble in a stock cube and bring to the boil for around seven minutes, until it's soft. *Note to reader*: check the instructions on the packet when trying things for the first time. The first time I tried to cook Israeli couscous, I treated it like ordinary couscous and waited for it to absorb all the water, by which time it was like frogspawn – huge, gloopy, and probably better for hanging wallpaper with than eating. It was even worse than the frankfurter kebabs that I served with it. You can use ordinary couscous but this type

really works well with the spicy flavours and is proper middle-class, innit.

6. Drain the couscous and tip it into the dish of roasted veg. Add a tablespoon of **harissa paste** (or more if you like it Detective Chief Inspector hot) and mix everything together. Serve the chicken on a bed of couscous and roasted veg. If you've got them, pita or flat breads go really well and you can mop up the spicy harissa and chicken juices. Alternatively, you can put the plate on the floor when you've finished and let the dog lick them up. *Note to reader*: don't do this. Cleaning up after a dog with explosive diarrhoea is less fun than you probably imagine. Your teenage daughter will be no help as she's too much of a princess to handle pet poop, and your elderly mother will suddenly look at her watch and decide it's time for her to go home.

Eat up, my lover, it's bleddy ansum!

Acknowledgments

This book was written in extraordinary times. The global pandemic has missed Penstowan completely, because we're all sick of hearing about it, but I can't ignore it here.

I've spent the last 14 years or so living between New Zealand and the UK. I moved hemisphere for the final time (or at least, the final time until I can afford a Cornish farmhouse or a Venetian palazzo) in 2019. Any doubts I may have had about coming back to NZ evaporated pretty quickly around March 2020, when Covid-19 reached these shores. On Wednesday 25th March, Prime Minister Jacinda Arden and Dr Ashley Bloomfield, the Director-General of Health, put the whole country into a strict lockdown, which meant no leaving the house (except for exercise) for at least four weeks. It went on for rather longer, and it was harsh, but it worked, and I'm writing these acknowledgments now in October 2020 from a country where life has more or less returned to normal.

During lockdown I was unable to work — my day job relied very much on the shops being open — but the government quickly put wage subsidies in place. Thanks to these 'Jacinda bucks', as my son immediately dubbed them, I didn't have to worry about my financial situation. And that meant that when, two weeks into lockdown, the lovely folk at One More Chapter offered me this book deal, I was able to concentrate on writing and not worry about paying bills. In effect, the New Zealand government paid me to write this book, so it would be churlish not to dedicate it to them! Thank you, Jacinda and Ashley, and thank you New Zealand (the 'team of 5 million'), for playing by the rules, being kind, and crushing the coronavirus.

This book is also dedicated, and written for, my mum and dad. My mum, Margaret, lives with my sister Sue in a little town in Devon, right on the border with Cornwall, and it's that town and others nearby which were the inspiration for fictional Penstowan. The OAPs coffee morning is real, and I've sat in that church hall drinking tea and eating Bourbon biscuits. I really did learn to cook by helping my mum, and I remember the dinner parties she and Dad used to throw. My mum is far less batty than Shirley, but she's just as warm and funny.

Like Jodie, my dad was an Eddie too. He wasn't a copper (he was a bricklayer, which may explain why, unlike Jodie, I wasn't so keen to follow in his footsteps), but he was big and strong. He was also completely soppy, and cried when he met his baby grandchild for the first time. I didn't get any detective skills from him, but watching him decorating and doing odd jobs around the house (occasionally turning the air blue in the process) has taught me when to DIY, and when to admit defeat and call an expert. He loved golf (and doughnuts), and his ashes are scattered on the 18th hole at Holsworthy Golf Club. I always give him a wave if I drive past the golf course when I'm visiting my mum, and I can't eat a bar of Cadbury's Fruit and Nut (one of his favourites) without thinking of him.

Okay, the sentimental bit is over. On with the thanks! I have such an amazing support network behind me, I am completely spoilt. Being a writer can be a lonely calling, so it helps to have other writers in your corner. I am blessed to have my Choc and Awe (the name's a long story) cheerleaders, Carmen Radtke and Jade Bokhari, who have my back whatever. Then there are my fellow Renegade Writers (yeah, that's another long story), Sandy Barker, Andie Newton and Nina Kaye. Thank you ladies, you are all awesome writers and amazing friends, and I love you!

Massive thanks also go to the super team behind this book. My agent, Lina Langlee at the North Literary Agency, has been a constant source of encouragement and support, and without her I would have given up. Hannah Todd, my editor at One More Chapter, and the whole lovely gang there, have been so great to work with, and without them there would be no Jodie.

And as ever, the last word of thanks goes to my husband Dominic and my son Lucas, because they're the reason I get out of bed in the morning.

ONE MORE CHAPTER

YOUR NUMBER ONE STOP

FOR PAGETURNING BOOKS

One More Chapter is an
award-winning global
division of HarperCollins.

Sign up to our newsletter to get our
latest eBook deals and stay up to date
with our weekly Book Club!
<u>Subscribe here.</u>

Meet the team at
<u>www.onemorechapter.com</u>

Follow us!

 @OneMoreChapter_

 @OneMoreChapter

 @onemorechapterhc

Do you write unputdownable fiction?
We love to hear from new voices.
Find out how to submit your novel at
<u>www.onemorechapter.com/submissions</u>